The Stalking Darkness

The Void watched Citadel bend over the body and do nothing. That's how it had always been. Void's memory was full of times Citadel did nothing to prevent the loss of life. In fact, Citadel's job had been, so many times, to take life. To destroy the most precious thing in the universe.

He'd done it to Void. He'd destroyed her just like Ho Chi Min, Saddam Hussein, Gregor Valinski. Each was a fledgling dictator, stopped before they could become a threat to the United States. Citadel had been the weapon the USA pointed at anyone who might have caused "difficulties" for America or its allies. A one-man Normandy invasion force.

Void remained *despite* Citadel. He'd done his best to kill her, but she lived, wrapped around a core of the same force meant to destroy her. She lived, if only as a dark stain on the motel office ceiling, hidden among the shadows there, looking down at the man she desperately wanted to kill.

Citadel stood suddenly, his head achingly near her, oblivious to her presence. He had always been so stupid. So careless. He didn't see the threat that hovered inches from his fragile brain.

Tendrils of shadow extended from Void, swirling a hair's breadth away from Citadel's long gray hair. Before she could act, he moved away, heading for the door to wait for the doctor.

In truth, Void still didn't know what she was going to do with Citadel. She didn't want to just kill him. She wanted him to suffer. She wanted him to know why he was dying. As it was, he knew nothing. He didn't even remember her. She would have to remedy that before she took any decisive action.

She would have to watch and see.

From the shadows, of course.

HEROES OF F.O.R.C.E.
BY ALEC GUNN

UNBREAKABLE

ALEC GUNN

Unbreakable

Copyright © 2020 Nick Marsden
All Rights Reserved
1st Print Edition
Published by Pencastle Publications
www.pencastlebooks.com
Cover and Interior design Copyright © 2020 Nicholas Marsden
ISBN: 978-1-7360973-1-1

Contents

Forward

This is a work of fiction.

This is also a book of alternative history. I've included several "real" people to ground the story and give it a certain feel. However, these representations of real people are fictionalized to the point that they can't possibly represent the real thing.

People like Zak Williams, Bill Murray, Sheppard Smith, and others are merely around as sort of easter eggs for the astute reader to point to history or reality and see a glimpse of the alternate.

In this world, "Superheroes" have made war obsolete. Since Vietnam, the United States has used them to secretly prevent the major conflicts we know of in this modern age from happening. Just these changes have drastically altered who people are, or if they existed at all.

So if you are or know one of these people, don't take offense at any changes to appearance or personality.

I've tried not to make any of them *total* dicks.

-Alec Gunn

Alec Gunn

Prologue

Mr. President, this is Subject Alpha.

The first time Alpha met President John F. Kennedy, he was at least as impressed as Kennedy was with him. It was 1962, a year after he'd broken the back of George Hudson during the Virginia state wrestling finals, where Alpha flipped the two-hundred-thirty-pound teenager onto his back and slammed him back to the mat hard enough to shatter bone.

Mr. President!

Why was he in Dallas that day? Dr. Morrow instructed him to follow the motorcade along with the Secret Service detail. He was just a kid. Still barely sixteen. But he'd done it. When the report of the gunshot reached his ears, he acted without thought. He threw himself at Kennedy, the only obvious target. He was fast enough—just fast enough. The six-point-five-millimeter round hit his shoulder and broke into thirty-seven pieces, none of which penetrated his flesh. One, however, ricocheted and struck Governor Connally in the front seat of the car, grazing the side of his head.

By the time the sniper had time to fire his second shot, Alpha's tall, lanky form completely obstructed Kennedy. That shot cracked against the back of Alpha's skull and ricocheted into Secret Service Agent Clint Hill, who was standing on the side of the car behind them. Hill fell from the car, his right knee giving way.

Someone knew Kennedy was in danger that day. Someone ordered Alpha to Dallas, even though he lived and trained in sub-basement three of the Pentagon building in Virginia, half a country away.

You want me to do what, Jack?

When you save someone's life, President Kennedy told him, you earn the right to call him by his first name.

It was April 22, 1964. Alpha strode along a winding river-bank in a hot, wet, foreign land. He wore loose camouflage pants and a brown, sleeveless shirt. The shirt was ripped in several places, flaps torn from the shirt flopped wetly at his side.

Alpha didn't feel the shirt; he didn't feel the heat. He didn't sweat. He hadn't felt heat or cold against his skin in almost three years.

He did smell the smoke, though. It smelled of diesel fuel and oily rags burned with too much heat. Behind him, the plumes billowed into the damp air, fighting the humidity to rise into the sky.

In front of him, weapon emplacements tracked his progress, waiting for him to get close enough for their fifty caliber rounds to do damage. If he spoke Vietnamese, he might have told them the barrels of the weapons would have to be two feet from his skin for those rounds to penetrate, let alone kill him.

When the jungle trees to either side of the river opened wide enough, Alpha saw the buildings of Hanoi rising on the horizon. He was almost there, almost to his target.

The thump of a mortar came to his ears. A patch of dirt to his left exploded and rocks pelted him. The fifty cals opened on him, peppering him like golf balls thrown by seven-year-olds. He felt those, but only as ripples on his flesh akin to the quick strikes of a masseuse.

The mortar was a bigger problem, however. He'd never been struck by high explosives before; he was pretty confident he would survive, but his wounds might hamper him for too long before they healed.

Rest break was over.

He spied the two machine gun nests a hundred feet away. The mortar would be nearby, but he couldn't see it. He rushed the nests, reaching them in three leaping bounds. The operators couldn't track him fast enough, so their rounds went wide of him. On the final leap, he landed in the midst of one. The two operators shrieked in alarm.

Alpha snatched up the gun up by its barrel; the red, glowing metal hissed as it evaporated the moisture on his skin in an instant. He swung it like a scythe, the metal of the receiver ripping through sandbags and flesh with equal effect.

Blood spattered on Alpha's skin unnoticed.

After the operators were dead, Alpha twisted the weapon in his hands until it was a useless coil of metal. Then, he threw it at the other nest.

That nest went up as if he'd thrown a grenade into it. Sand exploded everywhere. The screams of the operators were cut short. One of them climbed up onto the remains of the sandbag wall, his face covered in blood, one hand a mangled stump.

Alpha ignored the wounded man. He shut out the screams of agony as he scanned the jungle for the mortar nest.

It thumped again. Alpha noticed a shift in the foliage as the round jumped into the air. He leaped out of the machine gun nest just before the mortar struck and exploded, destroying whatever Alpha left behind.

He landed ten feet away from the mortar. The two operators, perhaps witnessing what happened to their comrades, screamed and fled in opposite directions. Alpha moved to the nest and crushed the mortar tube in his hand; for a moment, he considered tossing it after one of the fleeing North Vietnamese Army soldiers. Instead, he left the ruined mortar where it was and moved on, heading northwest toward Hanoi.

On the river behind him, miles back, American and South

Vietnamese boats followed him. He had to be swift now, or surely, they would catch up to him. They'd only given him two days head start and clearing the NVA defenses along the river took precious time.

He picked up the pace, turning his long-legged stride into a pace he thought a jog, but his trainers considered an Olympic sprint. It was hard here. Foliage threatened to tangle his legs. Despite his strength and agility, tripping was still a danger over this terrain.

Alpha might have been the most physically powerful human on the planet, but he was still a seventeen-year-old boy who had spent the last three years mostly cooped up in a concrete training facility. Sometimes he was overconfident. Sometimes he didn't think things through completely.

Sometimes he didn't consider landmines.

The explosion, combined with his momentum, threw him high into the air and a dozen yards into the brush. He hit the muddy earth face-first and slid several feet until his head thumped against a thick vine. He rolled onto his back, thankful there wasn't anyone else around to see such an ignominious stumble. He sat up and wiped mud from his eyes.

Then he looked down at his legs.

His boots were obliterated. About three inches of black leather and frayed laces remained on his right ankle, but the left boot—the one he landed on—was completely gone. His legs were peppered with shrapnel, blood rimming the wounds. Already, his enhanced endurance was closing the skin around the shrapnel.

His left foot was bare, bloody, and about half its normal size. The shock of the explosion mixed with his natural pain-suppression ability made the amputation painless. As he watched, the shattered bones mended and grew. A couple of minutes and the foot would be back to normal.

But that was a couple of minutes Alpha had to spend sitting on his ass. The explosion would draw the attention of the NVA. They'd see his wound and put two and two together—a large enough explosion might actually kill him. He imagined the dozens of grenades they'd throw his way.

He pushed back, sliding on his butt toward the riverbank. There was only one way he could think to hide *and* give himself time to heal.

By the time he reached the river, he heard shouts from above, toward the jungle. His toe bones were beginning to form and there was a buzzing in his foot as nerves knitted back into place. He fell back into the water, pushing himself along the silt toward the middle of the flow.

Taking a deep breath, he let himself sink, heavy despite the air in his lungs.

Alpha held his breath as he sat at the bottom of the river. His wounded foot tingled—a good sign, he supposed. His eyes were shut against the muddy brown water. He spent time waiting for his foot to heal while plucking the shrapnel from his leg. It was only a momentary sting as the metal shards pulled out, then a brief tingle, and the skin was whole again.

When that was done, he waited. His lungs generated oxygen for him or some such thing; he could hold his breath indefinitely if he wanted to—his body would keep him going.

When he thought his foot was whole again, maybe five minutes after he'd dropped below the surface of the water, he reached down to feel it.

That was a mistake.

The toes bones were whole. Tendons had formed and the muscle was beginning to regenerate, but it was far from finished. In his fingers, his toes felt like odd sticks of gelatin in the water. He drew his hands back, grimacing.

Then the NVA found him.

The water exploded around him as the NVA soldiers emptied their weapons into the river where his trail ended. Some of the bullets tapped against him harmlessly.

He needed to take care of this. When the American boats came through here, this pack of soldiers would be sitting here waiting.

Injured foot or not, he had to move.

He crawled along the riverbed toward the shore and the

NVA soldiers. When it was shallow enough, he pushed himself out of the water. He stood gingerly, aware the river silt was probably getting inside his still-healing foot.

The soldiers' eyes widened as he came back up into the air, water sluicing off him as he rose to his feet. In shocked reaction, some opened fire; the bullets shattered against his chest and face.

Standing knee-deep in water with a wounded foot, he couldn't move with the speed he was normally capable of. He limped forward. The nerves in his toe must be forming now, because he felt them dig into the silt, looking for purchase.

Beaches would never hold the same allure for him after that moment.

The soldiers backed away from him as he approached. They kept firing until their clips were spent, then they reloaded and fired again. When Alpha was out of the water, he glanced down at his foot. The flesh was red, inflamed—the skin was intact, but his body still needed to fight the infection caused by the open wound in the dirty mud and water.

But he could move now.

There were thirteen of them. Only three got away. They weren't running toward Hanoi, so Alpha let them go. In the distance, Alpha heard the buzz of motors. The boats were coming. With the defenses down, their progress was unimpeded.

Alpha picked up his pace.

You are nothing but a coward!

Ho Chi Minh's English was surprisingly good. Alpha expected a string of expletives in Vietnamese. He got those, too, but Ho Chi Minh stared at Alpha as the large American reached for him to do what he'd done to the others.

At the insult, Alpha paused. He was doing this to save lives. Thousands of lives. Seven Vietnamese lives, not counting the soldiers he'd killed to get here, in exchange for *thousands* of Americans.

The lives he would save—both Vietnamese and American—

were worth this.

Jack Kennedy said so.

You did good, son.

Alpha preferred those words come out of the mouth of his own father but hearing them from Jack was as good as he was going to get.

Upon his return, Alpha was told all record of his existence before 1961 was expunged. His father was ordered to stay away, and like a good soldier—a veteran of the Second World War and Korea—he obeyed.

Alpha would never see him again.

But Jack Kennedy would become a constant companion until his death in 1986 from pneumonia. He would be the father figure Alpha never really had. And there were worse people than a U.S. President to look up to.

There was a small ceremony in the Oval Office after the Vietnam operation. Jack, Vice President Johnson, and Dr. Morrow, the head of Project Brooklyn. Those were the only people who could know what happened. Even the Americans and South Vietnamese on the boats hadn't known how they'd gotten up the river without opposition. The raid on Hanoi was a cover for Alpha's mission: the assassination of Ho Chi Minh and the Central Committee of the Communist Party of Vietnam.

"The United States owes you a debt we cannot express," Jack said as he brought Alpha a small, thin box. He lifted the lid and showed Alpha the contents—a gold star-shaped medal with a blue ribbon bedecked with white stars.

The Congressional Medal of Honor.

"No one will ever know you have this," Jack continued. "There is no paperwork, no certificate. But I want you to have it. A feeble attempt to show you how much what you did means to this country."

Alpha lifted the box from Jack's hands. He nodded his understanding, though he was at a loss for words.

Jack turned to Mr. Johnson and Dr. Morrow.

"This boy…this *man*, has proven himself this nation's defender. He is our strong wall, our impenetrable fortress. He is our citadel."

Dr. Morrow smiled. "Then that is how he'll be known from now on, Mr. President. He needs a better name than 'Alpha,' anyway."

"Welcome home, Citadel."

AUPrimeNews Archive

(Posted: 12/23/2017)

TERROR IN THE HEARTLAND!

Ender, Oklahoma — A dramatic face-off with a speed-enhanced Super-Powered Individual (SPI) took place yesterday in this small hamlet in southern Oklahoma, resulting in the deaths of four AUSS heroes and one civilian.

The nine-day manhunt for Leonard Strange, 18, ended yesterday when the brave heroes of the AUSS cornered the vicious SPI in a closed bowling alley. Strange had taken three hostages, but our heroes infiltrated the facility and rescued two of them before Strange attacked, killing the third hostage and four AUSS agents. Strange was then subdued in a thunderous battle led by Agent Roger Hamilton, one of the AUSS's best and brightest.

Strange terrorized the little town of Ender for over a week before he was brought to justice. He revealed himself by beating a fellow classmate at President Andrew Marshall High School, almost to death. The young villain then ripped through the town, murdering the county sheriff—his own father—among others.

In the end, he had nowhere to run. The brave men and women of the AUSS closed in on him and took him down, some heroically sacrificing themselves to see the job done.

Memorial services for the slain AUSS heroes will be televised live on AUPrimeLive on Christmas Eve at 7 p.m., followed by a screening of *It's a Wonderful Life* at 8 p.m.

Leonard Strange will be executed on Christmas Day by enhanced hanging, pending the obligatory DNA screening.

The execution will be live-streamed on AUPrimeSports.com at 12:00 p.m. (CDT) prior to the Chicago Bears vs. the Tennessee Titans at 1:15 p.m. (CDT).

July 6, 2018 - 3:00 p.m.

Ender, Oklahoma

Since the days of the Chaos Years, when the U.S. government ran out of money for the military and the states ran out of money for police, Ender, Oklahoma was an island in an ocean of shit. It had rallied—circled the wagons, so-to-speak. With the County Sheriff gone, public utilities shut off or dwindled, gangs and worse rampaged through much of the state, but Ender had pulled together and protected its own.

A lot of that had to do with the fact that Ender had no resources, no money, and nothing worth stealing. But when a gang of looters had come through, hell-bent on razing everything in their path on their way north to McAlester, the people of Ender resisted. The average resident of Ender owned a gun—a hunting rifle, at least. When the gang arrived, Ender had stood tall and pushed them out.

The looters had decided it wasn't worth the trouble. So, they went around.

Ender became the only town in Oklahoma *not* to fall to the gangs of raiders and looters. Even cut off from the rest of Oklahoma and the United States of America lying dead as a corpse on Pennsylvania Ave, Ender had survived the Chaos Years unscathed.

When it was over, when Andrew Marshall led his army of coalition troops through what had once been the United States and swept the gangs away—taking out the trash so-to-speak—Ender had re-entered American society and went about its business. No memorial was erected. No monument to its success. No stories were told to the young.

So it was that the crowning achievement of Ender was swept under the rug like a family's shame.

Now, it was happening again. Instead of gangs and criminals, Ender now faced the might of Marshall's government, the American Union. While the people of Ender had yet to raise a weapon against them, one weapon and one alone, kept them at bay so the people could try and live normal lives.

That weapon was a man named Citadel.

Citadel stood on the corner of Main Street and Revell Avenue, his hands stuffed in his coat pocket, fingers fondling the cans of Coke he kept there. On his left, a Murphy's gas station squatted on the corner. In the same parking lot was a strip mall that included the Piggly Wiggly supermarket, the barbershop, and Dr. Posey's chiropractic clinic that now served as Ender's hospital.

On the right, Ender Lanes and its attached bar. That was where everything had changed for Ender. Where Leonard Strange had taken hostages. Where Agent Roger Hamilton and the AUSS had sparked a standoff that left people, mostly AUSS agents, dead. The parking lot of Ender Lanes was where Citadel had been confronted by the mysterious telepath, Exodus, and the memory of that fateful day in New York City was thrust back into his head like a bomb.

A nuclear bomb.

It was where Citadel unilaterally declared Ender off-limits to the American Union, a decision that had come in the heat of anger. He'd been violated. He'd relived his most agonizing memory as if it were happening right there in that moment. He'd retaliated by crushing the pavement with Roger "Rockhide" Hamilton's body until the poor SPI could barely move. The holes were still there. The rubble had been cleared away and bright yellow barriers now cordoned them off from the rest of the parking lot. The town didn't have the material to refill them, though. Street repair was something usually contracted out to a company in McAlester. Something the AU did caused that company to reject Ender's work order.

The AU had effectively cut Ender off. They'd shut down utilities—power and water. They'd arranged for regional services to stop serving Ender. The County Sheriff, if a new one had been elected following Reginald Strange's murder, was forbidden from patrolling in Ender.

Traffic still flowed. It was possible for individuals to go to McAlester, to buy supplies or go to the movies or whatever they wanted. Grocery shipments still arrived at the Piggly Wiggly. But that was the extent of contact the AU allowed. They could keep the other things quiet, but if they put up roadblocks and cut Ender off completely, word would spread, and someone would have to explain what was going on.

The buzz of generators hummed in the air now; all the businesses were powered by them. Piggly Wiggly had a few large, diesel-powered generators running the place. They kept the town livable, like the nearby river that provided the town's water. Most people preferred bottled drinking water, but the river provided water for cooking and washing, and boiled properly, it was perfectly safe.

Citadel preferred Coke. He reached into one of his deep pockets for his fifth can of the day.

He moved up the street, snapping open the can and taking a long pull of the lukewarm soda. With every step on his right leg, pain shot through his hip, quickly dulled by his enhanced endurance. It caused a slight limp that he'd used to good effect while hiding here, pretending he was a homeless beggar named Buck.

Citadel wasn't Buck anymore. Everyone in Ender knew that now. He no longer had to cover himself in the voluminous duster or hunch over to disguise his seven-foot-four height; he still wore the duster, but only because its pockets were large enough to carry three cans of Coke each.

It was three in the afternoon. The digital sign outside of Piggly Wiggly advertising Pork Chops and—*ugh*—Pepsi said it was ninety-four degrees. Citadel didn't feel it the way others did.

His enhancements regulated his body temperature in a way he didn't understand. He didn't sweat, he didn't overheat. He didn't get cold, either. No cool breeze could soothe his skin.

There was no discomfort, but there was also no comfort or relief from the weather like everyone else. It was what it was.

A shout from the direction of the bowling alley drew Citadel's attention. Ender Lanes was the only local entertainment establishment in Ender, and it was always busy lately. They had air conditioning.

The shout was followed by other, angry male voices—the bar attached to the bowling alley.

Citadel sighed and crushed the empty Coke can in his hand. He stepped off the sidewalk and onto the Ender Lanes parking lot, rubbing the mangled aluminum between his palms to roll it into a smooth, sharp dart. As he passed one of the holes in the parking lot, he flicked the little dart into it so that it buried itself in the dirt.

He stopped in front of the exterior door to the bar. The thick, frosted glass hid any view of the interior, but when Citadel heard what he needed to hear, he shook his head and stepped inside.

The Ender Lanes bar was a narrow strip in the shape of an L. To the right was the bar, backed by a giant mirrored shelf, stacked with booze. On the left were narrow booths meant for two people—one booth on the end could hold four. All-in-all, the place could hold probably a dozen people comfortably.

Bright sunshine swept across the dim bar before being blacked out as Citadel squeezed through the doorway. The strong breeze from the air conditioning ruffled Citadel's long hair, telling him that the some of it had come free from where he'd tied it back.

A group of three brawling men huddled together, arms locked about shoulders, free fists pounding into each other's faces and guts. They growled at each other, occasionally shouting obscenities.

"Rufus!" Someone shouted over the din. "Jimmy! Goddammit!" The shout repeated itself. Citadel traced the shouting to the bartender, a tough-looking woman in her forties. She was backed into the corner next to the door to the little kitchen that contained a fryer, but no grill.

Citadel closed the door behind him and planted his feet. The brawl continued in front of him, the combatants concentrated only on their foe. Citadel couldn't tell if it was a fist fight or a weird three-way wrestling match. He'd never seen anyone fight quite like that before—not that he could remember, anyway.

The bartender glanced at him, fear in her eyes. He tried a crooked smile and a shrug, but she didn't seem comforted.

"Boys," Citadel called calmly. His voice rose over their growls and shouts, but they didn't respond. One of them broke free and found a stool to use as a weapon. It was an escalation Citadel couldn't allow.

In two steps, he was within arm's reach of the man. As the man tried to swing the stool, Citadel grabbed it, stopping its motion cold. The man spun around and saw Citadel for the first time; the blood drained from his ragged face and he fell backward onto his ass. He let go of the stool in the process, leaving Citadel to hold it in the air.

"Jimmy!" The man cried out in warning, but the other two men were still engrossed in their own quarrel.

For a moment, Citadel considered using the stool himself. It would be easy to crush the wood and leather thing over the heads of these two nitwits. The stool would shatter and so would the heads—the temptation was frightening.

Instead, with his free hand, Citadel reached for the shoulder of the nearest man. At the touch, his target spun around and threw a punch. The blow hit Citadel in the sternum but he barely felt it. The man who hit him, though, howled in pain; he fell back, holding his right hand with his left.

Silence descended on the bar.

"Are we done?" Citadel asked. He loomed over all of them. The first man was on the floor still. The one who'd punched Citadel fell back into one of the booths, leaning on the table and cradling his hand. The one remaining on his feet gaped. His face was bloody, and he had a freshly forming black eye, but he didn't seem to mind in the moment.

They didn't answer him.

A wave of frustration forced Citadel to take a deep breath. It was all he could do not to stomp these idiots into the floor.

"What was this about?" Citadel asked, keeping his voice calm. He set the stool upright on the floor and sat. He leaned forward toward the others, hands on his thighs, and squeezed his fingers together hard enough that he could feel the pressure.

They didn't speak.

Citadel fought back the urge to scream. To keep himself from reacting poorly to the men's silence, Citadel looked at the bartender. "Are you okay?" he asked.

She nodded. "Yeah. These knuckleheads didn't do nothing to me."

Citadel smiled and turned his attention back to the men. He could do so now without wanting to kill them. He took another deep breath anyway. He forced his voice into a pleasantly moderate tone.

"Look, I don't care what you were fighting about. But if you need to fight about something, you take it outside. Look at this place." He waved an arm toward the floor, strewn with broken glass and stools.

The three men followed his gesture. The one on the floor pulled a shard of glass out from under his seat and tossed it aside.

"They call me the police chief here," Citadel told them. "I find that kind of funny, as I have no deputies and we don't have a jail in town, but I am responsible for keeping the peace. The Council wants me to make sure everyone is safe. That means safe from each other just as much as it means safe from the AU or whatever else. Do you understand?"

They nodded dumbly, glancing at each other.

"If this was some alcohol-induced argument or even a real disagreement that might be important, you guys have to put it aside. I know it's hard right now. We haven't seen it this hard in a while, but we have to stick together."

Citadel stood and moved his stool carefully to the end of the bar, putting it in what he guessed was its place.

"Like I said: I don't have a jail. No one is getting put in the drunk tank. But you three have a responsibility to this nice woman who didn't bother taking the baseball bat out from under the counter and beaning you all on the head with it." Citadel winked at the bartender, who looked at him, confused. She probably didn't have a baseball bat, but that wasn't the point he was trying to make. "I expect you to put your differences aside and clean this place up. If something is broken, it's your job to fix it. Sweep up the glass. And pay the lady, not just for the beers, but for the glasses you broke."

He waved for them to get started, then moved to the booth closest to the door and sat, pushing the table toward the other side to get a little more room for his large body.

Then he produced the last Coke can in his pocket and popped it open. He settled down to watch the cleanup. Eventually, after much glancing back and forth, Jimmy, Rufus, and the other man got to work.

Citadel was still sitting in the booth when the men were done. He stared into the mouth of his empty Coke can.

He'd wanted to kill those men. It scared him.

During the incident last winter, when he'd faced down the AUSS, he'd encountered someone from his past. A telepath called Exodus. Exodus had the ability to possess others, it seemed; he possessed the SPI called Rockhide. During their conversation, Exodus used his powers to tap into Citadel's hidden memories, the ones he'd forgotten since the explosion that destroyed New York City and should have killed him. Exodus had brought the memory of that moment to the surface, forcing Citadel to relive the pain. Even now, just thinking of it, a ghost of the pain returned.

But in the act, Exodus had done something else. The wall that held Citadel's other lost memories had cracked. Over the last months, bits and pieces of his past had returned. They were mostly incoherent flashes, mostly to do with his time with FORCE, which, admittedly, had been the majority of his life before the bomb.

But he remembered a time when he'd killed with abandon. He'd slaughtered hundreds, perhaps thousands, in the service of the United States of America, starting with that mission to Vietnam.

He'd been seventeen.

In his mind, the red of the Coke can bled onto his hand, covering it in dripping goo. Reflexively, that hand squeezed, obliterating the can. Bits of the ruined aluminum clattered to the table.

He'd been a teenager. He'd been a monster.

Now he was...what? Somewhere around seventy-years-old? His hands were much younger. His face might be a ruined mess of burn scars, but it wasn't old. His eyes, when he looked in the mirror, were sharp. His endurance enhancements, the same powers that had saved him from a nuclear bomb, kept him young. The only sign of his age was his long, dark gray hair, which he kept tied back now since he no longer had need to hide behind it. Maybe he'd get it cut like he had before—a sharp high-and-tight in the military style. But even the hair was healthy, despite every other strand grayed with age.

Even fifty-some years after the carnage in Vietnam, he was still a monster. Sure, he hid it well. He'd been nice to those men. But inwardly, he'd wanted to crush them into a paste that could be used to paint the walls of this place red.

What would happen when he couldn't contain his anger and frustration anymore? What if someone hit him like Rufus had, and Citadel snapped in response?

Someone would need a mop.

The bartender, Katie Newstead, put a sweating glass bottle of Coca-Cola on the table in front of him. Citadel raised an eyebrow at her.

"I figured you weren't much of a scotch guy," she said.

Citadel chuckled. "No. Not much alcohol can do for me and it all tastes like shit. No offense."

Katie laughed, too. "None taken, man. I appreciate what you did. You could have made things worse, but you didn't. There was a second where I wondered."

Citadel nodded. It was like she'd been in his mind. He dropped the aluminum scrap on the table and reached out for the bottle.

"Don't break it," Katie said, moving the glass bottle into his palm.

Citadel's hand wrapped around it. He barely felt the difference in temperature, though he knew the bottle was ice cold. "I'm careful," he said. Then with a glance toward the remains of his can, he added, "Most of the time."

Katie gathered the aluminum, careful not to cut her hands.

"What time is it?"

"Almost happy hour, five o'clock."

"Oh, well, I'll get out of your way. I doubt I'm a welcome guest when you should be having other customers. I have an appointment anyway. How much do I owe you?"

"Don't worry about it," Katie said.

Citadel nodded and stood. Standing next to Katie, he realized she was a tall woman. She came up to his chest. Not many women did.

"Thank you," he said.

He took the bottle with him.

July 6, 2018 - 5:30pm

Eric Sumner finished his run and flipped the off switch on his power. With the rush of warm air, his lungs forced him to take deep breaths to renew the supply of oxygen in his blood. Sweat popped up on his skin.

These simple things, air and cooling, were absent when he "ghosted," which was what he called his power. His ability to shift his atoms out of phase with the world around him allowed him to walk through walls or evade injury. But while he was in such a state, he could not take in air. If he stayed that way for too long, he'd suffocate and pass out, causing his body to revert to its normal state.

He also recently discovered, mostly through the cardiovascular exercises Citadel had him doing, that quite a few of his other bodily functions ceased to function in his ghost state. He couldn't sweat, for one. In the instant he returned to normal after exerting himself, his body ran incredibly hot.

It was both uncomfortable and potentially dangerous.

Still, once a week, he practiced running while ghosted. It was to measure his cardiovascular progress and measure any improvement in his ability to hold the ghost state for longer periods. The training might one day save his life.

Today, he'd been able to run the length of the field before his vision began to compress in a tunnel and white flickers of light burst in front of his eyes—the cues that Citadel insisted he take as a message to stop. It was a first for him and a good sign that the training was helping.

He turned to Citadel, a grin on his face, but the big SPI wasn't paying any attention to him. He sat on his chair under the RV's awning, facing the length of grass Eric had run, but his gaze was down in his lap at the empty glass Coke bottle he cradled in both hands.

Citadel's addiction to Coca-Cola amused Eric. As an endurance SPI, neither the sugar nor the caffeine would affect him. He just loved the taste. He always carried a six-pack in the voluminous pockets of his long coat, and the refrigerator in his RV was always stocked. Eric still hadn't discovered the source of the soda. He suspected Citadel stole it from Piggly Wiggly or the truck that came once a week, despite the so-called embargo on Ender.

"Are you okay?" Eric asked, setting himself on a pile of firewood across from Citadel. He was sweating profusely now. He took a swig from the bottle of water he'd placed nearby and wiped the sweat from his eyes with his fingers. Next week, he'd bring a towel as well.

"They used to make these in glass bottles," Citadel said, holding up the Coke bottle.

"Yeah," Eric said. "Still do."

"I'd forgotten."

Eric wasn't sure what shocked him more, that Citadel's amnesia was so bad that he'd forgotten such a simple thing, or that he was beginning to remember things he'd forgotten.

"It's coming back?" he asked.

Citadel shrugged. "Bits and pieces since Exodus..." He trailed off, obviously not wanting to relive what Exodus had done to him.

"What's it like? Not remembering things?" Eric asked. Citadel looked up at him, his eyes haunted.

"What was the first word you ever said? And who did you say it to? What was their reaction?"

"I don't know."

"*That's* what it feels like. Most people remember the general events in their lives after a certain age. I lived fifty years or so before 9/11, but I don't know what I did for the most part. There must have been important moments. People I knew, important conversations—it's like I never knew any of it. When something comes back, it's sort of...embarrassing, I guess? Like forgetting for a second what two plus two is. When you remember, you kick yourself for not knowing. It's also frustrating when I know I should remember something, but I don't."

Eric was silent for a while. He couldn't imagine what it must be like, even after hearing Citadel's description. He basically remembered everything he needed to. It was part of his intelligence enhancement. He didn't have perfect memory, but who did?

"I'm afraid," Citadel admitted, finally raising his head and straightening his back. "I'm afraid of what I'll remember next. How many people have I killed besides those in New York? What kind of a person was I?"

"I'm sure you did it for the right reasons," Eric offered.

Citadel chuffed. "When did you become the voice of positivity?"

"Kristin is constantly amazed at my faith in humanity, despite the fact that I can't handle crowds, or new people, or people in general, really." Eric shrugged.

"Kid," Citadel said, shaking his head, "Some things don't change. Like the government using SPIs to do their dirty work."

"You think there are more than Hamilton?"

"Most likely. But I don't understand how they can be loyal to the AU when all the government wants to do is kill them."

"Maybe some people hate themselves so much that they'll turn on their own people."

"Maybe."

"But not us, right?"

Citadel cocked an eyebrow at Eric. "Kid, are you trying to psychoanalyze me?"

Eric grinned. "I thought that, you know, with my social anxiety and horrible people skills, it might be the perfect job for me."

"Thinking about the future?"

Eric wasn't fooled by the attempt to change the subject, but he let it happen. "Well, I think college is out of the question. The only place I have a hope of getting an education without risk of losing my head is in the EUP."

Citadel's mouth twisted. They'd discussed the Estados Unidos del Pacificos, the EUP, before. Citadel didn't like them. The only excuse he gave was not trusting its leader, the SPI Mental Block. But Eric guessed there was something else.

No matter what it was, the EUP was out of the question for Eric. If Citadel wouldn't go, neither would Eric.

"There's not much here," Citadel said. "Not in the state Ender's in. The AU has your number. Do you think you'll be able to find a job out there?" Citadel waved his hand in the direction away from town. "The minute your name comes up on a background check, that's it."

"Yeah, I know. Mr. Turner wants me to become a great scientist. He says I'll be one of the greatest minds in the world one day."

"Your science teacher? Does he know about you?"

"I don't think so, but sometimes I wonder. He could be keeping my secret."

"A secret you don't need to keep anymore."

"Mom wants me to hold onto it until I'm out of school. Fewer problems that way. Leonard Strange might be gone, but that doesn't mean every hateful person went with him."

"Sounds like a good idea." Citadel considered for a moment. "Even as an adult, it's not easy. The Council forced me into a position of authority because of what I did, but that doesn't make everyone suddenly like me. If they aren't outright afraid of me, they're resentful. Of course, some of that might be because I'm directly responsible for the state Ender's in."

"Ender's free," Eric said, a bit more vehemently than he meant. "Having to work a little harder is a small price to pay for that."

"Tell that to Dr. Posey," Citadel said. He set the Coke bottle aside carefully and popped open his ever-present cooler to retrieve a cold can. "Tell that to anyone who had money before this all happened."

Eric thought about Kristin. His girlfriend was rich, or she would be when she turned eighteen. She was majority owner of the software company, DraftTech.

Could the AU somehow take that away from her because of what Citadel did?

Should Eric hate Citadel, too?

AUPrimeHistory: True Conspiracies

(Airdate: 6/24/2010)

INTRODUCTION

<Narrator over True Conspiracies intro graphic>

Tonight, on *True Conspiracies*, we cover the "dark age" of modern American society: The five-year period Americans now call, "The Chaos Years."

<Archive video of the walled city of Denver, 2003>

Between the collapse of the United States of America in the latter half of 2002 and the Marshall Coup in early 2007, there was a dark age of sorts across the center of the American continent. For nearly five years, lawlessness and violence ruled from Washington D.C. to Los Angeles and everywhere in between.

This episode of *True Conspiracies* will examine how chaos engulfed the continent and what happened when Andrew Marshall mobilized the fledgling American Union to save it.

<Commercial Break>

July 6, 2018 – 6:30 p.m.

Eric grinned at himself in the foggy mirror of the medicine cabinet. The blurry image of himself was nearly a perfect representation of him while ghosting. He wasn't using his power now; it was just the steamy result of his hot bath.

He had a new respect for how people lived before modern plumbing. It took ten four-quart pots of boiling water to fill the tub enough to bathe in. You had to make sure the first nine were boiling hot when you dumped them in, because the water cooled as the tenth was heating up. But if you made that tenth one nice and hot, it warmed the water to the perfect temperature.

The worst part was carrying the water from the stove in the kitchen to the bathroom. Normally, Eric would have ghosted through the wall, but water, especially hot water, didn't ghost. The molecules of the water were already vibrating rapidly. So, Eric had to go around the long way, the large, two-handled pot held safely away from his body.

By the time he could sink into the tub, his arms were exhausted. The heat helped then, but he needed to wash quickly, or the water would get cold, fast.

There was also the problem of rinsing off. He had to have a separate pot of water for that. This one was cool by the time he finished. By then, he was glad to have the cool water pour over his body.

All the work it took to take a bath kept Eric from doing it more than once or twice a week. Tonight was special, because he was going to dinner at Kristin's house. Gillian and Kristin's grandfather, Henry, would be there—a real family affair. It was something they did every week since the incident with Leonard Strange. At first it was about making sure the Matthews were coping with the loss of Kristin's grandmother. Then, it just became a relaxing time among friends.

He reached into the medicine cabinet, his hand ghosting through the glass and metal into the chamber beyond. He felt around until he found the plastic tube of toothpaste, then drew it out. This was a new trick he was beginning to master. When he first manifested his powers, he wasn't able to ghost anything he wasn't wearing. Then, with Citadel's help, he'd realized that if he could ghost his clothing, he could do it to other things as well. The knowledge saved his life against Leonard Strange, but the practical uses of the trick were something he'd worked on for months to get right every time. This was one of the first times he'd pulled out the toothpaste tube without rattling the cabinet door.

"Are you done yet?" Gillian asked from the other side of the bathroom door.

"Just a minute," Eric said.

"You didn't drain the water, did you?"

Eric looked back at the milky bath water. He shuddered to think of his mother using it. "Are you sure?" he asked.

"Give me the pot."

Eric jammed his toothbrush into his mouth and lifted the pot from the floor and ghosted it through the door. Once he felt Gillian take it, he let it go. She would be going into the kitchen to fill her own bucket and boil it since the water came from the stream about fifty yards behind their house. They were lucky to have a water source so close. But that water had to be boiled, whether it was being used for washing or—*ick*—drinking.

He hurried to finish brushing his teeth and shaving. That

was new, too. He had to shave almost every other day now. He considered growing a goatee like Jason, but he didn't think he had enough coverage for even a partial beard. He dressed and opened the bathroom door.

"I could go get you more water," he offered Gillian as he went into the kitchen.

"Don't worry about it," she said with a grin. "We had to do this when you were a baby. It's fine."

"Really?"

"Yeah, the power and water pressure stopped for almost a year. No one was maintaining the facilities. I guess someone got sick of it and went out to restart the power station and get the water flowing again. Both came back on within a week of each other just before the Marshall Coup."

Eric stared at his mother. This was the first time he'd heard anything about the Chaos Years from his mother. She was always tight-lipped about it, not wanting to relive that time of her life.

"Okay, but if you contract botulism or something, don't blame me."

Gillian put the pot on the boil.

"No one is going to contract...botulism?"

"Or *something*."

Gillian shook her head with a smile. She pulled him to her and kissed his forehead. Then she straightened his still-damp, black hair. He wore it long, letting it fall almost to his shoulders.

"I talked to your teacher today," she said.

"Which one?"

"Ben Turner."

"His name is Ben?"

"*Mr.* Turner has a lot of faith in you."

"He doesn't realize my brain is enhanced."

"You're a smart kid, kiddo," Gillian said, punching him softly on the arm. "Enhancements or not, that's as much a part of who you are as your nose."

"Both inherited from my father."

Gillian laughed loud, putting her hand to her mouth.

"Oh, kiddo," she said, shaking her head, "your dad was not that smart."

Eric was glad she could speak about Steven Sumner and laugh at the same time. She'd spent the last decade since his suicide nursing a bottle to try and escape the pain. Now, she was finally healing. He hadn't needed to do a sweep for alcohol in weeks. She'd fallen off the wagon a couple times since she decided to stop drinking, but it had been a long time since the last time. Eric was proud of her.

Gillian took the boiling water off the stove and carried it to the bathroom, closing the door behind her. Eric stood by the door, wanting to continue their conversation.

"I ran all the way across the field while ghosting today," Eric said. "It's the first time I've done that without passing out."

There was a pause and the ripple of water.

"You don't think he's pushing you too hard?" Gillian finally asked.

"I don't think he's pushing me hard enough. He makes me stop the moment I break a sweat sometimes."

"What you can do is dangerous, kiddo."

"I know that. God, I know that." He thought back on all the times in the last year that he thought he was going to die. He'd nearly shaken himself apart in the boys' bathroom at school. He'd nearly trapped himself without breath while ghosting in the ruins of the old toolshed he used to practice in. Then, there was the time he'd caused his entire body to harden so he could knock the wind out of Leonard Strange. That in itself could have killed him instantly. He still didn't know how it hadn't. "I'm learning a lot, though. I'm starting to know my limits and what I can do to push past them, like the running. I'm getting better every day."

Gillian didn't reply to that. Eric wondered what she was thinking. He knew she didn't approve of Citadel, but he hoped she understood that he needed someone to help him who understood what it was like to be a SPI.

When she didn't say anything after several minutes, Eric sighed and went to his room to finish getting dressed.

"And then, she says, 'That's not the way it works, Henry.'"

Henry Matthews laughed from his belly. The old, dark-skinned man had tears in his eyes as he told the story about his wife, Charlotte, who died at the hands of Eric's nemesis, Leonard Strange.

The four of them sat at the large dining table in the Matthews' house: Eric, Gillian, Kristin, and Henry. The house was larger than the Sumner house, but felt homey. Charlotte had decorated it with a grandmother's eye for nostalgia. There were photos of Kristin everywhere, scattered among images of Charlotte and Henry—always in the photos together—and even a pair that must be Kristin's parents. Kristin's dad had been a nerdy-looking guy with bright orange hair and a mass of freckles that made half his face nearly brown. Next to him was one of the most beautiful women Eric had ever seen, a dark goddess who should have been a model. Instead, she'd married the geek who eventually became one of the most powerful men in an industry.

Kyle Byrne had made something great for himself. He'd written several architecture applications and bundled them under the name DraftTech. His company had grown with the computer revolution in the construction industry. His software was used by architects, drafters, engineers, and even construction companies all through the building process. Now, DraftTech was the biggest computer-aided drafting company in the world.

And it all belonged to Kristin. Or it would, when she finally turned eighteen next year.

Eric glanced at Kristin, who sat across from him at the table. She was picking at her food. Eric couldn't remember if she'd actually taken a bite yet. His brow furrowed. He thought she'd been getting better. Her grandmother's death hit her hard, especially as it happened right in front of her. He knew she had nightmares. She didn't like to talk about them, but Eric made her. She'd relived that moment often in the months following Leonard's capture and execution.

But in the last month or two, since the end of their sophomore year of school, she'd brightened. She became more of her old self, teasing him and brightening his day whenever he was around her.

He wondered if Henry's story disturbed her. Was she thinking of that moment the gun had gone off? When a bullet she'd thought would be meant for her had instead taken Charlotte from the world?

Eric wanted to cry thinking about it. Instead, he reached across the table and held his hand out to her.

"Kris?" he said, "Are you okay?"

She nodded but didn't take his hand as he expected she would. He slowly withdrew it.

"Yeah," Henry said. "That." He laid his utensils down and wiped his hand with his cloth napkin.

"Henry?" Gillian asked. "What's going on?"

Kristin looked at Henry. Eric thought she looked afraid.

What the hell was going on?

"Well," Henry said self-consciously, "we've been talking about this for a while now." He chuckled to himself. "Sometimes screaming is a better word for it, eh, Kristin?"

"Pops..." Kristin said.

"Yeah, well." Henry was still wiping his hands on his napkin, wringing them together with the napkin in between. "Things haven't been good for DraftTech. I suspect the AU is having a go at us because of the company's ties to Ender. We've lost some contracts. Strangely, none of our government contracts, but some others—our more lucrative ones—have vanished with no good explanation."

"Is it that bad?" Gillian asked.

"Not yet," Henry admitted. "There is a small window to fix it, but it'll close soon." He seemed to realize what he was doing with his napkin and let go, folding it carefully before placing it on the table. "I was CEO of the company before my stroke last year. I worked remotely. It was a good situation. I could keep my hands on my granddaughter's future and still raise her someplace where she wouldn't get a big head." He grinned at Kristin.

"Are you still CEO?" Eric asked, guessing where this was going.

"Technically. I made a rather quick recovery. The stroke wasn't debilitating. The board hadn't gotten around to replacing me permanently. There's an interim, of course, but I think I can take my job back."

"But you can't do it remotely anymore," Gillian said. "Not with the power situation like it is, and not having internet."

"There's also the matter of the company's connection to Ender," Eric said. "If you continue to work from here, the AU will only push harder against DraftTech, right?"

Eric looked at Kristin. She avoided his eyes. That's when it hit him.

"You're leaving," he said. The words came out in a hot breath as his lungs tightened around them.

Henry nodded. "We have no choice, son."

Eric stood. He didn't bother pushing his chair back. He ghosted through the table instead. The glasses on the table hummed for a moment as Eric's frequency adjusted.

"Eric!" Gillian scolded.

Ignoring her, Eric turned and walked back through his chair and through the nearest outside wall of the house. He found himself in the backyard, an expanse of perfectly trimmed grass. A dozen yards to his right was a wooden deck. The yard was bordered by tall, narrow evergreen trees instead of a fence. Their trunks were set close together and their needle-laden branches provided all the privacy the Matthews would need.

Eric ambled toward them, not meaning to leave the yard, but just pacing. Kristin was leaving.

She hadn't told him. She hadn't warned him.

Henry said they'd been talking about it for a while. Why hadn't she given him some sort of sign that this was coming?

Why hadn't he seen this coming?

He'd thought that part of his life was over—the part where people left him. Gillian had come back from her near-endless drunken stupors. Eric had made friends. And even when the possibility that he would leave Ender came, his friend Jason had stuck by him. He wouldn't be alone. He still had Jason, but Kristin was *different*. They'd had their problems, but Eric had thought them over. He'd expected happily-ever-after.

How stupid was that?

What had he expected? That they'd grow up together? Get married? Have happy little SPI children?

He was sixteen-goddamn-years-old.

This was inevitable. It would *always* be inevitable. He'd known that once. It was a fact of life for him. Somehow, he'd forgotten.

"Eric?"

Kristin's voice seemed to come from far away. He ignored it. He knew he was being petty and childish. He didn't care.

He didn't feel more than a breath of sensation through his shirt when she reached out to take his arm. At that touch, he activated his power. Her arm, meant to lock around his affectionately as she'd done hundreds of times before, passed through him. She stumbled, surprised she had nothing to grip.

He didn't look at her.

"What the hell, Sumner?" she said. "You gonna be a baby about this?"

He didn't answer her. So, what if he was?

"I fought this," she said, coming around to look him in the face. "I don't give a shit about this damn company. The AU can bury it for all I care. I wanted to stay. I wanted to give up DraftTech to stay. But I'm seventeen-goddamn-years-old. I don't get a say."

Tears poured from her eyes as she screamed into his face. He watched her, finally understanding that she was hurting as much as he was.

"Neither of us get a say, Eric. We're just kids."

"We could run," Eric finally said, his voice quiet, simple. Kristin stared at him, her anger turning to shock. "We could go west. The EUP. Anywhere but here."

Her answer was equally quiet. "You are the most selfish son of a—" She took a deep breath. "You want me to leave my grandfather. You want to leave your mother? Both of them alone. Do you realize what that would do to your mother? Did you even think about that before you said such a stupid thing?"

No, he hadn't, but right now, he didn't want to. He wanted to find a solution. He saw a puzzle, and if he put the pieces together just right, everything would work out. But nothing worked. Any solution would leave someone heartbroken.

He just didn't want it to be him.

She was right. They were just kids.

July 7, 2018 – 10:20 a.m.

Citadel watched from his lawn chair as Eric's blue and silver bike emerged from the trees at the edge of the clearing. He didn't bother using the path anymore. As soon as his bike was clear, his misty form solidified and became clear.

The bike skidded to a halt next to the RV and Eric dismounted, sweating from the exertion of pedaling through the trees.

"You need to watch yourself," Citadel said. "You're going to overheat. Last time I was by the sign, it said eighty-five, and that was at seven this morning."

"I'm good," Eric said, clipping his words short. "But give me a Coke, okay?" The kid reached out his hand.

Citadel scowled. He opened his cooler and retrieved a bottled water. He tossed it to Eric gently. Eric caught it and returned Citadel's scowl.

"Drink it," Citadel said. Eric complied. At least he still knew how to take an order from his mentor. "Sit. Tell me what's going on."

"What do you mean?" Eric asked. He sat on the pile of firewood, hiding his expression behind the water bottle as he tipped it up.

"You're being self-destructive. Exerting yourself needlessly. Speaking to me in a tone I've never heard from you. Something's obviously going on."

"I'm fine."

Citadel waited. He snapped open a new can of Coke and sipped, his eyes never leaving Eric's face.

"Kristin's leaving town. Going to Chicago."

That would do it. That girl was the boy's lifeline to humanity. Without her, the kid was practically a robot, all mind, no heart. Citadel hoped some of her had rubbed off on him permanently, that she had taught him something about relating to people.

"Is this going to break your focus? Can you train with this in your head?"

"If you give me something else to think about. Why do you think I'm here and not moping around my room?"

Citadel bristled at the boy's tone but considered. Then he stood and walked over to the stack of tires that lay under a bright blue tarp. They were the wheels for the RV. Citadel had removed them years ago to protect them from the elements. The RV stood on blocks, a mix of concrete and wood to keep the vehicle off its axles and level. It had been that way for nearly ten years now.

There was something Citadel was hoping to work on this week regarding Eric's ability.

"This ought to keep that mind busy." He tapped the blue tarp. "I want you to work on bringing things with you when you ghost. Take the top wheel from this stack without moving the tarp."

Eric raised an eyebrow. "You realize I probably can't lift one of those tires by myself, even if the tarp wasn't there."

Citadel nodded. "There will always be seemingly impossible tasks that you have to figure out. Your mind is more powerful than your muscles. I'm confident you'll figure it out." He crossed his arms over his chest. "That's what you wanted, right? A puzzle?"

Citadel figured it out already, with what he knew of Eric's powers. The test wasn't really about lifting the tire. He didn't have to lift the tire. He could push it or pry it off or whatever.

But he had to affect one tire—just the top one. That was the trick.

Eric made his first attempt. He passed his hands through the tarp and gripped the top tire in both hands. The tire was big. His arms were held out wide to hold the whole thing. He heaved.

The tire shifted a little, but he couldn't lift it. The leverage was bad; he couldn't bring all his strength to bear on it with how wide his arms were.

He let go and stepped away. He glanced at Citadel, who tried an encouraging smile.

Then, the bright mind engaged. Citadel could see it in the kid's eyes. A flicker of glee kindled there, and Citadel let one corner of his mouth twist up.

Eric reached into the tarp again, careful not to disturb it. He felt the rubber tire beneath it. He set his right hand on top of the tire, then, moving his left hand down and around, he ghosted it through the second tire in the stack so he could get a grip on both sides. He stood like that for a moment, then the excitement in his eyes vanished, replaced by frustration.

"Tell me what's going on," Citadel said. But he already knew. This was the whole point.

"I can't get a grip on the top tire while ghosting through the next one down. The materials are the same."

Eric pulled away from the stack and stared at it.

"Can't do it?" Citadel asked.

"All the tires are the same material," Eric explained. "Can't phase through one while holding onto the other."

"Then you'll have to find another way to grip it."

Eric nodded and tried again. This time, he took an awkward hold of the tire along its circumference again. Citadel saw Eric's power buzz through the tarp. The tarp fell through the tire all the way to the ground. The tire Eric held stayed in place. He sighed.

"Can you—" Before Eric finished, Citadel yanked the tarp out from within the tire stack. When Eric let go and the tires returned to normal, Citadel threw the tarp across them again. He tried to restrain his mirth but failed. Eric murdered him with a glare.

"You're a smart kid, you'll get it," Citadel reassured him.

"You planned this, didn't you?" Eric asked.

"I'm not as smart as you, Ghost. I was hoping it would be like this, but I didn't know." He shrugged. "Sometimes a hunch is all you need. And sometimes a puzzle is what *you* need."

Eric clenched his fist at his side. Citadel's suppressed laughter turned to concern as Eric's hand came into ultra-sharp focus, the sign that he had turned it diamond hard. That was an ability he could only summon when angry.

"Eric," Citadel prompted.

The kid nodded and unclenched his hand while taking slow, deep breaths. The hand softened. Eric shook it to urge the blood to flow. Then, Eric's face split into a sudden grin. The flicker of excitement returned to his eyes.

"It's heavier," the boy said as he looked at his hand.

"What?" Citadel asked.

"My hand. When I make it dense, the hand doesn't compress. It stays the same size, and it's heavier."

Citadel shook his head, not understanding. The kid was going to start babbling science stuff. Again.

"Weight's just the pull of gravity on the mass of an object. Part of mass is density. Make something denser, and it's heavier—like lead or gold."

He went back to the tire stack, his smile widening.

"Make it less dense…" Eric's arm passed through the tarp and the rubber all the way to his shoulder. His stance forced him to crouch almost to his knees, his shoulder under the top tire. He closed his eyes and Citadel would have sworn the kid was meditating. His face was blank. For a moment, the tarp buzzed, the metal wheel hummed.

Then all was silent.

The tarp shifted for just an instant, then fell through the tire again. But instead of falling all the way through, it settled on the next wheel in the stack. Eric lifted with his legs and the wheel, steel and rubber, rose with him, misty and blurred by Eric's power.

Eric rose to his full height, holding the wheel at shoulder level as if it were a tin pizza pan.

Citadel's jaw dropped when Eric turned to him, eyes flashing, teeth showing through his ecstatic grin.

"Okay," Citadel croaked. "Not what I was expecting. You can put it down now."

Eric grinned and tilted the tire until it slipped off his hand. As soon as his hand lost contact, the wheel snapped into focus. It fell heavily onto the ground, bouncing on its air-filled rubber tire just as it would if it was lifted and dropped normally.

Citadel trapped it with one big hand to keep it from rolling away.

"What was that?" he asked.

Eric laughed uncontrollably. He jumped up and down, pumping his fists. His dour mood of a few minutes ago vanished entirely.

"That was super strength!" Eric said, a grin spreading his lips to their limit. "My God, Citadel! That was awesome!"

"But..."

"It's a bunch of science stuff that'll bore you to death," Eric said. "I basically made the tire lighter. So much lighter, I just lifted it off the other tires. Then I phased it through the tarp without worrying about the others."

"So, you basically broke the laws of physics," Citadel said. "As I understand them, at least."

Eric's mouth snapped closed. "It was my hand," he said, his voice suddenly soft and wondering. "It didn't change size, so I must have added atoms to it. Then I took atoms away from the tire." His face tightened in concentration.

"Where did they go?" Citadel asked. He gripped the tire in one hand and hefted it up to the top of the stack again. This was something brand new. At least with the ghosting ability, there was some semblance of real-world explanation. But this was next-level stuff. What Eric had done was physically impossible. What else could the boy do?

Eric shook his head, unable to answer.

"Take the rest of the day off," Citadel said.

"But this is incredible! I need to work on this."

"No. You need to take a step back. Think about what you did and how you did it. When you've figured out the science behind it, come back and explain it to me. Until you can do that, you're done."

"Done?"

"No more training. We both need to figure out what's going on. I'm relying on you to do the bigger part of the thinking for me. Find out what you did and how you did it."

"But…"

"Take this seriously, Eric!" Citadel snapped, fear getting the better of him. "This is the biggest thing since a sixteen-year-old kid broke his friend's back in a wrestling match." The words just came out—a stream of consciousness that cracked open a memory Citadel once forgot. He reeled back and stumbled to his chair. Only long practice kept him from falling into it and breaking the thing.

George Hudson had been his friend, maybe his best friend. But that hadn't stopped a young Citadel from shattering his back with an ease that frightened him even now. George hadn't died, but, as far as Citadel knew, he hadn't ever walked again. That moment was the moment the world changed. The boy Citadel had been had become the world's first SPI: part lab rat, part government black-ops agent.

Nothing had been the same since.

Eric stared at him, something that could have been fear or worry on his face.

"Get out of here," Citadel croaked. Eric didn't question. He gathered up his bike and walked it out to the road.

Alec Gunn

AUPrimeMovies — In Theaters Now!

DON'T STOP ME NOW

Don't Stop Me Now is an examination of Queen, their music, and their extraordinary lead singer, Freddie Mercury. Freddie defied stereotypes and shattered convention to become one of the most beloved entertainers on the planet, only for him to vanish mysteriously in 1991. The film traces the meteoric rise of the band and reveals, for the first time, Mercury's secret connection to the USA terrorist group, FORCE.

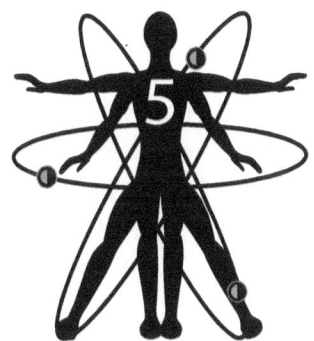

July 12, 2018 – 10:45 p.m.

L illy Tate opened the door to the motel office. The place
was warm, a remnant of the day that lingered long past
dark. The room was well lit, but the lights were fitful. Lilly heard
the buzz of a generator motor coming from the open back door.
It was true: There was no electricity anywhere in this podunk
town.

The bell tied above the door jangled when it opened. If she
wanted to be stealthy, that would have ruined everything. But
this time, she decided on a direct approach.

A middle-aged man stood from his chair and stifled a yawn.

"Coming in late and nowhere else to go?" he asked her.

"Just passing through," Lilly said as she did at every fleabag
motel between Miami and this hole. "I need one night."

The clerk cocked his head. *Kevin Duncan from Oklahoma,
right?* A small man with slicked-back dark hair said in Kevin's
memory as Lilly watched, like a small-town show on the television. The man held out his hand and the memory faded.

"Where are your parents?" Kevin said. "They'll need to sign
in."

"I'm old enough," Lilly said. She produced an ID from her
wallet. It was a Southeast Region card. He glanced at it and his
eyebrows rose.

Where'd you get that? The young boy asked in an impressed whisper. A young Kevin looked down at the flimsy card in his hand, a fake ID with Mississippi in huge letters at the top.

"Sorry about that," Kevin said through the old memory. "You look—"

"Young for my age, I know. I'll be sixty and they'll still card me."

Kevin chuckled. She was twenty-two, but people still thought she was a child. It was genetics, nothing to do with her enhancements. Her mother had been small, too. When Lilly was twelve, she'd been at the store with her mother when they were both asked where their parents were. They'd had a good laugh over that one.

Well? Young Kevin said to the bartender, who looked doubtfully at the fake Mississippi ID.

Lilly scowled as the memory continued to replay itself in Kevin's mind. He wasn't sure the out-of-state ID was real. It was.

Even when she was being honest, people couldn't trust her. Why did it always come down to this?

"I have cash," she said. She pulled out her wallet and drew out the faded gold and rose-colored slips of paper just a bit from her wallet. It was meant to be proof that she could pay, not a move to give the man money.

Kevin nodded, satisfied. He hadn't tricked the bartender that night more than twenty years ago. Perhaps he thought it was good turn-about to play along with her. He turned and picked up a key from the narrow strip of hooks.

"Well, welcome to Ender, Miss Tate. I wish we were better prepared for visitors, but we've had power problems for a few weeks now."

As he spoke, he picked room eleven out of twelve keys. A good distance from the office.

Perfect.

As soon as he placed the key on the counter, Lilly's hand reached to grab it. Simultaneously, she used her power.

She reached into Kevin Duncan's mind and isolated the

last few minutes since the bell on the door rang. She held them together in a mental grip, like hands cupped around a pile of marbles. She took the key and her ID and walked out the door. When she was gone, she shut away those minutes behind a wall Kevin would never notice.

He would never remember the young woman who had come to visit late in the night. He might even forget about key number eleven. In her experience, it worked like that. He'd just assume the key was there and, unless he consciously went looking for it, he might actually "see" it on the hook with the others.

"This place is a rathole," Lilly said to Trench when she stepped into Room Eleven alongside her client. "If I have to try and sleep through trains coming in the middle of the night, I'm gonna kill you."

"The trains don't run through town much anymore," the lanky man said. They'd been together for three months now. He didn't know that she knew his real name. He'd introduced himself as Robert Hernandez when they first met in Miami. It was a convincing enough name. He looked Cuban or Mexican, with short, salted black hair, full lips, and a large beak of a nose.

After they'd left Miami, Lilly stopped thinking of him as "Robert." She knew it was a fake name. But she didn't dare call him by his real name and reveal to the man how much she knew about him; the memories that loomed largest in his head were too terrible to linger on. She'd actively blocked his mind out after the first day of their partnership.

So, she called him Trench on account of the long, heavy, black leather coat he wore over his jeans and button-down shirt.

The room was dark. The lights from the street filtering through the windows were normally enough to see by, but this town was damnably dark without power. The moon was bright tonight, though, and it was tolerable once her eyes adjusted.

"It's no worse than any of the other holes we've been in since Miami, right?" Trench said after a brief inspection of the facilities. The toilet was cream-colored, and the shower didn't have too many rust rings in it.

"Yeah," Lilly said. Trench didn't remember any of those other places. "But this is going to be a longer stay than normal."

"Hopefully long term," Trench agreed. "But there aren't very many other options unless you want to move in with some family." Lilly didn't want to think how he imagined that would work.

He removed his long leather coat and hung it on a hanger in the closet. He ran his hands over his hair. His hand came away greasy, and he scowled. He disappeared into the bathroom.

"You really think you'll find what you need here?" Lilly asked.

A particularly powerful memory filtered weakly through her blocks. A toddler with black hair and an average-looking woman he thought of as beautiful.

"I think you will, too," he told her, his voice echoing from the tiled walls. "This is the one place in the AU I can guarantee you won't be killed for who you are." The bathtub knob squeaked and pipes banged inside the walls. "Shit!" The noise suddenly stopped mid-crash. A soft thrum pressed against Lilly's eardrum, making her yawn. Trench was using his power to cancel out the noise the empty pipes made. The unnaturalness of it sent a shiver across Lilly's skin.

"I don't know if I trust a guarantee from you," Lilly said after the pressure eased and it was still quiet. Did the motel manager hear the noise? Would he investigate if he did? No matter. She'd make him forget again.

Trench emerged from the bathroom. His smile seemed forced, a twisting of his lips that made his prominent Hispanic nose shift a little to the right.

"You've done an amazing job, Recall."

"Don't call me that," Lilly said. "I'm not one of your slaves."

"Only because you helped me cross the country without being seen."

"You were seen plenty, but no one will remember you."

"Same thing," Trench said as he dropped onto one of the

two beds, the closest to the door. "Things could have gone another way. If anyone else was sent to you, you'd have already been headline news for a day before dropping off the face of the Earth."

Lilly shuddered. He was right. Her survival came from luck. Luck that her powers were what they were, and luck that Trench needed those powers to get what he wanted. He'd offered her a choice. He'd laid it all out for her. He'd told her truths he said were never told to anyone until the day of their execution when a SPI was given the final choice of their lives.

"So, what's next?" Lilly asked. "Now that we're here, do you need me to follow you around town so no one remembers you?"

"I need one more pass from you. Get rid of today. I won't need you after that. When I step out that door tomorrow, I'll know where I am and what I need to do. After that, you can do whatever you want. Make some friends. Move into the place. Our deal is done. We've gotten each other where we needed to go."

"Yeah, I guess we did," Lilly said hesitantly. She really hadn't expected to be set free. It was jarring, even though she guessed that tomorrow he still wouldn't let her go. After all, he wouldn't remember telling her she could go.

She sat on the other bed. She stared at her hands for a while, wondering what was next for her. She turned to look when Trench rolled over on his bed. He looked at her gravely, but not in a way that frightened her.

"Thank you, Recall. I mean that. I couldn't have done this without you, kiddo."

She nodded at him, doubts still swirling in her mind.

"Sure, no problem." Then, as he closed his eyes and set himself to sleep, she gathered the last twenty-four hours of his life in her hands. Doing so butted right up against the limit of her ability, maybe even beyond, but she'd been doing this for months and the practice had helped her grow stronger. She'd pass out when she was done, but she was ready for bed anyway. She walled off the hours and felt herself spiral dizzily toward unconsciousness.

July 13, 2018 – 10:15 a.m.

The bowling pins leaped into the air, struck by a ball thrown with strength fueled by frustration. After the violent collision, the seven and ten pins remained standing, a large gap between them. The machinery moved to collect the pins and return Eric's ball. His hand hovered over the ball return.

"Did you think I wouldn't come in here after you?" A voice said over the noise of crashing pins and jangling video games.

Eric shut his eyes for a moment and took a deep breath. He turned to find Kristin standing next to the bench that wrapped around this lane's computer screen.

"I didn't even consider it," Eric lied.

"That why you're in the farthest lane from…?" she jabbed a thumb toward the far side of the room, where she'd lost her grandmother and Eric had defeated the speedster, Leonard Strange.

"It was the one available," Eric said.

Kristin scanned the other eleven lanes. Only two of them were in use.

"Why'd you make me come here?" she asked.

"I didn't make you do anything," Eric said. "I thought we said what needed to be said."

"Damn it, Eric," she said, then she rushed to him, wrapping

her arms around him. He hugged her back tentatively. He took a hard, deep breath and pressed his lips together, trying to hold back tears.

He hadn't thought about it when he decided to come here to blow off some of the anger that was festering in him the last week, since he discovered Kristin was leaving. But he knew she was leaving today. Maybe part of him was trying to hide, to prevent this very thing from happening.

Her hands raked through his long hair as she held onto him.

"I'm sorry," she said into his ear. "I'll come back. I promise."

"Don't promise that," he rasped. "Don't give me hope." Hope could be taken away. It would be taken away.

"I love you, Eric," she said.

She kissed him.

He couldn't speak. Then she was gone. He stood staring at the door long after she left. He hadn't said he loved her too. He should have said it.

Why didn't he say it?

He turned back to the lane. He snatched his ball up from the return. It was light in his hand. Power buzzed down his arm. He took his approach and threw the ball hard.

When it left his hand, it returned to its normal weight. It skipped across the polished wood of the lane and struck the ten pin. The pin broke into three pieces as the ball jumped and struck the back of the lane. A piece of the pin the size of his fist hit the fat part of the seven pin, knocking it over, too.

"Damn, that's impressive," a new voice said over his shoulder. Eric whirled to see a small girl sitting on the edge of the bench in the lane next to his.

Her black hair was cut in a sleek bob, curling slightly to catch at her jawline. She had a vague Asian look about her, though her skin was pale. She looked about Eric's age, but Eric had never seen her at school.

"I've never seen a bowling pin actually shatter."

Eric glared. He was angry at himself, though. He'd used his power in public. He shouldn't have done that. Maybe he had no control. He didn't remember consciously making the ball light, like he did with the RV wheel. He was angry, emotional. By all rights, the ball should have become super dense and heavy. He'd thought the key to control was his emotional state. He was wrong. He just didn't understand how his power worked, apparently.

He shook his head and returned to the lane. The pins were reset, a new ten pin replacing the old, broken one.

"That was a bad breakup, wasn't it?" The girl asked. "I mean, it didn't look like it, but I could tell by your faces."

"It's none of your business," Eric said. His ball came back through the return. Eric picked it up and spun it in his hands. It didn't seem damaged, though there was a mark on it where it struck the pin. He wiped at the mark with the heel of his hand.

He took his approach and bowled the ball again, this time carefully holding onto the off switch on his power. The ball slid down the lane and sheered the left side of the pins away, leaving most of them standing.

When he turned around, the girl was standing in front of him, blocking his way back to the ball return. She was short, maybe five feet tall, but her confidence and poise made her seem taller.

"It hurts, I know," she said, her voice raspy like she was trying to whisper, but she still put too much of her voice into it to be heard over the sounds of the bowling alley. "What if I told you I can take that pain away? Make you forget all about that girl."

Eric didn't like where this was going.

"I'm not looking for a replacement," he said. He pushed her aside, moving again to the ball return. "God, who the hell are you that you'd jump in not five seconds after she leaves?"

The girl smiled and shook her head.

"That's not what I mean," she said. "I mean I can literally make you forget her."

Eric felt a buzz in his head. The feeling was familiar. Exodus had tried the same thing to him that day in January. The girl was a telepath and she was trying to get into his head. It sent a chill down his spine even as he grabbed hold of his power quickly to cancel it out. Telepathy was a type of vibration Eric could cancel out by vibrating the atoms in his brain opposite, like noise canceling headphones.

Eric turned slowly to the girl. She wore a look of surprise, bordering on shock. *What did it feel like for her?* He wondered. Did it hurt when the telepathic wave vanished like that?

"If you touch her in here," Eric said, tapping his head, "I will kill you."

"Um, nevermind," the girl replied. She started backing away from him. Eric felt the buzz in his head again, this time it was a fierce press against the inside of his skull.

With a thought, he canceled that out, too.

She turned and fled, heading for the door at a fast walk, careful not to draw attention to herself by running. Eric made to go after her, but something in the air prevented him from moving in her direction. She was telekinetic, too, then. When she was out the door, the barrier vanished, but by then, it was too late to try and chase her.

Trench sat on a stool in the arcade, watching the interaction between Recall and Eric Sumner. Bells rattled in the pinball machines. Voices called out from video games ("FIGHT!"). Explosions and laser beams blasted around him. But Trench paid them all no heed.

Eric was in pain. He was angry. The other girl, the one he'd said goodbye to just a few moments before Recall made her move, did serious damage. It was in his voice, which Trench heard clearly, even from here.

Trench had watched Recall do this several times as he'd followed her in Miami. It was part public service, part grift. She had something of a moral code. She wanted to help people, but her fear of being discovered compromised that.

It went like this: Recall went to a public place and looked for people with problems. She then offered to help, either to restore a lost memory or hide an unwanted one. Only when she got permission did she finish the job. Then she'd liberate what money she could from the mark, causing them to forget the entire encounter. She justified the con by telling herself that she helped the mark.

It was how she made her living. How she survived as a SPI and how they must have crossed the country together unnoticed, though Trench didn't remember any of that, thanks to her.

Recall stumbled backward after something Eric said.

She fled. Only when Recall was out the door did Eric step forward, then seemed to think better of it. He wore a thoughtful look as he looked around the room. His eyes paused on Trench, and for just an instant, Trench thought he might have been seen, but there was no recognition and Eric continued his scan of the room.

What powers was Eric gifted with? Was he telepathic? That would be impossible. Trench had witnessed the super-powered throw with which he'd broken the bowling pin. It was obvious he had strength enhancements. But his resistance to Recall's powers spoke of telepathic abilities, too. Never before had a physical SPI had mental gifts as well. Eric should be a third generation SPI, wielding abilities few others before him experienced. But third generation SPIs, at least those Trench knew about, didn't possess either first- or second-generation powers. The powers of each generation had always been exclusive before. Had that changed with Eric?

Trench left his questions unanswered and rose from his chair, moving toward the door. Eric sat on the bench in his lane, staring blankly at the digital scoreboard of his game.

Trench paused, suddenly hesitant.

For a moment, Steven Sumner considered going to his son. His boy needed him. But there was a right time for that, and this wasn't it. Steven was still a danger to the boy.

He took a slip of paper out of his coat pocket and examined the three names on it. He knew two of them, but the third was unfamiliar. All three were keys to Steven being able to see his family again.

Trench sighed and took a short pencil off the high table next to him, meant to hold drinks for those playing games. He slashed the lead through the middle name on the list.

Alec Gunn

AUPrimeHistory: True Conspiracies

(Airdate: 6/24/2010)

SLIDE INTO DARKNESS

<Archive video: New York City, 1995>

The date: *September 11, 2001.*

We all know the horrific events of that day and how they resulted in the eventual founding of the American Union. But what about the time between? What happened to drive American society into utter anarchy?

<Slideshow: Slide into darkness>

As the ash cloud over New York City began to settle, millions were suddenly homeless and desperate. The once-wealthy New York City elite had either been obliterated or rendered destitute. Having been conditioned to seek restitution from the government, victims of the SPI attack on New York began to seek redress in the already overloaded federal court system. Suits and demands for trillions of dollars, on top of a suddenly crippled American economy, began to take its toll on a systemic level.

<Archive video: Bankers in chaos>

As the money ran out, and international lenders refused to prop up America with no hope of payback, federal and state governments sunk into chaos. Essential services: police, fire, and mail, went unfunded. Government paychecks bounced. Most who served in the most important functions simply quit. Police officers and fire-fighters abandoned their duties.

<Archive photo: Abandoned military truck>

On a federal level, law enforcement agencies collapsed. Soldiers, sailors, and airmen walked away from their posts, sometimes leaving their equipment on the side of the road. State-run National Guard troops went home. For the first time in the history of the United States of America, the nation was wholly unguarded. Only the two oceans and friendly neighbors protected the country from instant invasion.

<Slideshow: Anarchy in the USA>

In September 2002, a year after the disaster in New York, American news agencies declared the United States of America "effectively an anarchist state." They urged Americans to arm and protect themselves by any means necessary.

<Commercial Break>

July 13, 2018 – 5:00 p.m.

Along Main Street, a block away from the bowling alley, a large house stood with open doors. Once meant to be the abode of a rich coal trader, now it served as the home of Ender's richest resident.

Samuel Blue Hawk could trace his ancestors to a time before Europeans came to the shores of Massachusetts. The Choctaw tribe of Native Americans was one of the most successful tribes in the nation when it came to maintaining their own sovereignty and culture. Despite hundreds of years of government land-grabs, the Choctaw retained a sense of who they were. The largest Choctaw Nation finally settled on reservation land in Oklahoma. When the AU took control, nothing really changed for the Choctaw.

They were Americans, always had been.

Samuel's family had made a fortune in reservation coal from McAlester in the early twentieth century. His father sold it all to some big corporation in the 70s, setting the Blue Hawks up for life.

Samuel himself had served on Ender's town council since 1988. He was the longest serving member and the one people turned to when a consensus couldn't be found. He was trusted, respected, and even loved. He was one of the last good people in the world, it was said.

During the Chaos Years, it was Samuel who came up with the plan that would keep Ender neutral and safe. Under Samuel's leadership, Ender continued to function almost normally for those five years.

When Citadel unilaterally took Ender back into the Chaos Years by his expulsion of the AUSS, it was Samuel who'd had the idea to make Citadel the town police chief.

Samuel reasoned that the damage was done. If Citadel stood by his decision, then there was nothing any of them could do to stop him. They had to make the best of it. They'd asked Citadel into Samuel's house and spoke with him. Citadel stood firmly behind his decision, so Samuel held him accountable. If Ender was to give up the support of the AU, they needed someone who could protect them and keep peace.

Samuel re-instituted the rules he'd set up during the Chaos Years. *Everyone* is responsible for the town. At the same time, anyone who wanted to could leave.

When the town gathered in the Piggly Wiggly parking lot, all 4,687 residents, Samuel explained the situation. When he declared anyone could leave, only three people walked away. Two were a couple who'd moved to Ender after the Chaos Years, and the third was the town's Catholic priest, a white-haired old man who declared his retirement and desire to move to Florida.

The town had to be re-organized. Ender didn't really have a centralized government system. Sure, it had a council and a City Manager, but those were basically work from home jobs. There wasn't a town hall, or any place people could go for government business.

Samuel opened his house for that purpose. During business hours, his front door was propped open, welcoming any to come. The Council met there every day.

With the opening of a town hall, the Council needed a clerk. Someone who could record Council meeting notes and act as gatekeeper for anyone who sought a hearing with the Council.

The first volunteer was Gillian Sumner.

Gillian dove into the task of city clerk as if she had nothing else to live for. She arrived early in the morning and left only after everyone but Samuel himself was gone. Occasionally, Samuel had to kick her out.

So, it was at 5:00 p.m. that Gillian was still behind her computer when Ben Turner, the newest and youngest member of the Council, passed by her desk. He stopped in front of it and stared at her.

"You know, we're just going to shut off the generator at five from now on."

"Don't you dare," Gillian said. "I'll lose everything I'm working on." As if in defense of just that, she saved her spreadsheet with a quick keystroke.

"See? Now you can pack up and go home. Or better yet, come have a drink with me."

"I don't drink," Gillian said too quickly.

Ben nodded as if he understood. Gillian looked up at his face. He looked a little like Steven, her dead husband. His skin was a soft brown. His nose was prominent on his face, but not with the Hispanic/Southern European hook that Steven had. He might have Middle Eastern ancestors, or maybe South Asian. It was hard to judge.

"Sorry," Gillian said. "Didn't mean to snap. Recovering alcoholic. I don't want to be anywhere near that place."

Ben grinned at her. He set his fingertips on her desk, hesitating, then he nodded and moved to the door. Gillian watched him go, speculatively. That last bit of hesitation. Had he wanted to say something more? He *had* asked her to drinks. Was he interested in her?

Gillian's speculation was rudely interrupted as the door opened before Ben could get there. Ben froze as Citadel's gigantic form filled the door frame. The smaller man suddenly had the same posture as a frightened deer. Quite a few people had that type of reaction around Citadel.

Citadel set his hand companionably on Ben's shoulder and nodded his head.

"Councilman Turner," he greeted with a friendly smile. He moved out of the door and let Ben move past. "Have a good night."

Gillian caught Ben's face as he turned back to return Citadel's greeting with a silent nod. The look there was one of confusion and relief. It lasted for merely an instant, then Ben turned and let the door close behind him as he left.

Ben Turner descended the front steps of Samuel's house with a troubled expression on his face.

He hadn't sensed Citadel coming. That was new. Citadel had no resistance to telepathy. In fact, it was quite the opposite. If anything, Citadel had always been more susceptible. It was how Project Brooklyn planned to control him if he ever got out of hand.

The only explanation was that Ben lost focus. Gillian. It had to be her. He sighed and hoped that wasn't going to be a problem.

How much did the old man remember now? For an instant, Ben thought he saw a flash of recognition in Citadel's eyes, but a quick scan told him that must have been a misperception. Citadel had no idea who "Ben Turner" was. Using that name might not have been the best idea, but when it was chosen, Ben wasn't aware that Citadel was here. It was a good thing that Citadel's memory loss was as complete as it was. Ben's efforts would be for nothing if he were discovered.

What would Gillian think if she knew? She already held little regard for Citadel. Would she hold any more for him if she knew who he really was? Ben had been part of all of it. He held just as much blame for what had happened as Citadel, maybe more so.

She was an impressive woman. Ben knew a little of what she'd endured over the last decade. She had her weakness, sure, but she fought and took back her life, all for her son. That was what being a mother was about, wasn't it?

His attraction to her might be a little dangerous, given the task before him. He had to be cautious.

It was that caution that drew his attention back to the foyer of the Samuel's house. Citadel and Gillian were arguing over Eric. Something had happened. But despite his power, he didn't have super-hearing and his ability to read surface thoughts was limited. His abilities leaned more toward emotions and deeper subconscious thoughts.

Ben began walking away, moving to the corner of Main and Revell. He'd get caught up later. He could get Gillian to confide in him. It wouldn't be hard, though he was reluctant to use his power on her in that way.

He stood on the corner and turned in a slow circle, scanning around. The sun was at mid-height in the western sky. There were still almost four hours of daylight left. Still, the people of Ender chose more often lately to spend days indoors. Figures moved behind the glass front of the Piggly Wiggly. A single car was parked at the pumps of the Murphy's gas station. Ender Lanes would hold the rest of them. The older folks would be staying home. Very few people wandered the street.

This was the best place to get a feel for the town. It put him roughly at the center of the population. On one side, in the direction of the Town Hall, were the larger homes—the middle class and the rich. The schools lay in that direction and the calm green lots and family homes of the neighborhood surrounded them.

On the other side of Revell, past the train tracks and the broken-down motel, lay the older subdivisions, once the home of workers who commuted either to McAlester or to the mines and quarries in the hills to the west. The park was out there on Saints Drive, and it was where Gillian and Eric lived.

Ben stood on that corner of Main and Revell and closed his eyes. He tried to do this at least once a week. It might look strange for anyone walking by to see a grown man standing on a street corner with his eyes closed, but it was a risk he took to learn what he could about what was going on in town.

Waves of emotion filled the air above the town. It was like this everywhere, like radio waves. If they were radio waves, Ben was the antenna. He could reach out with his senses and tune himself into the miasma of emotion. The spectrum ranged from the calm, pulsing signals of worry, sadness, and companionship to the sharp, beating spikes of pain, fear, and passion.

One such spike rammed into him suddenly from not far away. He heard the swift slap of sneakers on pavement.

His eyes snapped open. He watched as Ken Hunter sped by across the street, fleeing, it looked like, from the rundown motel across the train tracks. Ben focused his senses and felt terror and desperation. Something bad had happened. Something unheard of in this little town.

Ben sighed and sent Ken an urge to turn his steps toward the town hall. He'd find Citadel there. It was all Ben could do without revealing himself.

If only he could do more.

Citadel let Councilman Turner go. He wasn't here for the Council. This was the only place he could be sure to find Gillian without running into Eric at the same time. Not to mention she'd banned him from the house. She didn't like him, and he didn't have the courage to ask her why.

"What do you want?" She asked. "Council's gone. Samuel's locked himself in his bedroom for the evening."

"Good. We need to talk about Eric." He reached into his duster pocket to retrieve one of the fresh cans of Coke he'd gotten from the Piggly Wiggly on the way over here. He held it out to Gillian. She paused for a moment, then shook her head.

"You know my thoughts about what you're doing to Eric."

"What I'm..." He growled. He took a deep breath and calmed himself. "I'm not going to rehash this argument. I've suspended his training for the time being."

Gillian's brows rose. "Really?"

"Not for the reasons you wanted," Citadel said. He cracked open the Coke and took a long pull on it, mostly to delay. When he was done, he looked back at her. "He discovered a new aspect of his power and it scares me."

"What. Did. You. Do?" Gillian took a step toward him with

every word. Her face was darkening in the dim light of the electric chandelier above them. She wasn't afraid of him like everyone else in Ender. She was barely tall enough to reach his sternum, but she was fierce about protecting her son. It was this that let her push away her alcoholism and become something for the town, even if it was only a government clerk.

Citadel stood his ground and let her approach. He let her put her fists on her hips and glare at him. He kept his face calm. He should have been angry at her for blaming him when she didn't even know what happened, but he just looked at her and let her be furious for a moment.

He was pretty proud of himself.

"I didn't do anything," he said when he saw a slight relaxing of her shoulders. "This is a natural progression in his powers. This type of thing happens to new SPIs. They find new ways to control what they can do, and their abilities become more versatile. In Eric's case, with the nature of his powers, the results are just a bit more...extreme."

"'Extreme' how?"

"He used his powers to simulate enhanced strength. Somehow, he is able to affect the things he touches to make them lighter. Then when he lets go, they return to their normal weight."

"That's not possible," Gillian said.

"Why do you think it scares me? I told him there will be no more training until he can come to me with a scientific explanation for what he's done."

"He'll do it. He'll tell you some bullshit about something that sounds scientific just to get back to training. Then, you'll keep pushing him into things that could kill him."

"Or he'll continue training on his own, which would be even more dangerous."

Gillian spun around in frustration. "Goddamn it, Citadel!" She said. "You are going to end up killing my son!"

"Stop this!" Citadel thundered. He took an involuntary step toward her, his hands flexing into trembling claws.

She froze like a rabbit faced with the sudden appearance of

a wolf. Her eyes widened. The terror in her face froze him in turn. He dropped his hands to his sides and slowed his breathing. For a moment, he even closed his eyes. Damn his pride. He thought he'd overcome the anger, but no. He was just holding it down until it broke free.

When he opened his eyes again, Gillian's fear had lessened, but her voice was hot with anger. "What was that?" She asked. "Were you going to kill me to shut me up?"

Citadel struggled to control his own fury, which still seethed inside him. "I am not responsible—"

The front door slammed open. Citadel's frayed nerves spun him around, ready to fight. But it was just Ken Hunter, the former compatriot of Leonard Strange, who was doing his own penance, acting as runner and courier for the town council. The job was a necessity without working cell or phone service. Even radios were problematic between poor signals and batteries being at a premium.

Ken was breathing heavily, his curly brown hair and dark skin both wet with sweat.

"There you are," he said before he'd entirely taken in the situation. When he saw Citadel's stance and face, he shook himself, squaring his shoulders. It was an instinctive reaction to danger. The kid had a fight or flight response that skewed toward fight in almost every situation, it seemed, even while facing a powerful SPI.

"What is it?" Citadel asked, hoping the growl he heard in his own voice was a product of his own imagination. Probably not.

"You need to come to the motel," Ken said. "Lacey Duncan found her husband...dead."

July 13, 2018 – 5:15 p.m.

Why aren't we running?" Ken Hunter asked, even though he had to jog to keep up with Citadel's long strides.

"He's dead, right?" Citadel asked.

Ken nodded.

"He's not getting any deader, kid."

They crossed at the corner of Revell and Main. Main was nearly empty, though there were half-a-dozen cars in the Piggly Wiggly parking lot and a similar number in the Ender Lanes lot. Someone was pumping gas at Murphy's, but they paid no attention to Citadel and Ken as they passed.

"I like running, though," Ken said. "I should have been a football star. I'd have been the star running back at school if Leonard hadn't been faster."

Citadel let the kid talk. It was nervous energy. The kid was facing his first glimpse of mortality. By his age, Citadel had already seen more than his share of death, but he understood a little of what the kid must be feeling.

"Georgetown sent a scout to look at me a few months ago. They even gave me a tour of the campus, but I guess they didn't pick me up. I never heard back from them about the scholarship. Can you imagine, though? Washington D.C. There's so much history there—it would have been a blast."

"Sorry about that," Citadel said. It was probably his fault if the AU got their mitts into Georgetown's selection process.

But Ken shook his head. "Eh, I might be hot shit here in Ender, but I probably don't match up with the city kids."

Citadel frowned. Who would have guessed a kid like Ken Hunter would have self-esteem issues?

They crossed the train tracks and approached the motel just on the other side. There were no cars in the lot. All the rooms appeared empty, which was no surprise. Who'd want to spend even one night in Ender with no reliable power or running water? Maybe Kevin Duncan killed himself.

God, if people started offing themselves...

They entered the motel office. Ken wretched almost instantly. Citadel wrinkled his nose. Any gag reflex he had was countered by his enhancements. But smell was smell, and this was foul; the room must be warm. Kevin couldn't have died that long ago, could he? His wife would have reported it sooner.

Lacey was nowhere to be seen. That was understandable.

Flies were jumping into the air behind the counter. Citadel followed them to find the body.

Kevin hadn't killed himself. There was no weapon, but there was plenty of blood, mostly around his head. He lay on his side, curled into a fetal position. His arms were raised to his head, as if he'd been held at gunpoint.

Citadel crouched near the body and turned the head to see the other side. There was no wound, neither gunshot nor stab wound. As far as he could tell, all the blood that pooled around the head came from his natural orifices. Trails of blood congealed around his nose and ears. There was even some at the corner of his mouth.

Citadel pressed his fingers around Kevin's neck. Memories of Vietnam came back to him, the feel of Ho Chi Min's limp body in his arms after his neck had been broken. There is a feel to a broken neck, a lack of support for the head. It took a lot of power to kill someone by breaking their neck, like Citadel had done to Ho Chi Min. If Kevin's neck was broken, then the murderer was almost definitely a SPI.

But it wasn't. Kevin's neck was intact.

Citadel crouched over the body, his arms resting on his knees.

"Well?" Ken croaked. Citadel looked up to see the boy peering over the counter. He still looked green.

"I'm not a cop," Citadel said, shaking his head. "I'm not a doctor. To tell you the truth, I have no idea what I'm looking at."

"Dr. Posey?" Ken asked. He must not want to open his mouth too much for fear of what might come out.

"Yeah," Citadel said with resignation. "Go get the doctor. Maybe he can make sense of this."

Ken left at a run.

The Void watched Citadel bend over the body and do nothing. That's how it had always been. Void's memory was full of times Citadel did nothing to prevent the loss of life. In fact, Citadel's job had been, so many times, to take life. To destroy the most precious thing in the universe.

He'd done it to Void. He'd destroyed her just like Ho Chi Min, Saddam Hussein, Gregor Valinski. Each was a fledgling dictator, stopped before they could become a threat to the United States. Citadel had been the weapon the USA pointed at anyone who might have caused "difficulties" for America or its allies. A one-man Normandy invasion force.

Sure, there were others over the years. Wall—a SPI whose Endurance nearly matched Citadel's, Tempo—the first speedster, Alacrity—a gymnast with the rare enhancement combination of Strength and Agility. All had served under Citadel. All had died under his command. Then there were the last ones: Rumble, Jitterbug, Mental Block. The only ones normal people actually knew about.

All dead, just like every other SPI that served with Citadel.

Only Void remained, but that wasn't because of anything

Citadel did. In fact, Void remained *despite* Citadel. He'd done his best to kill her, but she lived, wrapped around a core of the same force meant to destroy her. She lived, if only as a dark stain on the motel office ceiling, hidden among the shadows there, looking down at the man she desperately wanted to kill.

Citadel stood suddenly, his head achingly near her, oblivious to her presence. He had always been so stupid. So careless. He didn't see the threat that hovered inches from his fragile brain.

His face was scarred, a waxy layer that covered him like a mask. He'd been handsome once, but the bomb had done what no human or SPI could ever do. It had revealed the ugliness underneath. The vile man that only Void could see.

Tendrils of shadow extended from Void, swirling a hair's breadth away from Citadel's long gray hair. Before she could act, he moved away, heading for the door to wait for the doctor.

In truth, Void still didn't know what she was going to do with Citadel. She didn't want to just kill him. She wanted him to suffer. She wanted him to know why he was dying. As it was, he knew nothing. He didn't even remember her. She would have to remedy that before she took any decisive action.

Maybe the coming confrontation with the one who had destroyed the motel owner's brain would reveal those secrets to him. She would have to watch and see.

From the shadows, of course.

Dr. Posey arrived after another hour. Citadel leaned against the office doorframe, facing the parking lot. The smell was beginning to waft outside. It was almost unbearable inside. Citadel had checked the generator at the back of the building. It was out of gas. There would be no air conditioning.

The doctor drove up in an SUV. He backed it into a parking spot near the motel office.

Ken was in the passenger seat. As Ken exited the car, Citadel saw that he carried a box of lawn bags under his arm.

"Doctor," Citadel said as Posey came around. "I hope you haven't eaten lunch yet."

"This isn't CSI, Citadel," Posey said. "Shut your trap."

"No, really," Citadel started as Posey swept by him. As soon as the doctor opened the door, he gagged. He turned to one side of the door and emptied his stomach on the concrete step. "You might want a mask," Citadel said.

Posey was one of those Councilmen who blamed Citadel for screwing up his life. Before Citadel, Posey had been the town's chiropractor. He'd worked maybe four days a week for a few hours a day. Now, his clinic was a mini hospital and he was forced to work, or at least be on-call, seven days a week.

Now, he'd been promoted to coroner.

"Keep the damned door open," Posey said in a weak voice. Ken pressed his sleeve to his face as he followed Posey into the office.

Posey tugged on a pair of latex gloves, breathing shallowly through his mouth before circling around the counter to where Kevin Duncan lay. He only looked at the body for a few moments before gesturing to Ken.

"Get him bagged up. Citadel can help you carry him to the car." He stood and stripped the gloves off. He hadn't even touched the body.

"Well?" Citadel asked.

"Well, what?" Posey countered. "He's dead. That's all I can say for now. I'm a chiropractor, not a forensic specialist. I'm just the only idiot who got a medical doctorate in this damn town."

Citadel followed him out of the office into the fresh air. Once outside, Posey took a deep breath.

"I'll take him back to the clinic, get him cleaned up and see what I can see. I probably won't find anything that will help you, though, so don't get your hopes up. I'm not even a damned general practitioner." He said the last in an angry mutter.

Citadel returned to the office as Posey dropped into the driver's seat of the SUV. Ken did his best to wrap Kevin in the black plastic lawn bags. He tugged one over the man's head and the other over his feet. They overlapped in the middle, where

Ken wrapped a third bag around the body like a belt, which he cinched tight.

Citadel lifted the body off the floor himself. Ken was spattered with blood. He hadn't been able to keep it off himself while wrapping the head. He nodded gratefully to Citadel and led the way out the door. Posey unlocked the back hatch from inside and Ken swung it open for Citadel to place the body within. The entire back half of the SUV was covered in plastic from floor to ceiling.

"I'll send Ken out to get you if I find anything," Posey said. "But don't get your hopes up."

Citadel shook his head at the retreating vehicle. The doctor was going to be useless. He imagined the chiropractor giving the body a spinal adjustment and declaring that was all he could do.

When they were gone, Citadel scanned the gloomy office again, his tongue wiping across his teeth. What kind of murder was this? The body dead with no apparent wounds and nothing at all out of place in the—

Citadel's eyes locked on the key hooks.

Room Eleven's key was missing.

EUP News Archive

(Posted 3/24/2009)

FORCE LEGACY STOPS AU INVASION

The heroes of FORCE Legacy, the west coast protectors lead by former US operative Mental Block, have stopped an invasion by the aggressively advancing American Union Army who staged a "watch post" on the Nevada border. Having acquired intelligence that indicated an imminent attack by the AU base, FORCE Legacy moved to destroy facilities and equipment there.

The team consisted of Legacy members, Flight, Fight, and Freeway, in addition to Mental Block, who led the defensive strike. The team returned to Los Angeles with no casualties.

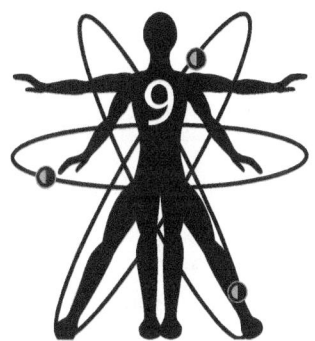

July 14, 2018 – 6:00 a.m.

The sun was beginning to lighten the sky when someone pounded on the door to the RV. Citadel's eyes snapped open. He was alert immediately, thanks to his enhanced endurance. That he was in bed at all at this hour was a bit strange; he usually only needed a few hours a night and couldn't quite remember when he'd gone to bed last night. The loss of that short-term memory scared him a little. Was his old brain injury causing him to forget current memories as well? Could Alzheimer's be a thing for him? What else was he forgetting?

The knocking on the door repeated itself, followed by a young voice.

"Are you in there, Citadel? It's Ken."

"Council meeting already?" He answered in a voice he was sure would carry through the plastic and metal walls of his home.

"They were already yelling at each other when I left."

Citadel sighed and reached for a pair of pants hanging on a hook near his bed. As he pulled them over the warped, burn-scarred skin of his legs, he remembered that day in the river outside of Hanoi. What was it called again? That, he couldn't remember. But he did remember picking mine shrapnel from his rapidly healing legs while submerged in the water. He ran a finger over a spot that would have had a short scar, if not for the greater damage done by the bomb almost seventeen years ago. Or maybe it healed without a scar.

Another thing he couldn't remember.

"Are you coming?" Ken called.

"Yeah, hold your horses." The RV rocked a little as Citadel rose from the bed. He was sure it sat sturdy and stable on its blocks, but the suspension still moved under his weight when he moved about.

He opened the door while he was putting his shirt on. He nearly skipped putting the large coat over it, but decided he'd rather be a little late than a little thirsty. He ducked back into the RV and filled the pockets with cold cans from the RV's ice box. He'd need to get more ice soon, or he'd have to deal with warm soda at home.

That was unacceptable.

Ken was hopping on the balls of his feet as Citadel emerged again from the RV. Citadel himself had unlimited energy, thanks to his enhancements, but he could never be in constant motion like Ken was. He shook his head and jerked it toward the path through the trees.

"Well," he teased, "what are you waiting for?"

Ken took off at a run. Citadel kept pace at an easy stride beside him.

"Why didn't you do something about this SPI?" Phil Bledsoe asked Citadel the second he passed through the door of the council chamber. "Council Chamber" may have been a little ostentatious of a name for what used to be Samuel's dining room. A long dining table served as the council table, and the council sat around it as if for Sunday dinner.

Phil sat across from Samuel, who, despite being the eldest and most respected member of the council, sat to the right of the head. The town manager, a too-corporate term for mayor, sat at the head of the table. Jacob Lane, a stocky, balding man in his forties was more comfortable crunching numbers than leading a city.

"SPI?" Citadel, standing at the foot of the table, looked from councilor to councilor. There were six in total. Samuel Blue Hawk, the aging heart of the council, was a full-blooded Choctaw Indian. His large nose and red-brown skin were surrounded by a thick mane of silver-white hair. Next to him sat Nakni Chunkash-Anli. If you didn't know Chunky's name, you might mistake him for another old, white politician, but what Chunky lacked in Choctaw blood, he made up in native fervor. He considered himself one of the last true natives to this land, though the Choctaw were pushed here from their true native lands to the east nearly two hundred years ago. Finally, next to Phil sat Dr. Posey, who looked uncharacteristically tired. He must have had a late night last night.

"There were no wounds on the body," Posey informs him. "What was inside the head was nothing more than a clumpy soup."

"And I was afraid I'd have trouble eating today," Chunky said.

"Could a telepath do that?" Samuel asked Citadel, who shrugged. He might have known at one point, but he couldn't remember anything like that about telepaths.

"No," Councilman Turner said. The entire council turned to look at him. Citadel started. He almost hadn't noticed the inconspicuous man. The man was so innocuous as to be almost invisible. He sat next to Dr. Posey, normally silent and contemplative.

"It's scientifically implausible," Turner continued. "Telekinetics might be able to crush something, but they have to be able to see it. Force is force. You can't reach beyond a barrier to affect something on the other side. The skull is a barrier. Unless the skull was also crushed, I can't see how any SPI we know about could affect a person's brain like that without also turning the skull to powder."

"I think I'm going to skip lunch," Chunky said, his face tinging green. "I wish I'd skipped breakfast."

"Have there been any newcomers in town?" Phil asked. "I mean, it can't be someone from Ender, right? It was Kevin at the motel. This stinks of a traveler."

"Leonard Strange was one of us," Jacob said. "That didn't stop him from killing his own father and a dozen AUSS agents. And he hid among us for years, using his powers to excel at sports. We can't rule anyone out."

"We need this SPI found," Samuel said.

Citadel shifted his feet. "I will not start lining people up to be tested," he said. "Even if we had the resources for that." He glanced at Dr. Posey, who shook his head in confirmation. "I won't start a wave of suspicion in this town over something that might not even be a SPI. It could have been some type of weapon. I can imagine a few contraptions off the top of my head that might be able to do this, and I'm not that imaginative. This could be a sadistic killer who wants to blame his murders on SPIs."

"You're reaching, Citadel," Dr. Posey said. "Are you trying to protect someone?"

"No," Citadel lied without hesitation. But if he were telling the truth, he'd have to admit he probably was. The only person he could think of that might be capable of this was Eric, or someone like him. "I'll find out what happened, and I'll take care of it. This is what I promised when I first came in here six months ago."

"You better," Phil said. Samuel glared at him; the first angry look Citadel had seen on the old Indian's face since he met him. Phil ignored it. "If this is because of you, we will find a way to eject you from our town."

Citadel mulled for a moment. Maybe that wouldn't be such a bad thing, to move on. But then he shook his head. "I follow through on my promises," he said, his voice deep and hard. "If this turns out to be my fault somehow, I'll submit to whatever you deem necessary, just like I did in January."

He wasn't concerned about that. He was already thinking about the consequences of this murder.

If this was something new, or if Eric had done something terrible, then things were about to get very complicated.

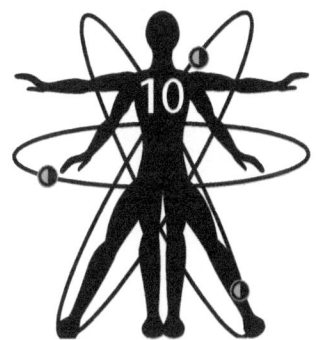

July 14, 2018 – 7:00 a.m.

G ood, I caught you before you left," Gillian said. Eric paused tying his running shoe and looked up from where he sat at the edge of his bed. Gillian stood in his doorway, dressed for work in black slacks and a loose pink blouse with tiny blue flowers on it.

"What's going on?" he asked.

Gillian glanced at Eric's shoes. "You weren't thinking of going to Citadel's to train, were you?"

"I was—"

"He told me what happened. That he cancelled your training until you could figure it out."

Eric took a breath. That was one thing he hadn't expected, Citadel and his mother working together to stop him.

"Well?" Gillian asked.

"What?" Eric replied.

"Did you figure it out?"

For a moment, Eric thought about lying. But he knew that's what they expected. He'd have to have a good, demonstrable explanation before he could make them believe it.

And he didn't have it yet.

He shook his head. "Not yet."

Gillian's eyebrows revealed her surprise, obvious enough

for even Eric to catch it. "Citadel is busy now anyway. There's been an incident."

"What kind of incident?" Eric asked.

Gillian was reluctant to answer, but she did. "Kevin Duncan was murdered last night. Citadel is leading the investigation."

"Then I can help," Eric offered excitedly. He cinched the knot he was tying and stood. "You know I'd be good at something like this."

Gillian stepped forward and put a hand on his shoulder. She smiled, but her head shook. "I know you would, but it's too dangerous. I won't have you out there hunting murderers."

"I did fine with Leonard Strange and he was a SPI."

Gillian's face darkened. She didn't like it when he spoke about what happened last winter.

"That was self-defense and you know it," Gillian argued. Her voice wasn't kind anymore. It was the voice of a mother trying to lay down the law. She wasn't good at it. "You're going to stay here. I have to go to work. No Citadel. No training. No running about hunting killers. Promise?"

Eric reluctantly nodded.

Satisfied, Gillian turned and vanished from the bedroom doorway. In just a few seconds, Eric heard the front door close behind her. He paced around his room in a circle, ghosting through his bed when it was in the way. He kept hearing one of the last things Kristin said to him.

Neither of us get a say, Eric. We're just kids.

Just kids.

No. If Eric was anything, he wasn't a kid. He was a SPI. He'd seen death happen in a split second. He'd fought for his life and the life of the girl he loved. That made him more than just a kid. Maybe he wasn't an adult, but he wasn't "just a kid."

His chest tightened as he paced. He circled around toward his bed again. When his leg swung forward to ghost through it, it stopped. The metal frame of the bed clanged. Eric didn't feel the impact. He stepped away quickly. The metal frame of the bed was dented where his leg hit it.

He was getting emotional. That was dangerous. Anger

flipped his power, making his limbs dense. Even with all the training and practice, even discovering a new ability, he still couldn't control his own body sometimes.

He closed his eyes and took deep breaths. If he left the power as it was, his limbs would freeze up. His blood wouldn't flow. He didn't know what kind of damage he was doing to his body.

He let his anger calm, and his legs and chest tingled. He relaxed.

Maybe he couldn't join Citadel in his investigation, but he wasn't going to stay here and stew in his feelings. In moments, he was on his bike and pushing the pedals with frustrated vigor as he banked out of the cul-de-sac and through the twisting streets. He passed by Saints Drive Park, where he'd discovered his power for the first time when he clocked Leonard Strange and broke his jaw.

He put emotion into his riding—something he'd always done. He used to race to school in the morning to let out his frustrations. The exercise now didn't seem as helpful, though. He was conditioned by his running practice. The bike didn't seem strenuous as it once did, but still, he had a lot of frustration to release now.

Kristin was gone. She promised to come back, but with the state of Ender, hearing from her again wasn't something he expected. Part of him didn't want to hear from her again. It would be better if he believed she was dead. He swallowed a lump in his throat at the thought.

Another part of him, probably the part that enjoyed pain, wanted nothing more than to hear her voice again, to see her chocolate chip freckles and her smile.

Yes, that was worse.

He pushed even harder on the pedals. Sweat broke out on his brow.

He found himself nearing downtown. He passed the motel, where the late Kevin Duncan had ruled over an oft-empty building. It looked the same as always, dark and empty. But the usual buzz of Duncan's generator was absent. He passed the Piggly Wiggly and Town Hall, trying not to think of what important things were going on in there.

As he approached the school, empty for summer vacation, he slowed, letting the bike coast. It wasn't the school he was heading for, but his destination was nearby. This was the "rich" neighborhood of Ender. The houses here weren't run down shacks, built in the fifties or sixties. The oldest of these homes was built maybe thirty years ago, when a second boom nearly doubled the size of the little town as job growth in McAlester led to good jobs and people willing to commute forty-five minutes to work them.

About ten years after 9/11, a family moved here from what had once been California. Zak and Ashley Williams raised their son Jason in this small, seemingly idyllic town, but they weren't here for Ender's wholesome image. They were spies from the Estados Unidos del Pacificos, the upstart nation most people called the EUP.

Washington, Oregon, California, and Baja separated from the American Union almost immediately after the new nation was formed. The EUP was supposedly ruled by SPIs, but Jason said that wasn't true. They had their own version of FORCE, led by the telepath Mental Block, who was the lone survivor of FORCE from the 9/11 incident. But FORCE 1, as they were called, was sanctioned and controlled by a normal EUP government out of Los Angeles, not its rulers. It was this team of SPIs that kept the AU government from swarming the separatists and retaking the west coast.

Jason was Eric's best—and now only—friend. His family was quirky, but he was a solid guy who always stood by Eric, no matter what was happening.

Eric needed that right now.

"Dude," Jason said. It was pretty much all he had to say.

Eric sat on a wooden desk chair, legs crossed. He picked at his shoelaces with one hand. Jason sat on the edge of his bed. Eric's friend was tall and rail thin. His chiseled face was framed by long blond hair that fell off his head in flat sheets. He had the fledgling strands of a goatee falling similarly from his chin. His wardrobe consisted exclusively of rock and roll t-shirts, mostly from bands only hipsters appreciated anymore, like Iron Maiden and Metallica. Today it was The Ramones, which he wore with a little embarrassment, since they were actually mainstream-popular.

"It's bullshit," Eric said. "I'm the perfect person to help Citadel with this murder, but I think Mom just hates Citadel."

"I wouldn't think your mom would fall for all that 'SPI terrorist' crap." Jason bit his lip with his bottom teeth and glanced at the partially open door. He lowered his voice. "That crap the AU spews."

Eric smiled. He got a kick out of what Jason considered a bad word. His mother made him paranoid about it. "I wouldn't either," he said, "but she used to watch a lot AUPrime back in her bender days."

"Maybe she's brainwashed, dude," Jason said. "Mom never let me watch AUPrime. She said it's all propaganda. Doesn't that mean they brainwash you?"

"Not really," Eric said, shaking his head. "Not like you mean, I'm sure." Eric shifted in his chair. He hadn't told Jason everything. Not yet.

"She gone?" Jason asked before Eric could think of what to say next. He didn't need to clarify who he meant.

Eric looked up at him and gave a short nod. "Yesterday."

"Dang, dude, I'm sorry. She was a cool chick."

Eric shrugged. "She's not saddled with me now. She can go back to being the popular girl."

"Dude, that's messed up."

Eric shook off his instinctual response. He put his foot back onto the floor and sat straighter in the chair. "What's messed up is that there's a new SPI in town. Someone who doesn't want to be noticed."

"Who?"

Eric shrugged. "I was at the bowling alley yesterday, blowing off steam, and this girl came up to me."

Jason cocked his head. "Dude, you moving on already? Good for you."

"No! Jesus, Jason, what do you think I am? Wait, don't answer that. *No.* This girl was a SPI. A telepath. I don't think she's from here. She said she could wipe my memory of Kristin. I blocked her, but that might have been a mistake 'cause it freaked her out. She probably thinks I'm a telepath, too. But with this murder thing..."

"You think she did it?"

Eric shrugged.

"You think she killed a guy because she's a SPI? Isn't that kind of...I dunno, like the AUSS?"

"No, she was weird. She was trying to...screw with my memories." Eric glanced at the door and paused, listening. Then he rolled his eyes.

He was getting as bad as Jason.

"You were about to say a bad word, weren't you? I think a swear jar would be better, but Mom doesn't agree with me."

"Is she even home?"

"I think so, but she's in the basement if she is. She's working on something tech-y."

"Without electricity?"

Jason shrugged. "I'm not the tech expert."

Eric thought differently. He knew Jason pretended to be stupid, but he was pretty good with mechanical stuff. If he tried, he'd probably be a pretty good engineer.

"What do you want to do about this girl?" Jason asked. "You want to go all gestapo on her?"

"No," Eric said, shaking his head. "I want to talk to her, though."

Jason grinned. He opened his mouth to speak.

"Damn it, Jason!" Eric said before he could say anything.

The bedroom door creaked. Eric turned and saw Ashley, Jason's mother, standing at the door. Her wavy blond hair was darkening from the roots. She hadn't been able to color it in months and it was naturally a few shades darker than she usually kept it. Still, she was an attractive woman with a soft round face. She wore simple black-rimmed glasses fit for working on small things. Jason told Eric one time that she'd been a child actor back in California in the 80s, but they never played her show anymore, surely not on AUPrime.

"You know I don't allow that kind of language in my house," she said. She jerked her thumb toward the hallway. "Get out if you're going to talk like that."

Eric cringed, then nodded. He stood to go. "You coming?" He asked Jason.

Jason hopped off the bed. "Eric's got a new girl," he said as he squeezed passed his mother through the door. "I gotta go meet her."

Ashley raised her eyes to the sky in exasperation, but she nodded, stroking her hand once down his long hair.

"It's not like that," Eric insisted.

"Go!" Ashley commanded. She seemed angry at him, but he knew it was only temporary. She was never angry for long. He'd be welcomed back in no time if he could watch his mouth.

Eric didn't have to get past her to the hallway. He went through the wall.

"Idiot," Eric breathed as they descended the stairs to the front door.

Jason grinned.

Alec Gunn

AUPrimeHistory: True Conspiracies

(Airdate: 6/24/2010)

ANARCHIST STATES OF AMERICA

<Photo: Crips and Bloods clash in Los Angeles>

At the collapse of law and order in the United States, criminal gangs quickly moved to take advantage. Prisons were left unattended and many violent criminals escaped to join compatriots. Once-furtive street gangs in Los Angeles, Chicago, and other large cities took control of the streets, carving out territory in the most violent way possible. Bodies piled up with no authorities to collect and bury the dead. Enterprising criminal organizations seized National Guard and military posts as their headquarters, gaining the use of military equipment and munitions.

<Video: Home is a castle>

Normal, law abiding citizens had to protect themselves any way they could. Many barricaded themselves in their homes. Others armed themselves and their families and defended themselves the best they could. Thousands died in urban and suburban areas in the first year.

<Slideshow: returning to normalcy>

After that bloody first year, things began to calm. Gang territory stabilized, though skirmishes still broke out frequently. People were finally able to live semi-normal lives, trading and working for food and goods. Daily life was still dangerous. At any moment anyone could be robbed, assaulted, or caught in a gang war crossfire. Almost everyone carried a weapon of some sort in urban areas.

<Photo: Grocery line in Chicago>

Food was scarce in most cities and towns along both coasts. The collapse of the economy and threat from gangs froze America's transportation infrastructure. Deliveries to urban centers stopped. Criminal smugglers made a killing on foodstuffs—sometimes literally.

But how did places outside of cities fare? After this commercial break, we'll examine how rural America fared during the Chaos Years.

<Commercial Break>

July 14, 2018 – 10:30 a.m.

Ender Lanes had only been open for half-an-hour when Jason and Eric pulled their bikes into the parking lot. Eric glanced at the pits in the asphalt as they passed, where he and Citadel had their encounter with Roger Hamilton and the telepath Citadel called Exodus.

They locked their bikes to the rack. Eric wouldn't put it over any of his school mates to go for a joyride on his bike.

Inside, the now-familiar jangle of video games and the rumble and crash of bowling games reverberated through the place. It smelled like cigarette smoke, even though it had been illegal to smoke inside since Oklahoma was part of the United States. Eric guessed the smell came from the threadbare carpet that hadn't been replaced since before the Marshall Coup.

There wasn't a trace of blood smell, which Eric thought should be much stronger and certainly more recent. But then, that was only in his head. It had been months since Charlotte Matthews had been killed here.

"You think she's here?" Jason asked.

Eric shrugged. "She might be looking for another victim to steal memories from."

"How do you think she does it?"

"You know more about telepaths than me. I didn't think it

was possible."

Eric strolled along the lanes, looking at each group as he passed. They were all familiar. He didn't know all their names, but he'd seen them all before—the kids at school, the adults around town.

Jason trailed him, brightening when they reached the arcade.

"Okay, spy hunter," Jason said firmly. "One thing I know about telepaths: if you go looking for them, they'll know before you see them and get the heck out of Dodge. We need to make ourselves inconspicuous." He pointed to one of the games. "Cops and Robbers," he said, though the title on the cabinet was *Virtua Cop 3*. "But you gotta try, no getting distracted, or she'll feel you thinking about her."

Eric scowled. He didn't know if Jason was being honest or if he just wanted to play the game. But he saw the logic in it, regardless of Jason's true intention.

He didn't get distracted.

In fact, he got lost in the game. He and Jason played together, teaming up with plastic laser guns against mafia bad guys on the screen. The game released during the Chaos Years and was one of the few gun games that didn't involve shooting SPIs with Electro-Guns.

Jason shouted a lot, calling out targets and even saying some words his mother would never allow when he got taken out. Eric laughed every time Jason shouted something that would get him grounded for a week back home.

They plugged several dollars into the machine before finally running out in the final stage.

When it was over, Eric leaned against the machine before sliding the improbably large pistol into its holster on the cabinet.

"You're a maniac," Eric said between chuckles.

"That game is a cheat!" Jason growled. He slammed his gun home after taking some empty shots at the demo screen. "We were so damned close."

"You just suck."

Jason scowled at him. "Sorry I don't have superhuman reflexes."

"Neither do I!" Eric looked around to see if anyone heard.

Jason punched him on the arm and smiled.

"Now," Jason said, "take a look around. What do you see?"

Eric did as he was told. The arcade was nearly empty, but he could see the tables around the snack shop and most of the lanes.

"Nothing," he admitted.

"She's not here, then."

"This was a waste," Eric groaned.

"No, it wasn't." Jason said. Without explaining what he meant, he started walking toward the front door.

"How was this not a waste of time?" Eric asked when he caught up with his friend.

Jason grinned his most mischievous grin. "You actually had some fun."

Eric stopped walking. "Did you do that to keep me from thinking about the girl or about Kristen?"

Jason turned around but kept walking backward. "What's the difference, dude? You've got your panties so far up your butt they're gonna get stuck in your throat. You need to unclench sometimes so they get a chance to slide down a little."

Eric considered this and decided Jason was right. He was trying too hard. He was an emotional wreck. He needed to start thinking logically again and not let his unease of that new girl cloud his judgement.

"You're a sneaky bastard," Eric said to his friend. "You know that?"

"I do my best," Jason said. "But I did get to thinking."

"Why try?" Eric shot.

Jason grinned and pointed at his friend, acknowledging the jab. "This girl is a stranger, right? You think she's sleeping on the railroad tracks? In the park?"

"The motel?" Eric asked. "Isn't that a little on the nose?"

"Occam's razor, dude."

"You watch too many movies."

Eric looked around quickly as they approached the motel office. There was no one around that he could see. He was anxious about running into Citadel. This was a crime scene and it was almost certain the guy investigating the crime would be here. He probably wouldn't be in a good mood or happy to see Eric.

"It's locked," Jason reported. "Do your thing."

Eric scowled, but he took one more glance around, then walked through the door and into the interior of the office.

A faint foul stench invaded his nostrils when he could breathe again. It was dark, even with sunlight streaming obliquely through the windows. The space behind the front desk, the furthest from the windows, was bathed in shadow from floor to ceiling.

He turned around and unlocked the door. Jason pushed it open from the other side. The bell hanging above the door clanged too loudly. Jason jumped in surprise, but quickly recovered and reached up to still the bell. Both of them froze in the open doorway, waiting for someone to come rushing at the sound of the bell.

They stood in the door silently, waiting for a sign of someone coming. Finally, when it was clear no one was near, Eric gently closed the door while Jason, who was taller, lifted the bell out of the way so it wouldn't ring again.

"Nice job, 'Ghost'," Jason said, using the name Citadel called Eric.

Eric shrugged. "I didn't see it. Lesson learned."

Jason nodded, his crooked smile not quite fading. He stepped away from the door and began walking carefully toward the front desk. Eric scanned the room himself, flipping idly through the flyers advertising nearby tourist attractions, which was mostly sites within the Choctaw nation. There was a flyer for Fort Gibson, which was hours away.

Ender wasn't close to the center of anything.

"Dude," Jason called. Eric lifted his head. Jason stood next to the desk, his hand and pointing finger held at shoulder level. Eric followed his finger to the row of twelve key hooks on the wall.

One was missing. Number eleven.

Eric moved. He ran from the office through the wall toward the rooms. He passed through each room in turn, starting with Room 1, which was adjacent to the office. Each was dark and perfectly set up for new guests. Daylight filtered through the curtains. Eric's passage, even ghosted as he was, stirred up dust in the rooms, creating a haze of particles in the filtered sunlight.

He counted up from one. The rooms were laid out in a row, allowing Eric to pass from one to the other in a straight run. The distance was almost as long as his weekly sprint in the field outside Citadel's RV. He reached Room Ten and stopped to catch his breath. Sweat broke out on his skin. The rooms were hot like ovens, unused and closed up.

Eric paused for a moment, letting his breath and heartbeat steady before passing through the final wall into Room Eleven, ready for anything. Like the other rooms, daylight passed through the thin curtains, giving him enough light to see.

Unlike the other rooms, though, this room was not immaculately kept. Both beds were unmade. A military-style travel bag lay next to one. A simple black backpack, the kind used for school, not hiking, sat next to the other.

Otherwise, the room was empty.

It smelled faintly of old sweat. The bathroom was not used, nor could it be. Sanitation was one of the hardest things about living in Ender these days. Without running water, toilets had to be flushed by dumping water into the bowl. Whoever was staying here wasn't using the toilet; they might be using the gas station or the bowling alley, then.

Eric was tempted to search the bags, to get some clue about who these people were. One was most likely the girl from Ender Lanes. But who was the other? He stopped himself from opening the bags, though. That might be noticed. He didn't want them to know they'd been found. They might run off.

Instead, he phased his hand through them and felt the contents. It was almost all cloth, with bits of metal or plastic mixed in. Clothing. In the military bag, he felt something different. It was a stiff, triangle-shaped cloth. He grabbed it and phased it out of the bag to take a look at it.

His skin, covered in sweat from his exertions, suddenly chilled.

It was a patch, green and black with an upside-down arrowhead design, like the old military units used in the United States Army. The figure stitched on the patch in black thread was a Vitruvian man, four arms and four legs outstretched. Around him swirled the symbol of an atom. Eric recognized the symbol from Jason's SPI collection. It was identical to the symbol used for FORCE before 9/11. Except on this patch, the letters AUSS were embroidered at the top.

The girl was an AUSS SPI, like Roger Hamilton.

That conclusion didn't make sense. The girl acted strange, sure, but above all, she was nervous and scared. Why would a government-trained SPI act like that? Why would she all but advertise that she was a SPI in the first place? In a public place, even. The risk of exposure was too great, and the repercussions if she were discovered would be disastrous. Citadel would go ballistic.

No, this patch belonged to the other one. This other one was the missing piece to both why the girl was here *and* who killed Kevin Duncan. The girl was a distraction designed to let the other one move unnoticed in Ender. And the motel owner had discovered them, so he'd been killed.

There were two new SPIs in Ender.

"You're sure that's what you saw?" Zak Williams asked after the second time Eric told the story. "Do you have the patch?"

"Yes and no," Eric said. "I put the patch back. I didn't want them knowing they'd been found."

Zak nodded. The Williams patriarch didn't look anything

like his son. His face was square and expressive. His hair was a dirty blond, almost brown, and crows' feet were forming at the corner of his eyes. The four of them—Eric, Jason, Zak and Ashley—sat at the Williams' kitchen table. Zak had made sandwiches, not so large as he used to make before the loss of power and water, but still pretty substantial.

"Do we tell Citadel?" Jason asked. He didn't look like he wanted to be the one to break the news that the AUSS had a presence in Ender again.

"I don't think we want to do that," Ashley said. "He'd go running off on some half-cocked mission to tear down Exodus and the AU."

It was only what he promised to do if Exodus sent anyone into Ender again. Eric had asked him once if he was serious about that. Citadel, his face stony, had nodded. *"I don't make promises I won't keep,"* he'd said.

"That won't solve anything," Zak said. "Let's keep this among us. We need to figure out who this other SPI is and why they're here. I'll go talk to a few people in town and see if they've noticed anyone new in town. You boys take your bikes and ride around. See if anyone new stands out."

"See if you notice someone who doesn't know their way around," Ashley added. "Or who keeps to themselves too much, especially in a public place. We're a small town and people know each other. You might even notice an outsider by how the people around them behave."

"Come back here if you find anything," Zak said. "Are you gonna stick around, Ash?"

Eric noted that he didn't tell her to stay. That said a lot about who was in charge in that relationship.

"I've got work to do," Ashley said. "And I have to check in on Anne." Eric didn't know who Anne was, but Zak nodded and shrugged it off, so Eric didn't consider it important.

July 14, 2018 – 11:45 a.m.

Anne Bancroft turned the ceramic bowl in her hand. It had a chip off one edge. Someone had broken it and not told her.

Hmm, who might that have been?

Twenty years ago, Anne Halston married Thomas Bancroft and forever gave others a reason to confuse her with the famous actress from the dawn of cinema. She wasn't half as beautiful. Her mousy brown hair curled in at her neck and hung over her forehead to hide her high hairline; it was just beginning to gray in her forty-fifth year. Her friend Ashley Williams told her that was a great reason to try another color, maybe blond or red, but Anne refused. She'd look silly. She wasn't glamorous like that other Anne Bancroft.

Thomas wasn't able to give her children, so they stopped trying nearly ten years ago. He was a good man, but their mutual disappointment at their failure to get pregnant had chilled their marriage.

So, Anne drowned herself in her career. She was a human resources trainer for Sears. She traveled the country to train employees of all stripes on the subjects of equal opportunity and harassment.

Thomas stayed home; he was the franchise owner of the

Murphy's gas station in town. He put almost as much time and energy in that place as she did in her own work.

She placed the bowl her husband had chipped on the counter. She wouldn't put it back into the cabinet. She was loathe to throw it away, though. She finished cleaning the rest of the dishes. She'd figure it out later. Maybe she could find the chip fragment and repair it.

She finished by wiping dry the crystal wine glass she'd used last night to polish off the bottle of rosé. As she reached up to return the glass to its place in the cupboard, she paused. The stem of the glass buzzed in her fingers. She brought it down and touched the bowl of the glass with her fingers.

It was electric, like a strange static electricity was running over the outside of the glass.

She smiled in wonder and shook her head. She'd heard that crystal had weird properties, like when you ran a wet finger over the rim to play a tone. She wondered what it was that made the glass buzz now.

Then, the buzzing was gone. She laid her hand over the glass, but it was still, as inert as it always was. Maybe it was the humidity. It had been warm and dry for weeks now. That might be it. Maybe it collected a static charge and all her touching dispersed it.

A knock on the door startled her as she was staring at the glass. She shook her head firmly and returned the glass to the cupboard.

The knock came again—probably Ashley.

"I'm coming," she called out.

They were the last words she'd ever speak.

July 14, 2018 – 5:35 p.m.

Citadel ducked under the doorframe of Samuel's house, Ken Hunter at his heels. The boy had to run to keep up with

Citadel's long, swift strides. He was sweating but didn't seem to mind it. Citadel, of course, didn't sweat, even though the digital board outside the Piggly Wiggly claimed it was ninety-five degrees.

Gillian Sumner stood near her desk, rubbing the back of a clearly distraught Ashley Williams.

The only reason Citadel knew Ashley was because of Eric. He knew she was a spy for the EUP. They'd been sent to Ender ten years ago to keep an eye on Eric and Gillian on behalf of Mental Block, Citadel's former companion in FORCE.

Citadel didn't trust them.

Now, with what Ashley claimed to find, Citadel's trust was tamped down even further.

"Mrs. Williams," Citadel greeted, keeping his voice even. "I understand there's been another murder?"

Gillian glared at Citadel as if he'd accused her of the deed right then and there. He ignored Eric's mother. That part would come later.

Ashley pulled herself together. She hadn't been crying, exactly, but her eyes were puffy and her face pale. Her long, two-tone blond hair was mussed. She squared her shoulders and tried her best to give Citadel an even stare.

Citadel read a certain enmity in her eyes. He wondered for a moment if she knew that he was aware of her true affiliation.

"My friend, Anne," Ashley said, her voice uneven. "I was going over to her place for a visit. She's not home much, so I try to see her when I can. But she was on the floor. There was blood..." She trailed off, taking a deep breath and pressing her lips together.

"Is she still there?" Citadel asked, glancing at Gillian.

"Dr. Posey is already on his way over there to collect the body," Gillian said. Citadel shrugged. He wished there was one law enforcement type living in this town.

"What did she look like?" Citadel asked Ashley. "What was her condition?"

"She was laying on her side," Ashley said. "Like she had gone to sleep right there on the floor." Anne pantomimed her hands cradling one side of her head like a sleeper. "But every-thing around her head was covered in blood. I think she was struck on the head."

"You saw a wound?" Citadel asked.

"I don't know," Ashley said. "There was a lot of blood and…" She shook her head. She'd been upset at finding her friend dead on the floor. She wasn't concerned with analyzing everything.

Citadel looked down at Ashley's hands. They were knead-ing each other at her waist-level. There were dark stains under long nails. Flecks of blood were still stuck in the creases of her knuckles.

Blood on her hands, but there was a good possibility this was only because she'd tried to resuscitate her friend. Citadel chose not to mention it.

So far, what Ashley described jived with what Citadel had seen in the motel office: hands up near the head, and lots of blood.

He'd check with Dr. Posey. The doctor would have a more observant nature. He would be able to confirm Ashley's story.

"Did Anne know Kevin Duncan?" Citadel asked.

"About as much as anyone, as far as I know," Ashley said.

"They weren't friends or work together or anything?"

"Anne was an EEO trainer," Ashley said, her tone impatient. "She traveled a lot. If she was going to cheat on her husband, she'd have done it outside of town."

"That's not…" Citadel stammered.

"Yes, it was. My best friend is dead, Citadel. If you don't find out who did it, I will."

"Don't butt in on this investigation, Mrs. Williams."

Ashley shrugged off Gillian's arm. She took a step toward Citadel, glaring up at him. "I won't if I don't have to. Do your damn job."

With that, she slid past him and out the door.

Citadel sighed and looked around for someplace to sit. He dropped into a low padded chair set against one wall. He de-liberately uncurled hands he hadn't realized he'd clenched into fists. If he could get a headache, it would probably be splitting by now.

"I don't know if I can do this," he muttered.

"Don't look at me for support," Gillian said.

Citadel glanced up. Gillian was leaning on the edge of her desk, watching him.

"What do you have against me?"

"Besides you putting my son's life in danger every time you see him?"

Citadel narrowed his eyes at her. Was there something more to it?

"I won't try to rehash this argument again," he told her. "But the boy is sixteen-years-old. He lost his first love. No matter what you want to make yourself believe, your son is a SPI. He's dangerous, not just to himself, but to everyone around him until he learns to properly control every part of his power. He's getting there, but only because he's been working at it. Are you prepared for the day your son destroys a city because he couldn't figure out how to stop himself?"

"Don't you bring Russell into this!"

"Only to press home the seriousness of Eric's condition. Of who he is. Both of the people who might've helped him best are dead. I'm all he has. I've a mind to let him come back and train again. It's too important. We can't let him try to figure all this out on his own." Eric still hadn't come up with a rational reason how he could change the density of objects. Citadel now thought it didn't matter; he could do it, and that had to be dealt with.

"You are the dangerous one," Gillian said, but with the tone of someone who'd lost the argument.

"Dangerous," Citadel mused. "What about Jason Williams? Are you going to forbid your son from seeing his only remaining friend because of who his parents work for? How is that not dangerous?"

He pushed himself to his feet, waving away any response Gillian might offer. The question was rhetorical. No matter what Gillian tried to do in that department, she wouldn't be able to keep Eric from seeing his friend. He was Ghost.

There would be no stopping him.

Citadel still had a job to do. He needed to verify Ashley's story, which meant an unpleasant visit to Dr. Posey.

Not an improvement over his present company, honestly.

AUPrimeTV
CASTING ANNOUNCEMENT

AUPrimeTV has cast Dave Bautista in the role of Uncle Cedric for its controversial sitcom, *My Favorite SPI*, a reboot of the famous 1960's television series, *My Favorite Martian.*

Synopsis: Ten years after 9/11, the infamous SPI, Citadel (Dave Bautista), is found by AUPrimeNews reporter, Tim O'Hara (Eddie Redmayne), in a ditch in rural Illinois. Hijinks ensue when Tim tries to hide his buffoonish "Uncle Cedric" from his neighbor, the local sheriff (Victor Garber).

July 14, 2018 – 6:00 p.m.

Before you even ask," Dr. Posey said as Citadel entered the examination room, "it's the same thing. A SPI—it has to be."

Citadel sighed and looked at the padded adjustment table where the body of Anne Bancroft lay. She was short enough that she fit on the table without her feet hanging over the edge. A white sheet covered her, and the part over her head was stained with blood.

"Nothing new?" Citadel asked.

"I'd have to cut her open to find out more and I don't have the equipment, or the stomach, to do it." Dr. Posey's voice quieted for the first time that Citadel could remember. "There's a reason I'm a chiropractor and not a surgeon."

He turned up the sheet to expose Anne's head. Her head was shaved with clippers, leaving pale stubble on her pale head.

"I examined her scalp for damage," Posey explained. "I also checked her cranial orifices as best I could after cleaning them out. She bled out of her ears, mouth, and nose." He used a long cotton swab to point them out as he explained. "Everything was as you'd expect. Except…"

He took a deep, resigned breath, then inserted the stick, swab-side first, into Anne's ear as if he intended to clean it. But the stick became smaller and smaller, vanishing into the ear canal. "The membranes that would usually prevent foreign objects from penetrating the skull are gone. The ear drum, and a lot of the structures within the ear are just...I don't know."

He pulled out the stick and did the same with Anne's nose. "There is nothing blocking the aural and nasal opening from a direct passage to the interior of the skull. Even the sinuses are gone. Like the thin parts of the skull couldn't withstand whatever forces obliterated the membranes. The brain was liquefied."

"What can do that?" Citadel asked, not really expecting an answer.

"What do you think?" Posey growled, his ire rekindled. "SPI powers. It's either some screwed up telekinesis thing or something no one has ever seen before. No one knows much about the limits of..." He trailed off before he said whatever offensive slur was in his head.

With an angry flick of his wrist, he tossed the sheet back over Anne's head and dropped the bloody swab in the trash.

Citadel didn't react. He was beginning to agree with Posey's view about this. Knowledge of SPIs and their abilities was limited by what the AU chose to reveal, which was little. Now, that lack of knowledge was going to contribute to the people's fear as it started getting around what happened.

"Can you keep this all quiet, Doctor?" Citadel asked suddenly.

Posey's head snapped up. "Quiet? Why?" he demanded.

"Think about how you're feeling right now. Now, imagine everyone in town feeling the same way. What's the thought going through your mind right now, huh? Do you want to round up everyone in town and start testing them somehow for SPI abilities? Do you want to detain every remotely suspicious person you can find? Think of everyone in Ender thinking the same thing. The town would riot. Everyone would blame someone else. People could be hurt on suspicion alone. Lynchings, mob justice. The real murderer would vanish before anyone ever really suspected them. Then what do we have? A bunch of dead innocents and a murderer still free to do what they want."

Citadel stood up straighter and stared Posey down. "So, can you keep this all quiet? Only the Council, who will receive the same advice from me, needs to know. For the good of Ender, we need to keep this one secret while I figure out what is going on here."

After a long moment, Posey finally nodded.

"Good. Do we have any morgue facilities? Where did you put Mr. Duncan's body?"

Posey squirmed a bit before answering. "The cooler at the Piggly Wiggly."

Citadel sighed in frustration.

"Get them out of here, Doctor. Get them to a legitimate funeral home so their families can prepare for services." Shaking his head, he turned to leave.

This was going to be a mess. Whatever mortician ended up preparing the bodies was going to be curious about the manner of death. Whatever secrets the Council chose to keep, they wouldn't remain secret for long.

Time was running out.

Citadel wasn't surprised to find Eric waiting for him at the RV. It was part of the reason he hadn't gone looking for the boy.

Eric was pacing back and forth in front of the door. He'd helped himself to a Coke, which gave Citadel a spike of irrational anger that he tried to ignore.

"If you're here for training," Citadel said as he strolled toward his chair and flipped the lid up from his cooler. "I'm waiting to hear what you've come up with about your new ability." The ice inside melted a long time ago. Still, he fished a can of Coke out and cracked the tab on it. When he turned back to face Eric, he tried his best to wear a stern, but fair, expression.

Eric turned in a circle, his hand fiddling with the red aluminum can in his hand. Citadel realized the boy hadn't even opened it yet.

"No idea," the kid said finally. Citadel was surprised he hadn't at least decided on some bullshit explanation. "And I know you won't train me until I do. I'm not here for training, really. I want to help you with the murders."

"Kid, you know I could use your brain, but I don't need your mother hating me even more than she does. We're probably dealing with a SPI."

"That's why I want to help!" The words shot from Eric's mouth, clipped short when he snapped his lips shut. Citadel's eyes narrowed. No one but the council knew anything about suspecting a SPI for the murders.

Why would Eric? Was he somehow responsible for this after all? Was he trying to cover his tracks by influencing the investigation?

"What do you know?" Citadel asked, choosing to trust him. He couldn't imagine the boy who had faced down a powerful speedster to save the life of his girlfriend would suddenly become a murderer. He knew Eric too well to truly believe that.

In response to the question, Eric finally popped open his can of Coke and drained it slowly. He was buying time for his remarkable mind to figure out how much, or what, to say. There was something more going on, but Citadel couldn't figure out what.

"There's a telepath in town," Eric finally said. "She tried to get in my head when I was in the bowling alley. I was able to block her. She's staying at the motel."

"And you think this telepath is my murderer?"

Eric shrugged. He was hiding something. He was very bad at deception, which was surprising, considering how long he's been able to hide his powers.

"It makes sense, doesn't it?" Eric asked. "She comes into town and people start to die. And she's hiding from everyone. No one has seen her...or remembers seeing her."

That last sent a chill down Citadel's spine. Could a telepath make people forget?

"It makes sense," he told Eric. "I didn't see her at the motel when I was there."

"Her bags are there," Eric said. "Room 11." Again, he clipped his words short, as if he'd said something he regretted.

"What aren't you telling me?"

Eric put the Coke can to his lips again but scowled when he realized it was empty. Citadel absently tossed him another can. Eric caught it but didn't open it. He fondled the tab instead.

"So, this girl," Eric finally began. "She told me she could make me forget Kristin. She must have some memory thing. Make people forget. It's possible you have met her, but she made you forget." It made sense, but the idea terrified him. There was someone out there who could make him forget everything all over again.

He felt an irrational urge to find her and end her.

"But that's not all," Eric broke into Citadel's reaction. Citadel's head came up. "There's another one." Eric said it so quietly that Citadel might not have heard him if his senses were merely human. Eric glanced around, as if there were someone else around who could have heard. "I'm supposed to be out looking for him. The Williams…"

"You told them, and they said not to tell me." Citadel might not have an intellect like Eric's, but he wasn't stupid. "The other one is AUSS. Rockhide?"

"I don't think so. We'd have noticed if Hamilton was in town. A guy like that can't just wander around and not be noticed, and too many people here know who he is, especially since you pretty much showed everyone what he is." The story of Citadel striding out of nowhere and tossing around a few news trucks and the chief AUSS investigator had been the talk of Ender for months. "I don't think the girl is AUSS, she's too…I don't know. She doesn't strike me as a trained operative. This other one has stayed hidden."

"And killed two people so far," Citadel said. He was certain that this was his murderer. "The question is, why those two?"

"Two?"

"Anne Bancroft. A friend of your Ashley Williams. They found her a few hours ago."

"There has to be a connection, right?" Eric said, "I mean,

they're not important in the grand scheme of Ender. They're not council members and not influential. If they wanted to shut down the motel for some reason, he would have to kill both Kevin and Lacey Duncan. Who is Anne, other than Mrs. Williams' friend?"

"If these murders are rational," Citadel said, feeling like he and Eric were getting somewhere together, "which they might not be, there has to be some other connection between Anne and Kevin. Something that matters to Exodus."

"And possibly other people," Eric said, then stopped. "Don't go ballistic on this, okay?" Eric said suddenly. "They think you'll run off to go kill Exodus if you know about this."

Citadel considered this and sipped at his Coke. He'd been completely irrational when he'd said what he'd said to Rockhide. Some of those words could not be taken back. He also felt a need to follow through on his promise. Promises were important, especially threats. If you didn't follow through on threats, then you lost the respect of your enemies. But there were priorities here. People in Ender were dying.

Eric could be one of them if they didn't stop this other SPI.

"What's important to you, Eric?"

"Huh?" Eric said, confused by the change in focus.

"I've told you before," Citadel said, trying to explain, "that I keep my promises. The one I made to Rockhide isn't the only promise I've ever made. A long time ago, I made a promise to a man who was worried about his family. That promise was so important to me that I came here when I couldn't remember anything else about myself. Those kinds of things are what you need to make the important decisions in your life."

"You promised my uncle that you'd take care of me?" Eric said.

Citadel nodded. "I think Rumble knew, even before you were born, what you'd become. He was nervous because we were going on a mission and he had a history of screwing up. And he knew the consequences of his mistakes, as powerful and uncontrolled as he could be. He heard your mom was going into labor just before we left, I think. He made me promise to take care of his family in case anything happened to him. He was scared, I think. It wasn't something I thought much on at the time. I made the promise. Then what happened in the next few hours made it the most important promise I've ever made. It was the one thing I remembered when I could remember anything again."

Eric rocked back as if he wasn't sure he could keep his balance. Rumble had been the youngest member of FORCE, and the least controlled. He'd been the first recorded third generation SPI, and not much was known about the extent of his abilities. FORCE didn't know how to handle or train him properly.

They'd paid the price when his powers triggered an explosion that destroyed New York City.

"So, I ask myself now," Citadel continued, *"What is important?* The promise I made to Rumble is more important than the one I made to Exodus. *You* are more important than whatever revenge I feel I need to do. What is important to you, then, Ghost? What do you want me to do?"

"Stay here and protect Ender. It's all I have left." Eric said the last in a near whisper.

Citadel nodded, satisfied. "Then here's what we need to do: we need to find that SPI. I'll go talk to Lacey Duncan. We need to dive deep and find out what Kevin and Anne had in common. You take Anne. Snoop around like the Ghost you are and find something that links her to Kevin. Talk to her husband at Murphy's if you need to, but I'd rather you not let your mother know you're helping me. Then we need to find out who else in Ender shares the same connection and make sure they don't die."

July 14, 2018 – 7:00 p.m.

A new sense of purpose filled Eric as he pedaled his bike away from the RV. He was part of something important again. Despite Mrs. Williams' warnings, he'd put his trust in Citadel and been rewarded. Now, *together*, he and Citadel were going to find this mysterious SPI and stop them from killing more people here.

It felt a little like his life's purpose was being fulfilled. He'd felt a little bit of that when he saved Kristin from Leonard Strange, but this was different. He didn't have a personal stake in this. He was working only to protect Ender, not himself or one of his friends. It felt wonderful to do something so…not selfish. Almost euphoric.

He turned onto the Williams' street and coasted for the half-block until he came their house, standing on the pedals. He was sweating in the heat.

He scoped out the Williams' house as he passed. He checked the windows to see if Mrs. Williams was watching. Mr. Williams and Jason should both be out, hunting down the mysterious, murdering SPI. But Ashley said she was staying home with work to do. Usually that meant holed up in the basement with her electronics and tools, but that didn't mean she wasn't sitting at a window, watching at this very moment.

The Williams had an adjoining driveway with Bancrofts. It was separated by a narrow, neatly trimmed hedge. The two garages almost touched. Eric turned into the Williams' driveway and rolled all the way up to the garage. He dismounted and dropped the bike against the hedge, which held the bike somewhat upright in its thick branches.

Mostly hidden from the street by the hedge and the Williams house, Eric passed through the hedge, confident in his concealment. He jogged across the width of the Bancroft's driveway and slipped behind the house through the walkway between the house and garage.

The Bancrofts' backyard was small and unkept. Leaves from the previous fall lay rotting upon a lawn that was more weed than grass. A pair of rusted lawn chairs flanked a low metal table that had a hole in the middle for an umbrella. The umbrella lay against the house, unused. It looked like no one had enjoyed the outdoors in this house for several years. Certainly no one had thought to tend the place in any way in a long time.

Eric was happy to see this yard was separated from the others by a high wooden fence, providing complete privacy. Eric heard voices from the yard immediately beyond the far side. Unlike the Bancrofts, some people enjoyed the use of their backyards.

Thinking that it might be those lives he protected with what he was about to do, Eric slipped through the wall into the Bancroft's kitchen.

A single, red glazed, clay bowl sat on the counter, a chip on one edge. Otherwise, the kitchen was neat and tidy. So clean that Eric didn't want to touch anything for fear of revealing that had been here to Mr. Bancroft when he returned home.

The house was quiet. The voices from outside were muffled perfectly by the house's walls and the carpeting in the living room absorbed the ambient sound in the right way to make the entire place seem like a tomb to Eric, a place to be respected and revered.

The stain on the carpet near the front door amplified that effect. Someone died here. That wasn't to be taken lightly.

Eric crouched near the stain and looked up at the door. It was locked with the deadbolt from the inside. There was no damage to the doorframe or anything around the lock. It hadn't been a violent entry. But the murder itself hadn't been all that violent, right? Citadel had given him the facts of how they died. There were no bruises or signs of a struggle; they just dropped dead and bled out, causing the stains. Eric had seen the stain in the motel, too, dark and thick, just like this one.

Eric stood. The *how* of the murder wasn't what he was here for. He needed to find the why.

He looked around the room. It looked like every living room he'd seen on TV, but actually lived in. A plush couch and recliner combo sat in an L-shape across from a big-screen TV on top of a low entertainment center. A large bookshelf leaned against the opposite wall. One shelf was strewn with books, mostly fiction paperbacks, but the shelf below was lined neatly with what looked like binders with colorful spines. Each binder was labeled with a year on a little white card slipped into a clear plastic sleeve.

Eric pulled out one of the binders and opened it. It was an old school photo album filled with standard three-by-five photos as well as a scattering of Polaroids with a wide white border. They were all vacation photos. This one—the spine was marked "2007"—had pictures all taken in a desert. The Grand Canyon, maybe. Some of them were at an Indian Reservation; not Choctaw, but probably in Arizona or New Mexico.

2007 would have been smack dab in the middle of the Chaos Years. Somehow, the Bancrofts had found time for vacation in those desperate times.

Eric shook his head and found the latest binder on the shelf. It was dated 2016.

The photos were digital now, though still printed on the same size paper that the older photos were. Mr. and Mrs. Bancroft featured prominently in these, too, though several were selfies taken by Mrs. Bancroft. The background was Chicago. A baseball game at Wrigley Field, goofing off in the warped reflection of the Cloud Gate sculpture, a view of Lake Michigan from an extremely tall building. The Bancrofts seemed to be having a lot of fun. It gave Eric a pang of sadness, seeing this happy couple now torn apart by tragedy.

There was no binder for 2017. Had they not taken a vacation last year? Eric scanned the rest of the binder spines. There was not a skipped year among them. They went back to 2002, a wedding photo album. A simple wedding, to be sure, as this was the year before the Chaos began.

Eric examined the shelf with the paperbacks. They were all science fiction books, all well-read. Some were upright, but several looked haphazardly tossed on the shelf. Eric picked one up. Underneath was a small camera, hidden by its similarity in size to the books.

The camera still had some battery left. The screen on the back lit up and Eric scrolled through the pictures.

They were more photos. This time, however, they were all selfies by Mrs. Bancroft; Mr. Bancroft was nowhere to be found. The location was a ruined city. There were a lot of pictures of burned out buildings.

A staccato clicking rattled through the room, then a sudden creak as the deadbolt lock on the front door slid open. Eric spun around as the door swung open slowly.

Eric acted instinctively. He ghosted through the bookshelf, still carrying the camera. Just before his eyes became obscured by the books and wood of the shelf, he saw Mr. Bancroft appear in the doorway.

When next he could see, he was in the dark bathroom, standing partway-in and partway-out of the shower stall. He moved into the middle of the room so he could solidify and breathe again. He tried to get his bearings but realized he had no idea where in the house he was. He also had no idea where Mr. Bancroft would go first after returning home. He might very well come into the bathroom, or into whatever room Eric ghosted to from here.

Eric's heart pounded. If he made the wrong move, he'd be outed to Mr. Bancroft, who might tell anyone. If it came out that the murders were committed by a SPI, Eric would be blamed.

Ender would erupt in a firestorm on a hot day and Eric would be at the center of it. His mother would be fired from her job. The Sumners would be ruined in Ender and only Citadel would be able to protect them.

Footsteps thudded in the hallway outside. In his panic, Eric hadn't listened for Bancroft's movements.

Eric's logical mind speared through his panic in a bid for calm.

It's only one man, it said. *Just pay attention to where he is and go the other way.*

"Alan, I know it's hard," called a voice through the wall Eric had ghosted through. It was Ashley Williams, and she was in the living room.

"You don't know shit, Ashley," Mr. Bancroft said. His voice shot through the bathroom door, through Eric to Ashley on the other side of the wall. "I knew she was screwing around on me. But with that motel scum?"

Eric was trapped between them.

"Kettle black, Alan," Ashley said. Her voice was raised to reach him through the house, but it sounded very close to the wall. She was standing near the bookshelf. "She wasn't sleeping with Duncan. She was distant because she knew about you and that tramp bartender."

Only Mr. Bancroft's angry growl warned Eric in time. Eric dove through the sink and mirror into another room just as Mr. Bancroft opened the bathroom door.

Eric emerged in another dark room, this one lit faintly through closed drapes over a single window. Some sort of storage room.

Something about the conversation between Bancroft and Mrs. Williams struck Eric then. Bancroft thought his wife was cheating on him with Mr. Duncan, the dead motel man. Could they be wrong about the two SPIs in the motel? Could they have been at the wrong place at the wrong time? Had Mr. Bancroft killed Duncan and his wife?

Was that why Ashley was here?

"It doesn't matter now," Eric heard Bancroft say through

the wall. He didn't seem to be angry anymore. His voice was resigned. "They're both...dead."

What did that mean? That strange hitch at the end? Was he admitting to the murders?

Eric made his way to the door of this room. If his memory was right, the Bancroft's garage would be across the hall, through one last room, then out through the wall. A straight shot. He poked his head out of the door and into the hall to make sure it was clear.

It wasn't.

Ashley leaned against the wall across from the bathroom door, her face sad. She glanced toward him, possibly seeing his movement from the corner of her eye. Eric ducked back into the storage room.

Damn it! Had she seen him? It wasn't the end of the world if she had, right? But he was in this house for Citadel, and Eric wasn't supposed to be working with Citadel.

"It's not your fault," Ashley said, finally. "What do you think you could have done? Gone with her to D.C. and tried to make it like old times? That ship sailed a long time ago."

D.C.!

That was why the photos looked so familiar. Eric turned the camera back on and pressed the button to open the image folder.

There Are No Photos to View.

The screen flashed the sentence twice, then went blank.

The data card was wiped. He'd ghosted with it; that was another thing to consider when using his powers, then. He hadn't thought about the possibility that the change in vibration might affect electronics.

But the pictures had been pictures of Mrs. Bancroft on vacation, alone, in Washington D.C.

There was something here. Something about Mrs. Bancroft's solo trip to D.C. and Mr. Bancroft thinking she was cheating. Ashley didn't seem to believe he was the killer, after all.

The distraction was enough for him to miss the opening of the door to the room he was in. Only the increase in light spilling in from the hallway drew his attention. Eric's head jerked up and he saw Mrs. Williams glaring at him from the doorway.

She'd seen him.

Her jaw muscles squirmed as she clenched her teeth together, trying to hold back her anger. It struck Eric, then, how young she looked for her age. Her face was smooth, her cheeks rounded. Eric couldn't remember a time when he'd seen her smile, and this certainly wasn't going to be one of them, no matter what he did.

Her hand shot out and she pointed toward the shaded window.

"Out!" she mouthed silently.

Eric was going to hold out the camera, but it was useless now. He put it on top of a stack of cardboard boxes and tried his best apologetic look on Ashley, but she wasn't having it. Finally, he took a deep breath and ghosted through the wall to the outside after a quick peek out the window to make sure no one was there.

He raced to his bike and pedaled away. This wouldn't be the end. Mrs. Williams would surely have some not-kind things to say when he saw her again.

The trick would be making sure that didn't happen any time soon.

AUPrimeHistory: True Conspiracies

(Airdate: 6/24/2010)

SIEGE OF AMERICA'S BREADBASKET

<Re-enactment: Siege of Springfield>

While urban centers had to defend from internal gangs who had been largely present already, the criminal element in rural America became roaming gangs of raiders, who attacked farms and ranches looking for food.

Towns who still had a functioning government erected walls to protect against these external threats. These walls often did not prevent the attacks from happening, however.

Many raider gangs sought out the smaller towns as bases of operation in order to extend the range of their criminal activities.

In 2005, one gang of 200 raiders laid siege to the city of Springfield, Illinois. It was one of the most ambitious raids of the Chaos Years. The raiders quickly destroyed the walls and waged a guerrilla war in the streets of Springfield. Finally, the state capitol was captured, and the raiders successfully took control, ruling through force and fear.

This event wasn't the first or last of its kind. By the time the Marshall Coup began in 2007, hundreds of small towns and cities in what was once known as "fly-over" states were occupied by criminal elements. Others were merely raided periodically for supplies.

<Commercial Break>

July 14, 2018 – 7:00 p.m.

Citadel put the photo down and turned to Lacey Duncan. The woman he saw hardly looked like the woman in the photo; there was no smile on her thin lips and her dishwater blond hair was only half-up in a bun on the back of her head. The hastily tied thing had come mostly undone, leaving strands of hair running down the back of her neck to her shoulders. She held a cup of tea in both hands as she waited for Citadel to speak.

"It's a hard question, but…" He paused, trying to figure out how to be tactful about this. "Was there any sort of relationship between your husband and Anne Bancroft?" Instead of being shocked, as Citadel expected, Lacey scoffed.

"The actress?" she asked. She stood in the rundown living room of a rundown house just a block away from the motel.

"No, Anne Bancroft. She lived on Majority Lane up by the school."

"Lived? Oh my God, there's been another murder?"

Citadel nodded, silently cursing himself for the slip. He guessed it was either going to be that or Lacey would assume he was accusing Anne of murder. There was no winning in this no matter what.

"I didn't even know that woman existed," Anne said. "I

would have if Kevin was involved with her."

"You're sure about that?"

"Of course. We have what you might call an...open relationship." Lacey put her tea down and leaned both elbows on the counter of the breakfast nook that separated them. Her face tightened as she considered her next words. Then, she gave what appeared to be an "oh, screw it," shrug to herself and said, "In fact, I'm not his only wife. Kevin was polyamorous. His other wife lives in Kansas City. We tried to do it together at first, but Emily and I couldn't make it work. Kevin split time between us. He spends summers here, because he thinks he'll get the most out of the motel. "Oh God, she's gonna kill me. I know she'll blame me for what happened."

"So," Citadel cut in, "if he was to cheat on the two of you, he'd tell you?"

Lacey shrugged. "I think he would. He'd ask permission, at least. He's done it before."

Citadel shook his head. He couldn't wrap his head around that kind of relationship. What was the point of marriage, then? "Do you know Mr. Bancroft? He owns the gas station."

Lacey shook her head.

"Anyone else who might have a reason to hurt your husband?"

After a pause, Lacey shook her head again.

Citadel looked around the living room. It was lit by open windows only, the warm sunlight making the air smell thick. The furniture looked either second-hand or very old; the seating was worn in patches along favorite sitting spots. The couch had a wide patch of worn fabric that had to be where two people sat side by side, close. His eyes went back to the picture, an image of Kevin and Lacey standing side by side with the St. Louis Arch in the background, the optical illusion of distance making it seem like they stood under a much smaller arch.

Citadel's eyes narrowed.

"Have you and Kevin ever been to Chicago?"

Lacey cocked her head at the strange question. "No." She saw Citadel looking at the St. Louis picture. "We went to St.

Louis three years ago. That's where that picture was taken."

"Has Kevin ever been there alone?"

Chicago was the capitol. If Exodus and the AUSS had some connection to Kevin Duncan and Anne Bancroft, Chicago would be where it came from.

"I don't think so. He went to Washington D.C. with Emily in February, I think, but I don't think he's been to Chicago."

Citadel shook his head and sighed. He was getting nowhere here. "Did Kevin have a home office or someplace he might have papers or records?"

"No, he keeps all that stuff at the motel."

Citadel nodded, resigned that he'd hit a dead end. "I'll go check there again, then, if you don't mind?"

"Sure, I don't see why not. The place is empty." Citadel couldn't help raising his eyebrows.

"No guests?"

"Not all summer," Lacey said with a disgusted snap in her voice. "We're living on savings." She stopped herself. "*I'm* living on savings."

Something broke in Lacey. She dropped her head on the counter and hid it behind her arms.

Citadel watched her awkwardly for a moment, then let himself out.

The motel yielded similar results. There was nothing helpful in the office, which still smelled a little like bad meat. The blood stain had dried on the thin carpet, now a rust brown. All the records there were motel records. It verified what Lacey said.

They were broke, and there hadn't been any guest in months.

For a moment, Citadel considered heading to Room 11, where Eric said the girl was staying with her mysterious AUSS friend. He decided against it. Eric had defenses against her power, but Citadel wouldn't stand a chance against a telepath if she were powerful enough to wipe memories. If it came down to a confrontation, he'd need Eric backing him up. The thought scared him a little—the idea that he was helpless against a foe who could only be stopped by a sixteen-year-old kid.

Speaking of that kid, he should get back to the RV and find out if anything they'd discovered pointed toward another possible victim.

July 14, 2018 – 7:45 p.m.

Eric arrived at the RV before Citadel. He had pushed himself fast as he fled the Bancroft house. He parked the bike against the pile of tires and ran his hand along the tarp, remembering his bout with super-strength.

How had he been able to swap molecules in solid matter the way he had? Some of them had vanished completely, yet the tire was still there. Did it have to do with some sort of quantum shift? Was there a dimension the particles went where weight and density didn't matter?

The worst-case scenario was that he had obliterated the atoms and somehow recreated them in the exact same configuration. That was some next-level shit, even beyond quantum particle manipulation. He'd thought his powers were all about vibration; he could vibrate molecules out of phase with other matter. But if he could actually remove and recreate those molecules, what else was he capable of?

Nuclear fission?

He shuddered. This is what had scared Rumble so much. He'd discovered how far his powers to vibrate matter could go, and it scared the shit out of him.

Eric was pretty positive now that it was those powers that destroyed New York City.

Citadel and his mom believed that he was pushing his powers too far. That's why they both finally agreed on something: to stop his training. It was reason to pause and think. Getting those two to agree on anything was definitely a momentous event worthy of consideration.

He should be more frightened than he was; he should be huddled in a dark corner afraid to come out because of what he might do to the world on accident.

But he wasn't afraid. He was *excited*. He wanted to learn everything he could do. He wanted to push and test as far as he could go. He wanted to extend his powers.

Why didn't that scare him shitless?

He was scared to say hello to a stranger! He hated being around groups of more than three people. But he was totally confident that he *wouldn't* destroy the world with his powers.

Why not?

He dropped down on the collection of firewood he used as a chair when he visited the RV, chuckling at himself. He was a mental mess with a head for logic and science. He'd never be a psychologist, no matter how much he joked about it. People were Kristen's thing. She could see inside them intuitively, see what they needed and how to deal with them. She'd seen he needed a friend all those months ago, and she'd made herself his friend, whether he liked it or…Well, he had liked it.

To think he'd ever be able to fathom the complexity of human emotion like she could was a pipe dream. It wasn't the same as understanding the physical effects of hormones and chemicals on the brain. While it should all boil down to that, it didn't. There was something more that was unfathomable—to him, at least.

A shadow passed over him just before the lawn chair across from Eric creaked under the expansive weight of Citadel. How that thing never collapsed was another unfathomable mystery of the universe, almost as complex as human emotion.

"Nothing?" Citadel asked as he cracked open a Coke can. Eric shook his head.

"Anne and her husband were breaking up. He thought she

might be cheating on him with Mr. Duncan, but Ashley says that never happened."

Citadel huffed a laugh and took a drink. "It was exactly opposite with the Duncans. Duncan had another wife in Kansas City, but Lacey was part of it. If he had cheated on her with Anne, he would have asked Lacey."

"Really?" Eric asked, his eyes wide. What the hell was going on in people's minds? Was everyone crazy in one way or another?

"Don't look at me like that," Citadel said. "It baffles me just as much as you."

"That makes me feel a little better."

"I tried to see if there was some connection between Duncan and the AU, but he never had any connection to them. He's never been to Chicago, at least not in the last twenty years or so."

"The Bancrofts went to Chicago two years ago," Eric said. "Tourism stuff. But I guess that's not a connection. Last year, Anne went alone to tour the old D.C. ruins. She had pictures on a camera, but electronics don't like it when I ghost." He shrugged.

"Washington?"

"Yeah."

"Duncan went to Washington last winter with his other wife."

"That's a connection," Eric said. "But what does it mean? Why would Washington matter at all? The AU hates the idea of being in Washington almost as much as it hates SPIs."

Washington D.C. had been invaded by Marshall's Coup. It had been the first stop in that national tour. Marshall had torn D.C. to the ground and the AU never rebuilt it. It was just a tourist trap now. A place people went to witness the ruins of the old USA.

"That's the key," Citadel said. "It has to be. We'll get the Council to survey the town for who else might have gone to D.C. recently."

He sighed. Eric examined his face and realized Citadel was

tired. Maybe not physically, but he had all the signs of it.

"How is the killer figuring out who's been to D.C.?" Eric wondered. "There are a few thousand people here to sift through."

"We have to hope it takes time. If they knew who it was, the killings wouldn't have taken so long. Two in two days? The killer has to find them. Maybe that's why the telepath is here."

"In that case, we should see the Council first thing in the morning."

"I'll take care of it. Go home, Ghost. Get some rest."

Eric nodded. "You, too. You look tired."

"Not possible." Citadel glanced at Eric's doubtful face and shrugged. "Okay, I'll sleep if I can."

Eric took that as a good sign and left Citadel to his own thoughts.

Alec Gunn

September 23, 1992 – 12:30 a.m.

Y ou've never left this box?" she asked.
She was introduced to him as "Jitterbug," a new recruit to FORCE. But within minutes of their first conversation,
she'd told him her real name was Janet. Janet Turner. She was
a tiny thing, barely as tall as his stomach. Her auburn hair was
cut short. But as he looked at her, the hair morphed into a black
bob cut at her jawline. He blinked and it returned to normal.

Citadel grinned at her question. He'd never considered the
bunker to be a box, but he could see what Janet meant. It was
somewhat box-like: concrete and steel walls, thick pillars holding up the ceiling, and the only way out was a pair of brushed
aluminum elevator doors.

He had left the bunker several times over the last twenty
years. The Vietnam mission hadn't been his last—far from it.
But he'd never gone outside just to go outside. He'd long ago
forgotten why he'd want to. What would he do? He could watch
movies here. He could get coffee here. Everything he could ever
need was here.

Besides, if he left, he might hurt someone. That was what he
did when he left, wasn't it?

"What's so special about outside?" he asked her.

"You worry too much, Omar," she said. His eyebrow cocked.

When had he told her his name? "I know what you're afraid of."

Oh, she was part of the new generation, like Exodus.

"I'm not afraid of anything," he lied.

"Come with me, then." Her pretty smile told him she knew he was lying.

"They're not going to let me walk out the front door."

Janet's smile became a mischievous grin. When she did that, he couldn't refuse.

The elevator door slid open silently.

Janet pressed the button marked "1" with a star next to it. Citadel blinked and the number next to the button changed from "1" to "11."

He didn't feel the change in gravity as the elevator moved. He could have been going up or down, but in seconds, the bell rang, and the doors opened. For a moment, a room appeared beyond the doors that wasn't what should have been outside the elevator. It had a pair of beds and a large mirror over a squat chest of drawers. Citadel blinked and it was gone. It was replaced by a plain white hallway and black tiled floor. Only one in every three lights was on, just enough for the night guards to see.

They moved silently through the hallway, Jitterbug guiding Citadel by the hand, a child pulling a giant behind her.

He thought of her as a child often in those first days. It was her size. She was a woman, though, north of twenty then. Even if he was twice that age, she definitely was not a child.

They emerged from the narrow hallway into a large lobby. The tiles here were generally beige, but there was a symbol etched into them in black and silver at the center of the room. An eagle holding three arrows in its claws.

They sneaked out past the guard on duty. He didn't even seem to notice them there. Janet had never been a strong telepath, but she did have her talents.

When they emerged outside, there was a huge parking lot lit by orange lights. The building they just exited was huge—easily five stories high and stretched to either side of them for hundreds of yards in both directions.

The sky above was black and moonless, the stars obscured by the haze of light in the parking lot. It must have been summer because Janet wasn't wearing a jacket. But, of course, he couldn't feel the temperature.

They strolled into the mostly empty parking lot. A few cars still rested between the white lines. One of them might have even been Dr. Morrow's. Otherwise, they must have been late-working employees in the big building...

Citadel knew the name of the building. It was famous. He'd visited it as a kid when his father worked there, but for the moment, he couldn't remember it. All he could remember was Janet. That's all he wanted, anyway. He wanted to think about her, remember what they had together. The connection that formed that night as she snuck him out of the bunker and revealed that he was a prisoner.

She took him through the parking lot. Lots, really. There was a road separating the two. Beyond the flat sheets of blacktop, a copse of trees loomed, dark, but limned in light from beyond. Jitterbug dove into those trees.

Citadel followed.

The trees weren't deep. Very quickly, Citadel stopped to stand next to Jitterbug; they both stood above a riverbank. Across the water, a city glowed.

Citadel and Jitterbug looked at the city across the river. It was marked by a single, tall spire of white rock, a perfect square column tipped with a sharp-cornered pyramid.

"That's the center of everything," Jitterbug said, pointing to the monument. "The Capitol, the White House, the memorials and monuments. Almost like it's the center of the universe." Citadel listened to her speak, enraptured. She turned around and gestured back the way they came. "Even this is part of it. Just a few miles away is Georgetown, where most of the people who run this place learn how. Antonin Scalia, Bill Clinton..."

"Jackie Kennedy," Citadel finished. Jack's wife was a genius in Citadel's eyes. He'd idolized her as a young man, though he'd never truly met her until they were both at Jack's deathbed a few years ago. She'd never known who he was.

Jitterbug's eyes shone when she looked at him.

Citadel smiled awkwardly. "Most of my tutors came from there, back in the 70s."

"So," she said, her grin revealing straight, white teeth, "you're alumna, too!"

July 15, 2018 – 6:00 a.m.

Citadel jerked awake, making the bed in the RV creak under his weight.

Washington D.C.

All the talk of Washington the evening before brought him dreams of a past life. He'd been a prisoner there for years, let out only to cause death and destruction at the behest of the U.S. Government.

He remembered the Pentagon now. Jitterbug had shown him that night what was in the outside world. She'd given him something he never thought he needed. A taste of freedom that had led to...

He forgot. It was an important moment in his life, he knew, and not just because it had been the beginning of a years-long relationship with a wonderful woman.

Suddenly, Citadel sat up in the bed.

His mind clicked and for a moment, he almost knew what it was like for Eric when a puzzle was solved.

"He never left," he said to himself. He was up and dressed in a matter of moments, suddenly realizing why the connection to Washington was so important.

Georgetown.

In the next instant, he was out the door and moving at his best speed, hoping he wasn't already too late.

July 15, 2018 – 8:00 a.m.

Washington, D.C.

The Pentagon building, nestled between the George Washington Expressway and the Potomac River, was the only vestige of the old United States government remaining that wasn't toppled or collapsed. Even across the river on the old Mall, only twenty feet of the Washington monument stood upright. The remainder lay in several pieces on the cracked concrete and weed-thatched dirt that was once a perfectly tended park that stretched from the river to the Capitol building.

The Pentagon remained for one reason and one reason only. Edward Bradley, the man known in certain circles as Exodus, wished it so. Exodus had been the voice in the ear of then-Senator William Marshall when Marshall led the Canadian and Mexican armies against the Federal stronghold of Washington D.C. in September of 2007. Such an act would have been unheard of in the twentieth century, when American leadership in the world was secretly defended by four extraordinary men and women. But FORCE was no more, and American power had crumbled under the weight of financial and legal burdens more powerful than Citadel himself.

Marshall had sought to crush any remnant of what he saw as the irredeemably corrupt U.S. government. He used the power of the armies at his command to destroy the monuments and symbols of that power. The Lincoln Memorial, the Washington Monument, the Capitol building, the White House. All destroyed by explosives and artillery. What remained of the U.S. army out of the Pentagon was little more than a nuisance, and easily crushed.

But not the Pentagon itself. Marshall ordered that building remain untouched.

Now, Edward Bradly sat at his desk within the fortress he maintained and cultivated. The Pentagon was now Exodus' personal castle and fiefdom, separate from the American Union's government in Chicago and beholden to no one.

Here, Exodus reformed FORCE under his command. He built the team from the ground up, controlling them with his telepathic power and with promises of life in a world that wanted them dead. Now, FORCE was a power greater than it had ever been under Citadel's leadership.

A power Exodus had yet to reveal to the world; a power that would one day make the globe tremble.

The office Exodus now called his own had once been occupied by the Chairman of the Joint Chiefs of Staff. It was larger than any one man would ever need to work in. One wall hosted a bookshelf, the size of which would not be out of place in a university library. Where once it had boasted titles from the world's most prominent military strategists, the spines of the current collection were of a myriad of subjects: science, history, philosophy, and mathematics, just to name a few.

Exodus had written many of those books himself under several different pen names.

"I don't care, Jefferson," he told the man on the other line. "Just get it done. If you call me again whining about the electricity situation, you won't need to worry about any of it again. Which would you prefer?" He hung up without waiting for an answer. "That's what I thought."

He leaned back in his chair and closed his eyes. He imagined the lines of a complex mandala patterned against the flickering black of the back of his eyelids. He traced each line in his mind until the mandala was complete again. Within a few breaths, his mind was calm once more.

Order restored, the sudden knock on his office door didn't surprise him. He pressed the button that released the privacy lock with a soft buzz. The door opened to reveal Edward Bradley's secretary, a woman of middle years with curly black hair tied back to keep it away from the red-rimmed glasses she wore. Her suit was the same shade of crimson as her glasses.

"Mr. Bradley," Cheryl said as if he weren't staring at her expectantly. He had the knowledge to be "Dr. Bradley" a dozen times over, yet he never saw the value in wasting years of his life to get a certificate that mattered little in the big picture. There was only a minute tinge of resentment when people referred to him as "Mr. Bradley." He didn't mind *that* much.

"There is news out of Ender, Oklahoma."

Edward sat up straighter. He quickly probed Cheryl's mind and got the information he needed.

"Thank you, Cheryl," he said, waving her out. Only a wrinkling of her brow and a ghost of thought betrayed her annoyance at being dismissed before she could demonstrate her knowledge. The woman was too proud, but she was a valuable cat's paw when he needed her. He'd asked her to monitor the situation in Oklahoma and report any news. Edward couldn't spare the effort himself. There was too much else to do.

Two deaths in as many days, only revealed when the town doctor requested mortuary services out of McAlester. The question was "Why?"

Was the town breaking down from the isolation? Were people killing each other? Two fatal accidents in two days wasn't likely, but months without power and water and communication could fray men's nerves. The presence of a powerful SPI would also splinter the town. A decade of anti-SPI propaganda would do that. They hadn't turned on Citadel like he hoped, but that didn't mean the old man was completely welcome among his inferiors.

Then there was the boy. He hadn't revealed himself despite Citadel's protection. More needed to be known about that one, and the AU would need to step carefully around him until the extent of his powers were sussed out. The events in New York and Edward's own study of Steven Sumner urged caution. The third generation was poorly understood. Edward's experience with them only demonstrated how poorly.

Two deaths.

A closer look was warranted.

The news Cheryl gathered said nothing about who died or their circumstances, but those sorts of things were easily discovered. All Edward would need was to contact someone in town.

Luckily, he had three contacts.

Edward stood and moved to the opposite side of the office, where a zero-G chair waited for him. He sat and reclined until the weight of his body was distributed evenly across the chair's surface. When he closed his eyes, he felt as if he floated in space. The loss of physical perception aided the concentration he needed to extend his mental perceptions across the distance he needed.

In the darkness of his thoughts, Exodus produced the cloud of minds he kept at arm's length at all times. His collection consisted of dozens of people he had touched over the last twenty years and more. Dr. Morrow had been his first, but that one was long dead. Citadel was once in the cloud, but after New York, he'd vanished. Exodus had thought him dead, but the trauma of being destroyed and rebuilt must have changed the makeup of his mind. The memory loss was part of that, but Citadel was now a completely different person than he'd once been. Their brief contact in Ender last year proved that. Exodus had been able to reconstruct some of his memories, but Citadel would never be what he once was.

Exodus would never be able to categorize or order all the minds he collected. He found them through his eidetic memory. He remembered each of them, and the touch that sealed them to him. Usually, that touch was a simple handshake, like the one he found now, the polygamist who had come to Washington D.C. on vacation with one of his wives. Edward Bradley had met them at the airport under the guise of a tour manager. Mr. Duncan's handshake was firm and confident. There had been excitement in his eyes as Edward told him about the most interesting spots to visit that weren't in the brochures.

Despite the detail of the memory, Kevin Duncan's mind did not appear to him. Exodus' brow wrinkled. One of the dead was Kevin Duncan.

Coincidence?

The next touch he tried had been a quick, friendly hug. Edward Bradley had attended a human resources conference where he'd met a wonderful woman with the name of a classic actress. He'd smiled and greeted her warmly as the conference host. She'd returned the embrace almost eagerly. She was attracted to him; her marriage was on the rocks and she was lonely.

He hadn't taken the bait. He didn't want to leave that much of an impression on her.

That woman, Anne Bancroft, was also dead.

There was no chance that both the dead people in Ender would be his agents.

Had Citadel discovered them and executed them? No. It was something the leader of FORCE might have done when he was younger and unscarred, but this new Citadel...

There was still one more contact.

He chuckled when he remembered this one. He'd invited this one to Washington himself at the suggestion of the newest member of FORCE. He'd given the poor boy hope, then yanked it away. It was the kind of prank he might have played had he ever gone to college himself. The only touch he'd given the boy was a slap on the shoulder as he sent him back home to wait for word on his scholarship.

As the memory played back in his mind, it faded into a new awareness. The familiar feeling of transference pleased him. He began to feel the heat of the Oklahoma summer and the strain on his muscles as he ran down the street.

He was constantly running.
Running.
Running.

Ken Hunter ran as he always did. It was the one thing he was good at. The courier job was supposed to be a punishment for his friendship with Leonard Strange and his participation in the bullying of several of the students at Marshall High.

But Ken found that he liked it. It kept him in shape. Even the short sprints were fun. It was the long jaunts across town that allowed him the most freedom, though. He could only think clearly when his heart was pumping and his legs were moving.

The last two days had been a little crazy. The bodies and the blood. If anything was a punishment, that was it. He'd had to help the doctor carry the bodies back to the clinic both times. There was something unnatural about holding the shoulders of a person who was so...heavy. It was about more than the weight, though. It was about knowing the thing he carried had once been a living person, but it felt like nothing more than a hundred pounds of clay when carried.

Ken shuddered thinking about it.

He stopped at the corner of Wall and Ackerman, about three blocks away from the school. He needed to catch his breath. He only had a few more blocks to go, so he walked, letting his leg muscles cool. They trembled, but in a way that felt good.

Something about the run this time made his head ache. He probably wasn't drinking enough water. It was a pain in the ass to boil any water that wasn't bottled, then wait for it to cool. Most of the water he drank was warm. Sometimes he wanted to go to the river and drink right from the cool water.

That would be asking to get sick, though.

He touched his ear, wiggling his finger in it to clear the high-pitched whine. But that didn't work. The pain in his head was only getting sharper.

The whine itched both his ears now. He squeezed his eyes shut.

Louder and louder.

He put his hands to his ears. His head was pounding now. It was about to explode, he knew it. Ken dropped to his knees.

The last thing Ken heard was—

Exodus's body spasmed as he snapped his consciousness back before he followed Ken Hunter to his death.

Immediately, he returned to the mandala. 2,048 lines that were really one line drawn in what appeared to be a chaotic spill of whorls and spirals. Drawing the figure from beginning to end in his mind ordered the chaos and brought understanding.

As the final lines were illuminated in Exodus' mind's eye, the trembling in his arms and legs eased and his heart rate slowed. His shuddering breathing smoothed. He'd come within a hair's breadth of death, almost trapped in the mind of that boy as it was liquified to nothing.

Order from chaos.

Now three were dead in Ender. *His* three. The three spies he'd carefully cultivated over the last year to watch Ender for the boy, then to monitor the town and track Citadel's movements. All three were dead.

No one knew of them. No one could know.

How had they been targeted?

It wasn't too late. This could be salvaged. He needed to fall back on his original plan, but he had to act quickly. If he failed, more extreme measures would be needed.

And that wouldn't help anyone.

Alec Gunn

AUPrimeHistory: True Conspiracies

(Airdate: 6/24/2010)

RETURN OF THE WILD WEST

<Archive video: The Searchers (public domain)>

Life in the Anarchist States of America was dangerous and cruel. Only where communities could stick together and protect each other was there any sort of stability.

Some smaller communities were successful in creating what might have once been called communes. People shared supplies and helped defend each other from outside threat. Most of these communities were cut off from water and power for years, forcing them to live life as pioneers once did in the days of the American "Wild West." Water was found in dug wells and in contaminated rivers. Sickness was prolific, and medical help outside of gang-controlled urban centers was low-tech and hard to find.

<slideshow: American starvation>

What must that have been like? For the first time in its history, Americans faced hunger, disease, and famine as water sources dried up, and once-powerful farming corporations collapsed on top of the parched soil that was their livelihood. The loss of life was in the hundreds of thousands over the five years of chaos.

<photo: Citadel from FORCE presentation, 1999>

All because of one man's need for power.

More when we return.

July 15, 2018 – 6:05 a.m.

Ender, Oklahoma

Citadel watched from five hundred yards away as Ken Hunter stumbled and fell. The boy didn't even reach out to brace his fall. He was dead before he hit the ground. He hit the concrete of the sidewalk and bounced once.

Citadel was there before his body came to rest. Only then did dark blood, mixed with melted brain matter, spill from every orifice in his skull. Citadel paid no mind that it soaked through his jeans with the boy's head in his lap.

Kneeling on the ground with the boy cradled against him, Citadel looked around for anyone who could have caused this. There was no one. Shimmers from the heat rose from the empty street. A quiet breeze ruffled long, browning grass in Samuel Blue Hawk's front yard. They were smack in the center of town, steps away from the Ender government, and a boy was murdered in broad daylight.

Fury rose in Citadel unlike any he'd felt since Exodus had thrust memory back into his mind, forcing him to relive the moment New York City burned with him inside it. He carefully set Ken's head on the sidewalk and stood.

Just then, Gillian Sumner emerged from the front door of

Samuel's house. She stared at the scene for several heartbeats. Before she could make assumptions and accusations, Citadel shook his head. He felt the firmness in his face, the flaring of his nostrils and the tightness of his lips. He did nothing to hide his anger.

"I was too late," he said in a tone that rumbled through the air like quaking earth. *"Come out, you coward!"* His voice would carry to whoever was around, no doubt reaching the ears of the murderer who must be nearby. "See if your tricks will work on me!"

There was no answer. Doors all along the street began to open, their occupants peeking out to see what was happening.

Someone screamed.

No one came to face Citadel.

Finally, Citadel stepped over Ken Hunter and strode toward the town hall. As he approached, Gillian stepped back into the house, terror on her face. He was two steps into the foyer when Phil Bledsoe emerged from the council room. Gillian was pressed against the wall, trying to flee Citadel's wrath, but Phil stood his ground.

"Now what?" The councilman asked. "What is all this yelling?"

Citadel reached Phil and grabbed his shirt. The man yelped as he was lifted off his feet. Citadel didn't stop moving, holding Phil before him with an outstretched hand. He moved into the council room where four of the council members were still seated. He dropped Phil into a chair, expelling the air from Phil's lungs.

Samuel sat at the head of the table. He took in Citadel and his blood-soaked pants.

"What happened?" Blue Hawk asked.

"Ken Hunter is dead," Citadel said. "You need to conduct a survey of your people. Find out who has been to Washington D.C. or Chicago since last summer. Anyone who has is in danger."

"That will take days," Chunky said.

"Then you'd better get started," Citadel said, his voice low.

"If the pattern holds, there will be another murder tomorrow."

"You can do it faster than any of us," Phil said, his face pale, eyes wide.

"I have other things I need to do. Like find this killer. I will not wait for that." He had one last hope of doing that, but it would take time.

Time he might not have.

He turned before anyone else could argue further.

"We should do as he says," Ben Turner said. Citadel started at the voice. He hadn't registered Eric's teacher as one of the men seated at the table. The man was so ordinary as to be invisible. Something about that bothered him.

Could Turner be the killer?

He set that aside for the moment. He wasn't in a position to be throwing accusations around. He needed more information first.

Citadel passed through the foyer and noticed Gillian sitting on a bench not far from where she'd retreated when he stormed in. Citadel pressed his lips together and went to her. He crouched down. She raised her face to him, revealing red, trembling eyes.

"I'm sorry I scared you," he said. "My anger can get the better of me sometimes."

"I know," she said.

That was a strange thing to say. What did she know of him? What hadn't she said?

"Go home," Citadel said. "You'll be safer there."

"Like Anne was?"

Citadel took a deep breath. "Have you been to Washington D.C. in the last year?"

"Of course not," Gillian said.

"Then you are as safe as you can be. But if you stay around other people, you could become collateral damage."

She nodded, giving in to his argument.

"Make sure Eric doesn't leave the house. I'll check in when I have a chance."

She gave him a suspicious look, but he rose and turned away from it.

After Citadel was gone, Ben felt a weight slip off his chest. The man was beginning to suspect something. It was fortunate he had more important things to think about.

"I'll take the blocks around the school," Ben said absently. "We should each go door to door and ask everyone we can find."

"We should gather them all in one place," Phil said.

"How do you expect to do that with our runner dead?" Samuel asked.

"Oh, God," Chunky said. "We need to call Dr. Posey to pick up Ken."

"That'll be your job, Chunky," Samuel said. "You'll need to go to his office, then help him with the body."

"I don't have much gas left," Chunky protested.

"Then walk," Samuel said, his voice hard. Phil and Ben turned to look at Samuel, whose face had become as hard as Citadel's. The old native was furious but trying to hold it back. Ben could feel the anger coming off him as it threatened to infect him.

"Yes, sir," Chunky said, lowering his head.

"We should get moving," Ben said, standing.

He left the house quickly. Gillian crouched over Ken's body, straightening a sheet over it. She must have raided Samuel's linen closet. A small crowd lined the street now, their faces and auras fearful.

Ben turned toward the school and walked quickly. He wished he was like Citadel, or even Leonard Strange, able to move blocks in the blink of an eye. But he was not a physical SPI.

He found the house he was looking for and made a beeline to the front door. He wasn't ready for this, not by any means, but he felt like preparations needed to be made. It wasn't a premonition, exactly. But a feeling that he'd learned over the last thirty years not to ignore. He'd learned the lesson early, living on the streets of Baghdad in the late 1980s. He'd felt his own brushes with death several times in those days, and the only times he came away unscathed were when he listened to his gut.

Now, his gut was telling him it was time. Something bad was coming and the entire town needed to be prepared.

His knock was answered by the boy, lanky with straight blond hair. He didn't bother to vocalize. He sent an urge of welcome to the boy and brushed past him. He immediately felt the location of the other two down in the basement. They were arguing.

No time for that.

He made them stop.

He descended the stairs to find them gaping, confused with each other. Ashley Williams recovered first as he appeared in the cavernous basement unannounced.

"What...?" She trailed off as a wave of calm wrapped her like a blanket.

"Ben?" Zak asked, bewildered. After Ben explained it to them with a mental sending of understanding, Zak's mouth fell open.

July 15, 2018 – 1:06 p.m.

Citadel stood at the corner of Main and Revell, staring at the motel across the train tracks. The sign outside the Piggly Wiggly read 1:06 p.m., ninety-two degrees.

He reached into his pocket to retrieve a Coke. Pressed to one of the cans was the piece of paper he'd put there. He pulled the paper off before popping the can open.

Motel Room 11, the paper read in letters smudged by the condensation on the can.

He returned the paper to his pocket with the two other cans. He drained the open Coke, then he took a step toward the motel. Frustrated, he turned in a circle and glanced back at the Piggly Wiggly clock.

1:22 p.m., ninety-two degrees.

Sighing, he reached into his pocket and drew out another Coke. He felt the paper he'd put there crumpled like an old receipt. He pulled it out and unfolded it.

Motel Room 11, it read in crisp, black ink.

He drained the can and took a step toward the motel.

1:45 p.m., ninety-three degrees.

Motel Room 11, read the words on a torn sheet of computer paper.

Another can of Coke. He drained it.

2:30 p.m., ninety-four degrees.

He reached into his pocket for the last can. His pocket was empty except for a scrap of paper. *Motel Room 11: I think I'm wearing her down.*

Eric was right. The girl was powerful. But there was something she wasn't counting on: Citadel's patient persistence. When he put his mind to it, Citadel could out-wait the worst of them.

He moved again toward the motel. Instead of crossing the street, he hit an invisible wall. He smiled and pushed against it with one hand. It didn't budge, even under the immense pressure he brought to bear.

"What the hell do you want?"

The voice didn't come from the direction of the motel, but from behind.

He turned to find a tiny girl walking across the street from the direction of the Piggly Wiggly. Her stature reminded him of Jitterbug, who had barely topped five feet. In one hand, she carried a six-pack of Coke, sweating from the combination of heat and cold. She threw it at him. In one motion, he caught it and stripped the cans from the plastic rings, dropping five of them into his coat pockets.

She grimaced and held out her other hand. Her fist was stuffed with white paper. She opened her hand and at least a dozen small scraps of paper fell to the sidewalk.

"Neat trick," she said.

"You can't read minds, can you?" Citadel said.

"Just memories," she said. "You don't have many for someone so old."

"Still working on it."

"You want me to give them back to you? Is that what you want?"

Citadel's eyebrows lifted of their own accord. Had he considered that before she wiped his memories all those other times?

"They're gone," she said before he could ask her. "The parts of your brain that stored them have been destroyed, rebuilt by your powers as a blank slate. It's amazing you have what you have."

"I'm not here for you," Citadel said.

"You've said that so many times, but I don't believe you." *Then why are you showing yourself now?* He wondered.

"I'm here for the other one. The AU SPI." He sipped at the ice-cold Coke, ignoring the fact that it was probably stolen.

"Trench," she said.

"Is that what they call him?"

"No, it's what I call him. He wears a long coat, no matter the heat." Her lips twisted in a mocking smile. Citadel waved the flaps of his own long coat. "Yeah," she said, "Seems to be a trend."

"Who is he? And don't tell me if you're just going to wipe my memory again."

"I don't wipe memories, I block them away. I can block that one if you want—you know the one."

"Don't touch me, again," Citadel growled. "Who is he?"

The moment the name was off her tongue, Citadel vanished in a rush of wind.

Eric kicked a larger than normal rock. It skittered away, bouncing into the road, then hitting an odd edge and bouncing back to the shoulder.

After his mother had come home from work before Eric had even dressed properly, she'd told him not to go anywhere. After the news that Ken Hunter was killed—couldn't have happened to a nicer guy—Eric had acquiesced for the morning. But he'd grown restless. He knew it wasn't smart, but he had to get out. He'd slipped out his bedroom wall as he'd done plenty of times before.

His first stop was Saints Drive Park.

The park was strangely empty for the middle of the day. Maybe it was too hot for kids to play. He couldn't remember ever caring about that when he was a kid, though.

For such an innocuous place, this park was filled with momentous events. He'd learned about his powers here, when he'd done the impossible and laid out Leonard Strange. He'd had his first real conversation with Kristin here. He'd made the deal that effectively made him Citadel's sidekick here.

What was it that attracted history to this place? For that was what it was. *History*. The events that played out with Leonard Strange and resulted in the return of the most notorious SPI on the planet had begun here. Not the school or the bowling alley or wherever else the books might say it started.

It had started here, with a boy and a girl.

He missed Kristin more than ever.

Eric stood behind the bench he had vacated in fear when Kristin had come toward him. He hadn't realized at the time that she was coming to warn him of Leonard's arrival. His fear of her had pushed him right into Leonard's path.

He turned and stared at the patch of grass where he'd punched Leonard, breaking his jaw with a compressed fist. There was no sign that anything momentous ever happened there. The grass was grass. This summer, it was just more brown than green.

It all felt like ages ago.

He turned back to the bench to retrieve his bike before realizing it wasn't there. He didn't walk often—it felt weird.

He was growing up. Soon, the bike would be gone entirely. He'd get around in a car…like Kristin. He dropped into the bench. It was too much. He was happier before, he thought. He had been alone, but he hadn't had to think about what he'd lost. He had his classes, his books…

A dead father and an alcoholic mother. He stole money from his mother to get by most weeks. He had to step carefully in school to avoid that money being taken from him by Leonard Strange.

This was what growing up meant, maybe. Wishing you could go back to a time you fooled yourself into thinking was better. Being an adult was complicated; being a kid wasn't supposed to be.

Eric wasn't, either—he was between. His life was getting

complicated. Not just because of his powers or his friends, but because that's just the way things happened.

What do I have now that's good? he asked himself. He started counting on his fingers.

One: his mother was recovering. She was better and took care of him like a mother was supposed to.

Two: a best friend who looked out for him.

Three: his power gave him what he needed most. A new puzzle every day.

He sat for a while with three fingers up but couldn't think of another thing. With a sigh, he dropped his hand to his lap. He rose from the bench and saw a young family heading his way from the street. A small child skipped down the road with an eager look in her eye. He decided to go and let them have their fun without a moping teenager getting in the way.

It was time he went back home anyway. Gillian had probably noticed his absence by now.

The red Ford Tempo sat in the driveway as usual. There hadn't been much need for it these last months. A light dusting of dirt in the shape of rain droplets covered its body and windows; it hadn't rained in several weeks.

Eric's blue and silver ten-speed leaned against the garage wall. It was clean, of course. He never put it back dirty if he could help it. A long scratch marred the paint along one side. It took a bit of a beating last year. The sight of the damage panged Eric even now.

He opened the front door and crossed the living room, refusing to look toward the couch where he saw Gillian out of the corner of his eye. He waited for her to say something about him leaving the house.

"Not going to say hi?" said a voice.

Not Gillian's.

He stopped in his tracks and turned toward the speaker. Before he even noticed who it was, he saw Gillian sitting stiffly on the couch. She was still dressed as she had been when she'd come back from work. Her face was preternaturally still, her eyes focused straight ahead. One hand on her lap trembled.

On the chair next to the couch, facing toward the coffee table that lay in the center of the room, sat a man Eric knew only from a picture that hung on the wall to his left. The man was older now. His face harder, his skin rougher. But the dark skin and prominent nose was the same. His black hair was cut short in a military style and he wore a long, leather trench coat, even in the summer heat. Beneath the coat, the clothing was solid black and non-descript, almost like coveralls.

Steven Sumner, back from the dead.

Puzzle pieces from over six months of revelations flew together in Eric's head. It all came together to tell the true story of Steven's fate. The chaos years in Ender hadn't been easy. Eric saw that now, with Ender's current situation. Raising a baby during those years must have been even worse. Years earlier, the U.S. government came to take away Russell Sumner to train and help him control powers strong enough to trigger earthquakes. Now, it looked like the incoming AU government wouldn't tolerate SPIs.

Steven Sumner was a threat to his family in this new world order. Just before Marshall's Coup swept through the old United States and established the rule of the American Union, Steven left. He'd always hidden his powers, afraid of what might happen if he revealed them, but someone had found him, perhaps even Exodus himself. Like Leonard Strange had been manipulated by Agent Hamilton, so was Steven.

But Steven was a third generation SPI. He wasn't like Leonard.

Not at all.

"They threatened us," Eric said before he could even greet his "dead" father.

Gillian looked at Eric, her eyes wide. Confused. She didn't know what was happening, but she was shocked. Afraid. What did Steven tell her before Eric arrived?

"The uniform," Eric said into the silence, staring through the trench coat at the black uniform—no, a flight suit. Steven watched expectantly, evaluating Eric's words. "They took you, threatened us to get you to cooperate, then faked your death.

Must have been easy in the Chaos Years."

Steven nodded. "You were right, Jill. He's smart." He gestured to Eric. "Go on."

"You...You're the one who killed Mr. Duncan and Mrs. Bancroft and Ken." Gillian's eyes snapped to Steven in shock. "They'd all been to Washington D.C."

Eric looked down at the carpet. What was the connection? He still couldn't fathom it. "Did they have something on Exodus? Did he send you to assassinate them?"

Steven shook his head. "Information, Eric. *That's* your limitation. You aren't intuitive; you don't have the creativity to make an educated guess. You can only find the dots and connect them. When you don't have the right dots, there are no connections. Here is the dot you are missing: Exodus can see through the eyes of people he's touched."

"You didn't want him to see you here," Eric said, understanding now. "Citadel warned him off...Exodus doesn't know you're here."

Steven smiled, glancing at Gillian.

"You still murdered those people," Eric said. Eric remembered the murder sites, and what Citadel told him of how they died.

"I had to," Steven said, his voice on the edge of regret, but not quite. "I had no choice."

"Why are you here?" Eric asked. "Why now?"

It made no sense to him. Twelve years since Steven disappeared. What made now special? Citadel? Did he know about Eric's powers?

"I need..." Steven paused, rethinking what he was going to say. "You showed up last year. Did a good thing. You made Exodus and the AU very interested in you. Like me. You have a lot of potential."

Eric opened his mouth to protest, but Steven raised a hand.

"Even if it doesn't seem like it to you now, I started the same. I thought my powers were limited to mimicking sounds. I could throw my voice in a way street-magicians never could, but there is so much more that I'm capable of. FORCE showed me that."

"FORCE?" Eric said, surprised the AU would use the same name as the team that supposedly killed millions of people.

Steven shrugged. "It's basically the same idea. We're preparing for something…Something big. We have to be ready for it."

Eric shivered as the purpose of Steven's visit came to him. He wasn't ready for this. It was too early.

"It's coming," Steven said, "and it's coming fast."

"The evolution of the SPI gene," Eric guessed. "Citadel told me about it. The Physicals evolved into Mentals. Now there are SPIs like us."

"The third generation," Steven said. "Something else entirely—probably barely human. We can control forces that shouldn't be wielded by the will of man. It started with Rumble and me. We were the first. Rumble could barely control himself; he was a child in more ways than you know. When it all came to a head, millions of people lost their lives."

"It *was* Rumble who destroyed New York?"

Steven shrugged. "There is no way to prove it, but that is the most likely theory. He was capable. But we are not the worst of it. The evolution continues. Soon, even sooner than you can imagine, the fourth generation will be born. With the fourth generation, there will be no limit to their power. The cosmos itself will bend to their will. Primal energies. Gravitation. Time. Soul. We need to have control of that process. We need to prevent the fourth generation from coming into being, and if it does, we need to destroy anyone who exhibits that level of power."

Eric stared at Steven, stunned. His father killed three people for this? It made no sense. Eric's mind worked even as he spoke. "How do you know? Even if it were true, evolution takes eons."

"The first SPI, Citadel, was born in 1947. The first Mental was born in 1972. Rumble, the first of the third generation, was born in 1980."

Steven paused to let this timeline sink in. If this was true, the first fourth generation SPI could already be out there. Eric's breath caught, and his fear spiked exponentially, drowning out the puzzle he'd been working out.

"You think it's me."

Gillian's head snapped back and forth from Eric to Steven. Her lips moved but nothing came out. Steven was canceling whatever sound she was producing. He held up a finger to his lips, but he paid her no more mind than that.

"Eric," Steven said in a condescending tone, "*everyone* thinks it's you. The AU, the EUP, Citadel, and everyone who knows anything about this."

"Are you here to kill me, then?"

"No," Steven said simply. "I'm here to bring you in."

Gillian stood, or tried to; the air vibrated and thickened around her, forcing her back down.

"Stop it," Eric said in as hard a voice as he could muster. "You'll get no cooperation from me if you hurt her."

"I don't need your cooperation," Steven said.

"Citadel calls me Ghost," Eric said. "I'm untouchable. You can't kill me, even if you tried to scramble my brain like you did the others. So, yes, you need my cooperation." The words came out with more conviction than Eric actually felt. He didn't know the extent of Steven's power, but he was pretty sure Steven didn't know the extent of Eric's abilities, either. Hell, Eric didn't even know that yet. Eric was playing a dangerous game with his father.

On top of that, Eric guessed that the man in front of him was much smarter than he appeared.

Steven stood, his head hanging in thought. "Gillian, go to your room. Eric and I need to speak alone." He looked at Eric before adding, "You'll be safe there."

Eric didn't dare move close enough to help Gillian. She rose carefully, discovering that she could indeed move again, and circled around the couch. When she was facing Eric, with her back to Steven, she gave him a look of terror, the likes of which Eric had never seen on her face.

The last puzzle piece dropped into place and Eric's blood ran cold. If he was scared before, what he knew now almost froze him.

When she was gone, Steven took a step toward Eric around the coffee table. "I don't want to hurt you, Eric. I'm just here to take you to FORCE. Whether you are fourth generation or not, we need your abilities to help us prepare for the future."

Steven held out his hand toward Eric, inviting him to strike a deal: to join the AU and become a member of the new FORCE.

"My mother is off limits," he said. "This town is off limits."

Steven nodded at each of Eric's conditions. "You have my word."

Eric raised his own hand and moved to shake hands with the devil.

And, hopefully, save his father in the process.

AUPrimeMovies

CLASSIC FILM WEEK CONTINUES TUESDAY AT 8 P.M.

SANDS OF IWO JIMA
John Wayne at his best as the tortured Marine, John Stryker, as he fights the Japanese, and himself, in this Last War classic!

July 15, 2018 – 2:33 p.m.

Citadel burst through the door, ripping it from its hinges. In an instant, he scanned the room to watch as Eric extended his hand toward Steven. Steven's lips curled up in a cold smile that shivered Citadel's bones.

This was not right at all.

All at once, time resumed its normal beat. Citadel's senses slowed to a normal speed to match his physical speed. Citadel stopped in his tracks, translating the momentum of his run into force down his arms. They were extended before him, hands outstretched. Though Citadel stopped before hitting Steven, the force rippled the air between Citadel and Steven, hitting the other man like a battering ram. Steven flew off his feet and tumbled over the couch, knocking it over.

Eric turned to Citadel, shock on his face.

"I almost had him!" The boy's voice was desperate and terrified. A wave of fear rippled down Citadel's body, shivering his toes. It was an altogether unfamiliar feeling.

Steven rolled to his feet, shrugging into the long coat which had come tangled in his arms. He stood as tall as he could but couldn't match Citadel. He was barely taller than Eric.

"Get your mother," Citadel said. Eric stared at him for long moments, glancing back and forth between Steven and Citadel.

"I heard your memory is something of a mess right now," Steven said. "I'll forgive your mistake." He brushed off his uniform, as if he somehow got dust on it from his tumble over the couch.

"It wasn't a mistake," Citadel said. "You've killed three people in as many days. I'm going to stop you from taking more."

"Citadel," Eric said. "I've got this."

Citadel glanced at Ghost, shocked at the boy's furious tone. Had the boy's logic been overwhelmed by the emotion of his father's return from the dead?

"Are you saying your father did not kill those people? People who were not criminals, not SPIs, not anything more than people trying to live their lives in hard times?"

Eric pressed his lips together. He looked at Steven again.

"Get your mother," Citadel repeated firmly. "Before she becomes another victim, if she isn't one already." Had Steven killed her too?

At the implied threat to his mother, Eric retreated into the back hallway, turning toward the master bedroom. It was a little surprising that he hadn't ghosted through the wall. Was that a calculated move, or was he too confused to think?

"How much do you remember?" Steven asked. "Do you remember Russell?"

Citadel stepped toward the couch, intending to shove it aside so he could reach Steven. The mention of Russ stopped him. "Yes, I remember Rumble."

"Do you remember if you ever wanted to anger him or turn him against you? You were very careful about that. He was treated different than the others, different even than you. They treated him like he was bomb set to go off if touched wrong."

Citadel nodded. Rumble had always been assured that he was in FORCE voluntarily. He was never forced to do anything. He wasn't controlled like some of the others. Not overtly, at least. He was manipulated with promises and gifts.

Russell got the carrot where others got the stick.

"Do you remember why that was, Citadel?"

"He was dangerous. We didn't know enough about him."

Steven shook his head. "Oh, you knew enough. You might not have known the extent of his powers, but you knew enough. Russ had four years to develop his abilities, to get them under control. To learn everything he could do.

"I've had twenty."

Steven thrust out his hand. A cone of air rippled between Steven and Citadel. An instant later, Citadel's ears popped as a burst of sound—white noise static, like feedback from a concert speaker set to eleven—hit him like an elemental fist.

Citadel felt it, a rib-cracking thud in his chest. He was lifted from his feet and thrown across the room. He crashed through the wall next to the open door and landed in the front lawn next to Eric's blue-silver bike.

He looked up from the ground in shock, a hand going instinctively to his bruised chest. He knew pain. He felt it every day when he walked. His hip was permanently injured, a by-product of the nuclear blast in New York, but he rarely felt it otherwise. His endurance enhancements thickened and hardened his skin, burying his nerve endings deep in his flesh. Even simple touch denied him. It took great force for him to even feel a slap on the shoulder.

The impact of that blast of sound felt like a wrecking ball. He still felt it, even as his enhancements rushed to repair the damage.

The front of the Sumner house was ruined. Citadel's body had torn a ragged hole in the wood and glass. The opening looked as if someone had driven a car through the wall. Debris—wood and glass—littered the lawn. Electrical wires hung like a tangled web from the edges of the hole.

Steven walked into the gap, his long coat flapping around his ankles like a cape.

"I've ripped apart endurance SPIs. I've frozen speedsters in their tracks. I've shown strength SPIs like Rockhide just how weak they are. You're no different, Citadel. If you want me to show you, try and stop me from taking the boy."

Citadel almost wanted to give up. He was probably overmatched, that was true. Rumble had been a nuclear threat. It was possible that Russ was the one to cause the explosion that destroyed New York City. It was something the nerds in FORCE had theorized could happen but hadn't really believed.

Now, here was a living, experienced, third generation SPI. A being with powers beyond anything mankind had seen before. If he was only half as powerful as his brother, Citadel didn't stand a chance. It was only prudent to stand down, to let Steven take his son to Exodus and the new FORCE.

Promise me, Citadel. Tell me my family will be safe, no matter what happens.

It was the first time Citadel could remember hearing Russell Sumner's voice, but still he recognized it. That promise was why he was here. Why he found himself in Ender. It was a moment so ingrained in his being that he remembered that promise, or the intention of that promise, before he even knew who he was.

Citadel had told Rumble that he would take care of his family in Ender no matter what. Rumble had been afraid his unborn nephew would become like him, a slave to a power he could not control. He knew Citadel was the next thing to immortal. Even after Eric was grown, he could watch over the boy and protect him—from his own power, if necessary.

But instead, he was now forced to protect Eric from his own father. From a kind of slavery that not even Rumble had to endure. There was no telling what Exodus would do to the kid.

And Steven was a party to that.

Instead of standing down, Citadel stood.

Combining his enhanced speed, strength, and endurance, Citadel swung his arms back, then forward, slapping his palms together hard enough to create a thunderclap. He held nothing back, and only his extreme endurance kept his hands from shattering with the impact. Still, he felt a pain sharper than what he'd felt under Steven's first attack.

The force of the thunderclap lifted Steven from his feet and threw him backward. More wood peeled away from the house and the entire structure shuddered.

Citadel strode back through the hole, seeking his enemy.

Something changed within him. Thoughts of keeping Eric from harm vanished—his sole focus was Steven. Citadel had to find him quickly and crush him.

Steven slumped against the kitchen wall. He shook his head and rose slowly, blood seeping from a cut in his head.

Citadel didn't waste time, he rushed toward Steven at speed. The world slowed as he summoned every ounce of his enhanced alacrity. His mind adjusted to the motion of his muscles, giving him extra time to react and control himself.

He was two steps away from Steven when he struck something…

Or something struck him.

Either way, he found himself once more moving backward. His feet no longer touched the floor. Around him, the house disintegrated. The wood merely vanished, becoming what looked like smoke. Other materials—copper pipes, plastic, glass, and steel—exploded outward in the slow motion caused by Citadel's hyper-fast senses.

Citadel still flew backward. He heard a blast of sound like a jet engine. His eyes widened when Steven rose over him, his coat billowing, the air beneath him rippling. Then a burst of static, white noise.

All his senses, his muscles, his speed, returned to normal in a blink. The noise slammed him into the ground like a fly under a swatter.

Citadel hit the ground with bone shattering force. Pain exploded in him, his skin broke open as his bones broke and exploded out from within.

When he landed, he furrowed a ditch through concrete, earth, and asphalt. His head struck the side of Gillian's red Ford Tempo. The car slid sideways, its alarm barking its distress. Stunned, his body healing even as he came to a rest, Citadel stared into the sky.

Steven Sumner was flying.

Real, true flight—an impossibility made real before Citadel's eyes. His coat billowed around him, holding him aloft on ripples of air stirred by the jet engine sound.

Gritting his teeth, Citadel staggered to his feet even as the bones of his legs returned to their proper places. He snatched up the Tempo and heaved the car at Steven. It rocketed up as if inertia wasn't a thing.

The car shook apart before it could hit Steven. Parts fell to the ground and the steel and fiberglass panels were stripped of paint before being shredded by an indescribable sound that assailed Citadel's ears and vibrated his skull around his brain.

Citadel took a staggering step down the trench he'd furrowed in the ground. He didn't feel the pain of his hip. It was drowned beneath the pure agony he felt as his body struggled to fix itself.

Steven descended, landing smoothly at the source of the trench. The jet engine shriek died, giving Citadel some relief. Citadel stepped forward, fighting the pain in his legs and back as his wounds knitted together. By the time he reached Steven, his body would be healed and the man would get the beating he deserved.

"You still don't understand," Steven said, a hint of a plea in his voice. "No matter how much you fight me, your fate is sealed. You are a relic. SPIs like Sonic and the Sumner boy are the future's only hope. I can rip you apart; I can soften your skin so I can pierce it with a butter knife."

As Citadel grew closer, Steven shook his head more. "Fine. Here is how it's done."

Steven spread his hands to either side, his palms facing Citadel. A deep thrum pulsed in the air. The vibration buffeted Citadel, growing until it was like a wind, resisting his forward momentum. Citadel fought against it; his body was nearly healed now. He planted his feet into the earth with each step and pressed forward, pushing against the growing force. He felt the pulse against his chest like a twisted shiatsu massage.

Then he stood before Steven, within arm's reach. He reached out to grasp one of Steven's arms with the intent of pounding him into the ground like a wet rag.

"You're not taking me seriously, Omar," Steven said, his voice somehow audible above the thrum of his power.

Citadel froze at the name…His name. How did Steven Sumner know his name?

This briefest hesitation ended it. Steven reached out one hand and snapped his fingers. But instead of a flesh-on-flesh crack, the snap rang out with a dark, clanging musical note, like a string breaking off a guitar the size of a house.

A blow like a hammer struck Citadel in the chest. He stumbled backward, struggling to catch his breath. He looked down at his chest while his legs buckled beneath him and he fell to his knees.

A hole the size of a fist punctured the left side of his chest just at the bottom of his ribcage. It bled freely, a stream of dark red pouring from the wound like water from a hose that was just turned off. Whatever inflicted the wound – pure sound? – had driven through his bottom ribs and punctured his lung.

Steven watched him calmly while Citadel's vision dimmed. This was a death worse than the bomb. That was a gunpowder flash compared to this. He felt like he was being turned inside out slowly, his chest ripped out while his heart still beat. He felt light-headed. The pain was so beyond that he barely felt it. It was just *him*.

Steven raised his other hand, his fingers in a snapping gesture.

But then a hand fell on Steven's shoulder. Citadel's eyes widened as the boy he'd named Ghost appeared from nowhere.

"Give me my father back," Ghost said. A visible shudder washed through Steven Sumner, a vibration that blurred his entire body for a split second. Silence suddenly struck so hard, Citadel thought for a moment he'd gone deaf. Until that moment, Citadel hadn't realized Steven was producing some sort of ambient sound the whole time, a low buzz that filled the air at the border of human hearing.

Now, it was gone.

Steven's mouth dropped open. He stumbled back. He turned from Citadel to Ghost, then at the house he once called home more than a decade ago. Horror touched his eyes for a single moment.

Then his coat billowed out on the quickly building sound of a jet engine. He rocketed into the air, arcing away through the sky.

As soon as Steven was gone, Citadel slumped to the ground, the darkness taking him.

July 15, 2018 – 4:40 p.m.

Washington, D.C.

Exodus jerked upright in the zero-gravity chair. In response, the chair swiveled upright. His feet touched the floor of the office. He leaned forward, breathing deeply.

Rockhide, he called out. There was no response. After a moment, he realized he was alone in his own head. It had happened again—the boy had booted him from Sonic's body like an NFL punter. He would be without his abilities for several minutes, maybe even as long as an hour.

To fill the time, he stood and went to the bar in his office. He poured a drink, leaning against the bar as he sipped. Had he lost Sonic? Had the boy taken his father back, as Sonic wanted?

The whole point of luring Sonic to Ender of his own volition was to get the boy back to D.C., where he could be indoctrinated into FORCE. Edward almost missed his chance when Sonic nearly outwitted him. Now the chance was gone forever. The boy would never fall for the ruse again; he had intelligence enhancements as part of the powers he was gifted. His ability to piece together events on scant information was impressive. He would be on guard now for any other attempt to bring him into FORCE.

He'd need to be dealt with permanently.

Edward moved to the door and locked it. He felt alone, as if he existed in a void of silence. He wouldn't be able to hear the approach of anyone, which meant he was vulnerable.

The damn boy had made him weak!

Had the boy's attack dampened all his enhancements, including his intelligence? Was he stupid now?

No, that wasn't possible. He was just panicking, that was all. He needed to calm down.

He took his drink to his desk and sat in the office chair. He looked at the phone, something he'd had installed so he could communicate with those not on his team, who didn't know he was the director of the AU's FORCE team. Just as with the USA, only the President and the most senior commanders of the AUSS were aware of the Department of Supernormal Affairs. Even as far as the President was concerned, FORCE didn't exist. The DSA was the agency responsible for evaluating SPIs, providing intelligence to the AUSS, and deciding on the manner of execution for each captured SPI.

His hands hovered over the buttons, trying to think past his panic to remember the right button to push. Finally, he found it. He jabbed it sharply with a bony finger.

"Cheryl," he said in a voice he struggled not to choke on. "Get me Hamilton."

"Uh, yes, sir," came the mildly surprised voice. "I'll make sure he's here immediately."

While he waited for Rockhide to arrive, Exodus tried to relax. He guessed that if he could find some mental calm, his mind would heal faster. He quickly sunk into a meditative trance. He fell into a floating mental state, releasing all thoughts of Ender, Sonic, and the boy. He began to draw the lines of the mandala in his head.

So, he lost track of time when a rattle came at the door, followed by a knock.

Annoyance creeping into his calm, he rose and went to the door to unlock it. Rockhide was on the other side, confusion on his face as if the doorknob spoke to him like *Alice in Wonderland*.

"It's called a lock," Edward said, turning back into his office, leaving Rockhide to follow and close the door behind him. The big man engaged the lock again when he was inside, which actually made Edward feel better.

Roger Hamilton was short of six feet but built like a block of marble. His dark skin was taut over his chiseled jaw. Under his black suit and white shirt, his body was cut like granite and just as hard. He had the blocky look every bodybuilder had when dressed in a suit. A suit was great for hiding muscles or fat.

Rockhide opened his mouth to ask what Exodus needed, but Exodus raised a finger for silence. He felt the tickle of Rockhide's mind—annoyance, followed by sharp fear, followed by his own surge of relief. There was always the possibility that his powers might never come back. This was only the second time this had ever happened to him, after all.

"What did you tell Sonic?"

Rockhide's mouth fell open, but Exodus felt the steady flow of images rush to the surface. Even if Rockhide didn't want to answer the question, his mind did the moment he was asked.

The weight cracked concrete through the rubber mat as it fell to the floor. The bar was bent slightly. Every weight in the gym was threaded on it, leaving just a little room for gripping the bar. He also duct taped the heaviest dumbbells to it, but it wasn't enough. He scanned the room for more weight.

Instead, he saw a billowing coat and long legs striding across the room toward him. Sonic grinned at Rockhide in amusement as he approached, his eyes glancing from the stack of weight on the floor to Roger.

"Heard you had yourself an adventure," Sonic said by way of greeting.

"Fuck you, Songbird," Roger said.

"That bad, huh?" Sonic said with a laugh.

"He cracked my ribs," Roger said.

"Getting ready for round two?" Sonic said, kicking the weights.

They didn't even wobble on the floor. Sonic would have had trouble moving that with a forklift.

"More like round three." He began sifting through his options. Maybe he could strap the weight bench to the bar somehow, add a few more pounds to it. It might even keep the bar from bending, too. Alternately, he could lift the armored personnel trucks they kept in the garage.

"You fought him twice?" Sonic said, confused.

"He kicked my ass the first time. But Exodus wanted a shot, so he hopped on for a ride. Next thing I know, the damn kid kicks Exodus out of my head and Citadel is pounding me into the pavement. Again." Roger rubbed his chest as if experiencing the pain again.

"What kid?" Sonic's voice was tight.

"Rumble's nephew, Eric Sumner. He's got some weird trick."

Sonic only nodded. "He's the one you were there to push?"

"No, that was Lightning, the new guy. Speedster. The kid was a side job. Observe and report. Exodus said he's not ready for a push yet. But shit went south. Sumner kid's a third gen like his uncle. You know…" Roger gestured to Sonic to indicate the similarity. The third gens would be trickling in soon. Sonic was the first since Rumble himself. Now this Eric Sumner kid would be coming along, too. Eventually others would pop up. It was that evolution thing Exodus kept on about.

"Damn right," Sonic said, pride and arrogance dripping from his mouth. Roger gave him a sick scowl. When Sonic got friends of his own generation, things would get bad. Roger hoped Exodus would be able to keep all the damned third gens in line, like he did with Sonic.

Exodus smiled.

It wasn't a happy smile. It wasn't even a content smile. Nor was it an evil grin. Even to Rockhide, who wasn't great at picking up Exodus' moods, it was a smile that hid something terrible. Behind that smile, Exodus seethed with rage on the verge of breaking out.

He didn't like making mistakes, not when it was obviously

one he could have avoided. Citadel's appearance in Ender was wholly unpredictable. The unbreakable bastard should have been dead. No, that wasn't anything he could have anticipated.

But Exodus should've wiped Rockhide's memory of what happened. He should've known Steven would go to the musclebound freak to get info on his kid and the Ender situation.

He'd wanted Sonic in Ender, but he wanted it to happen on his own timeline, not Sonic's. When Sonic learned the kid had some sort of power over Exodus' ability, he must have jumped at the chance to free himself.

Somehow, he'd avoided Exodus' awareness and arrived in Ender. He'd also figured out the identity of Exodus' spies and dispatched them.

It wasn't Rockhide's fault that he didn't know who Sonic was, or where he came from. That was a secret Exodus kept close to his chest. The others only knew him as Sonic. Steven Sumner, Rumble's brother, didn't exist.

But it was Rockhide's fault that he'd said anything about a possible limitation of Exodus' abilities. The rock-head had to be taught a lesson.

"Go to Dr. Murray," Exodus started, lacing his words with compulsion. These were orders even the ever-loyal Rockhide might refuse. "Tell him that he better not fail this time. Then offer yourself as a test subject."

Rockhide's mouth dropped open, but he nodded at the same time. As he turned to go, Exodus stopped him. The man was the closest thing to a friend Exodus had, a loyal man.

"Think of this as getting what you want, Roger," he said without the compulsion. "If Dr. Murray succeeds, you'll have your rematch with Citadel." Exodus' lips tightened. "And if he doesn't…Goodbye. You've been a good man."

Rockhide nodded, but Exodus caught a glimpse of a glistening tear in his eye as he turned away. Fear drowned out his thoughts as he left the room to obey Exodus' final orders.

When Roger Hamilton was gone, Exodus took a deep breath. Then he slumped into his chair, willing his body to complete relaxation. He needed to think. He needed to adjust his plans. He couldn't afford any more mistakes.

Somehow, he needed to get through Citadel and remove Eric Sumner from the face of the Earth.

July 15, 2018 – 2:40 p.m.

Ender, Oklahoma

S he sensed his presence before he opened the door.
Lilly pulled the sheet over the bed and set it flat, finishing the bed by throwing the thin summer blanket over it and smoothing it out.

"You leaving?" Trench asked. She turned to face him, hands trembling. She'd heard what happened. The entire town—and maybe towns miles away— had heard. It hadn't taken much to figure out exactly what it was. Citadel ran off like a flash, and minutes later, all hell broke loose in that direction.

"You promised me this place would be safe," She told him, her voice sounding more confident than she felt. She threw her backpack onto the made bed and returned the few sundries she'd removed from it back into the bag. She pushed her fear aside, wishing for an instant that she could block her own memories off like she had so many others. "I thought you weren't going to…" She took a steadying breath. "I thought you were done."

Then she saw his face. Really saw it, for the first time since he'd come in. The light was poor, but in it, his face was ashen and his cheeks looked gaunt. His prominent nose stuck out like an axe blade.

"I need your help, Recall."

"You said I was free."

"You are. I'm not."

She stared at him; she couldn't read him. His mind was a fog. That wasn't unusual, but she couldn't even see his memories of the last hour. That meant he was an emotional wreck, not thinking of the past. He was afraid and desperate, thinking only of now. There were no memories for her to see.

"He found me. Exodus. He's the one who did that."

She saw a flash now, Trench floating above the ground, Citadel on his back, a hole in his chest. A hole. In Citadel's chest.

She backed away, only for the bed to find her legs and dump her onto the mattress.

"Oh, God..." she whispered, only because her breath couldn't move her voicebox hard enough to vocalize any louder.

"I need you to wipe me. Everything. Go all the way back to 1995. I don't care. I don't want to know them; I don't want to know what I can do. I don't want anything. I want to be blank."

"I can't," she said, only a bit louder than before.

"Please, Recall."

"Don't ask me to do that. Blocking off that much time would kill me, if it even worked."

Trench dropped onto the other bed. Lilly had made that one first and laid the green duffle bag on top at the foot. His arms hung limp on his knees and he hung his head.

"I had to watch as that bastard nearly killed my family, as he taunted my son. He made me kill Citadel."

"He's dead?" The thought that the implacable, unbreakable man could be killed was frightening. Sure, everyone thought Citadel was dead. But he'd survived a nuclear blast. She saw it in his memory. To think he might have been murdered so easily by the man with her was terrifying.

"I don't know. I think so. Even if I didn't, to know that I could...I need to forget that, at least. *Please.* Exodus could take me again at any moment and set me against them again. I can't bear to know if I kill my own family."

Tears poured from Trench's eyes, his face a mess of them.

"You came all this way for a reason. You risked everything, crossing the country for them. If I make you forget the last two days, or even the last two hours, what makes you think you wouldn't come back here and replay it all over again? That's the danger of forgetting, Steven Sumner." She put emphasis on his name, saying it out loud to him for the first time. He'd never given his name to her. She'd taken it. He had to remember that he was dealing with a telepath. "You don't learn the lessons you need to learn."

He stared at her, as if such wisdom should be beyond her years. She hated when people underestimated her because of her small size and apparent youth.

Finally, he nodded. "You're right. I need to learn this lesson." He stood, composing himself. In moments, he looked to be the man Lilly knew these last few months, straight-backed and confident. He considered the green duffle on the bed. "Hold onto that for me. I won't be needing it." Lilly watched, frozen as Trench strode to the door and opened it.

"Where are you going?" Lilly asked. "What are you going to do?"

"As far from here as possible. To do what I must."

He closed the door behind him. Moments later, the motel rattled as a jet engine screamed on the other side of the wall. It built to a crescendo, then receded into the distance.

Lilly looked around the suddenly empty room. Then she snatched up her backpack and the green duffle and abandoned ship.

AUPrimeHistory: True Conspiracies

(Airdate: 6/24/2010)

CITADEL

<Archive video: Citadel speaking to a reporter off stage at the FORCE presentation: 1999>

CITADEL

"I'm just here to protect America."

These are the only recorded words from the infamous SPI, Citadel, recorded on the day FORCE was presented to the world in 1999, a year after FORCE destroyed the town of Wichita Falls, Texas. Desperate platitudes coming from a man who has done nothing but kill and destroy to maintain his hold on the power he seized from within his secret government terrorist group.

Citadel's words sounded especially hollow during the Chaos Years, which were a direct result of his actions on 9/11.

<Slideshow: Mass graves across the country>

The numbers are uncertain, due to poor record-keeping during the Chaos Years, but estimates put American casualties from starvation, disease, and suicide at around 400,000. This doesn't account for the deaths caused by violence due to the gang wars and raider attacks we spoke of in previous segments. In all, at least a million people died unnecessarily during the Chaos Wars.

To stop the chaos, America needed a real hero. It took five years, but they finally got one:

<Photo: silhouette - President Andrew Marshall>

President Andrew Irvine Marshall.

More when we return.

<commercial break>

July 16, 2018 – 7:30 a.m.

Citadel opened his eyes, feeling like he'd spent a night tossing and turning instead of sleeping. But this time, his enhanced endurance didn't absorb the fatigue. Above him, thick timbers held up the ceiling and pipes twisted to and fro.

He was in a basement.

"He's awake," said a rough, feminine voice. Gillian, nearby. He turned his head to see her sitting on a chair above him. He was on the hard, concrete floor.

"How'd I get here?" He asked. "Where is here?"

"Eric was able to lift you into Ben's truck," Gillian said with some trepidation. "Now we're in the Williams' basement."

"The Williams...? Ben Turner?" His mind wasn't working right. He was so tired.

How? He yawned.

"Ben?!" Gillian called, her voice urgent.

Citadel pushed himself into a sitting position, finding the effort strangely hard, as if he were pushing himself through mud. He found a nearby wall and slid over to it so he could lean against it.

Ben Turner appeared from around a corner. They'd stuck Citadel in an alcove, so he was away from the larger part of the basement. This was probably where a laundry room should have been, but the walls were bare.

"What's wrong?" Ben said.

"He yawned," Gillian said.

"Of course, he did," Ben replied, "He's—" Ben's eyes widened. "You're tired." Ben told Citadel in a hushed voice.

"What's wrong with me?" Citadel said. He put his hands against his chest where the hole had been punched through. There was a puckered divot there, the skin tender. He lifted his hand away as if he'd touched a hot stove, suddenly terrified.

"I can feel it," he said. His breathing quickened and his eyes teared. "My enhancements…They're gone."

"Is that possible?" Gillian asked.

"We haven't seen any evidence," Ben said. He reached forward and touched Citadel's leg. Citadel jerked it back, staring at Ben.

"Who are you?" Citadel asked, suddenly sure the question was important.

Ben Turner stared at Citadel for a long moment, then turned to Gillian.

"Can you check on the others, please, Gillian?"

Citadel noted the expectation of obedience in Ben's voice. Gillian looked from Ben to Citadel, then nodded. She stood and walked away toward the larger part of the room.

Ben turned back to Citadel.

"My real name is Benjamin Maxwell, Citadel." A chill ran through Citadel's body, another alien sensation after all the others of the last few minutes. Suddenly, Citadel saw Ben with crisp clarity and understood why it was so hard for him to notice the man before.

"Mental Block," Citadel felt tears run from his eyes. Before, he was afraid to meet this man, the man who held the key to so much Citadel was missing. After 9/11, Mental Block *was* FORCE. He was the last of those who knew everything, Exodus excluded.

"I was afraid, too, Omar. I didn't know how you would respond to me or what you thought about what happened."

"You know my name," Citadel said in wonder. "What is my

name?"

Mental Block stared at Citadel for a long time as his form blurred in Citadel's vision. He couldn't hold back the tears now. Why had he been so afraid?

"Omar Bradley, Jr." Mental Block said. "Your father was General Omar Bradley. When you were sixteen, your enhancements manifested, and you were taken away. Your existence was scrubbed from every record; no one outside FORCE knew you existed for four decades."

"Jack Kennedy."

"You remember?"

Citadel shook his head. "Not everything. Hardly anything. I dream of things sometimes. Hanoi. Jitter. I remember the moment the bomb exploded—thanks to Exodus—but nothing immediately before or after."

Mental Block dropped into the chair Gillian had sat in. "I was hoping..." He sighed. "You said his name over comms right before the explosion. Exodus. I thought maybe you could tell me why."

Citadel shook his head.

"He must have been there. Probably possessing someone in the building. But why? He wasn't part of the op. He hadn't been a field member of FORCE since Wichita Falls."

"I don't understand."

"Exodus—Edward, as he prefers most of the time now—was 'promoted' past field duty after the Wichita Falls incident. The DSA wanted to keep him back and use his enhanced intellect more than his telepathic abilities. He became a suit. I think he had ambitions beyond the DSA or FORCE. That sort of panned out. Exodus is the director of the DSA now, at the least, and probably the hand that guides the puppet government of the American Union."

"You think he planned it all?"

"Destroying the USA to rebuild it as an oppressive dictatorship?" Mental Block shrugged, shaking his head. "I don't know. I never would have imagined he'd do that. Sure, he was capable, but I can't imagine he would betray us like that."

"Then...what?"

"I think he took the opportunity 9/11 afforded him and did his best to salvage what was left."

"You think he's doing this because he's a good guy?" Eric Sumner broke in as he rounded the corner. Citadel watched Eric. There was a stiffness in his posture and a look of plain disgust on his face.

Mental Block stood and moved away. "We'll talk more later," he said to Citadel. Then he vanished back into the basement proper.

"What's your problem, kid?" Citadel asked Eric when Block was gone.

"He lied to us," Eric said, taking the chair, flipping it backwards and straddling it, putting the chair back between him and Citadel. Citadel looked into the kid's eyes and understood.

"He lied to *you*, you mean."

"He's been in Ender for years, pretending to be a science teacher. He sent the Williams' here, then didn't tell them he'd be coming, too. What has he been doing to our heads that entire time?" Eric's words were hot, but his face was sullen. He idolized Ben Turner, the science teacher. Now, his hero was the closest thing to a villain he knew outside of Exodus himself.

"You're right," Citadel said. "He was keeping himself from us, and probably using his powers to do it. But I did the same thing until I couldn't hide anymore. I did it because I was in enemy territory, and the wrong person knowing the truth meant me ending up locked in a concrete room in D.C. for the rest of my life." Citadel watched Eric's face carefully as he spoke. There was no softening of his expression, so Citadel decided he needed to hit him over the head with one more truth. "You've been doing the same thing to everyone in Ender except for your family and friends. You haven't come out, even now when you know it would be safe. The people of Ender have been living with at least one known SPI in their midst for the last six months."

"But my mom..."

"Your mom has never been able to stop you from doing anything, Ghost."

"I don't even know who he really is anymore."

"Probably much like the man you knew," Citadel said without hesitation. "Like you said, he's been here for years. You don't infiltrate someplace for years by lying to people. It's too easy to get caught in your own lies. You blend in by being yourself as much as you can, so you can remain consistent with your story."

"You were the one who said you didn't want to meet him because you couldn't trust him."

"And I still can't, but knowing he's been Ben Turner this entire time makes me feel a little better. He's done no harm. He hasn't kidnapped you and taken you back to the EUP." Citadel shrugged.

He still didn't know what to think of Mental Block. He remembered next to nothing about the man; he remembered Rumble and Jitterbug, at least a little, but he couldn't think of any memories around Mental Block. Part of him wondered if that was by design, if Ben was manipulating his memories like that girl somehow.

Suddenly, Citadel chuckled. "I never did trust telepaths," he said, even as the realization came to him. "That I remember. FORCE used them to keep the first gens in line..."

Was that how Mental Block had been used?

He pushed himself to his feet. He was surprised to find his legs held his weight. He still felt weak, though. He was half-afraid that without his enhanced strength, he wouldn't be able to move. He rubbed the palms of his hands together, and for the first time in his memory, he felt the friction and heat.

Maybe this wasn't such a bad thing.

He put his large hand on Eric's shoulder. "Give the man a chance. I will. I have a feeling he's not all bad."

"No one is all bad," Eric admitted.

"Not even Exodus?"

"You can be a complete asshole without being all bad."

Citadel grinned. "Let's see what we can do about your father and find out why Block chose now to reveal himself."

Eric stood and followed Citadel into the larger part of the basement. A large, rectangular table was set up in the middle of the room. Around it sat all three of the Williams, Gillian, and Mental Block. Another chair was empty.

Eric brought the last chair to the table and sat. Citadel remained standing. He felt like he needed to keep moving.

"What do you think?" Gillian asked Ben.

"I think his endurance enhancements are working too hard to heal what's been done. They're taking energy away from him, sapping his strength and speed. I'd guess Citadel was in a similar state for a while after recovering from New York." Ben looked at Citadel for confirmation.

Citadel shrugged. "I don't really remember. I was in something of a fog for several years after I regained consciousness. A lot of that time is still a blank."

"Regardless," Ben continued, "he will recover, I expect, and his normal enhancements will return. It will just take some time."

"Unfortunately, I don't know if we have much of that."

Eric stared at Mr. Turner—Mental Block—when he made such a leap in logic. It was one more thing that proved Mental Block and Mr. Turner weren't the same man. Not at all.

"Over the last few days," Mental Block continued, "I've been feeling a build-up of emotion. That's where my talent lies, by the way. I can feel, and manipulate to some extent, human emotion. Since the AUSS came to town last year, I've felt an undercurrent of fear building in Ender. It's only logical that this would happen, but over the last week, that fear has been building to terror."

"Why?" Citadel asked.

Eric tried not to glare at the big man. It sure as hell didn't seem like Citadel was untrusting of his old comrade. And indeed, Mental Block seemed to meet the question with trepidation.

"Well, there is something I've learned over the years, especially since the founding of the EUP." He paused, seeming unsure what to say. "The powers and abilities we've been granted," he indicated himself and Citadel, "don't come from nothing. No scientist whipped up a magic potion to suddenly give everyone super strength and telepathy. That's why it didn't work in the War. They wanted to give the Normandy landing party a distinct physical advantage, but it didn't work. What they did was rewrite the potential of those men's genes. Their children, or children's children, were genetically different than what they would be naturally."

"And your point?" Eric said. He couldn't help himself. It was like Mental Block was teaching a science lesson. Gillian flashed him a scowl, but he ignored it.

"The point, Eric, is that even the mental powers that were unlocked in the second generation are latent in every human being on the planet. We are all connected by low-level telepathy and empathy. Even telekinesis was once studied as a real phenomenon, but the abilities of even the strongest telekinetic wouldn't be enough to do more than influence a compass needle before Project Brooklyn. Another ability that has been recorded throughout history is precognition—the ability to intuitively predict the future."

"Are you saying there are second gen precognitives?" Zak blurted. "True oracles?"

Mental Block shook his head. "Not even FORCE was able to determine that. There are none on record, anyway. My point is that every human has this ability latent within them at some level—it's your gut feeling, or your intuition. When you feel the emotions of every person within a five-mile radius like I can, you experience the 'gut feeling' of a thousand people combined." He paused to let that sink in. "Right now, the people of Ender feel something bad is coming. Something catastrophic. It's been building for six months, and in the last week, the feeling has become…urgent."

"The AU is coming," Eric said. If he took Mental Block at his word, that was the only conclusion he could come to, short of a completely accidental natural disaster. The entire table turned to look at him. "It started when Hamilton and his crew were in town and it reached its peak when my dad came and killed those people. It's all connected to the AU—to their FORCE team. Exodus."

"Frankly," Zak said, "I'm surprised they haven't already. I expected tanks and soldiers a long time ago."

"Which I would have promptly ripped apart," Citadel said. "If Exodus thinks I'm wounded or dead after what he did to me using Steven's body, then he might allow the AU to pull the trigger on that."

"What do we...*can* we do about it?" Ashley asked.

Eric shuffled his feet and rearranged his hands on the table. Everyone looked at him expectantly. Why did they think he had the answers? It was a moot question.

He actually did have the answer this time.

"Since Citadel is out of commission for a while," Eric began, "we need someone who can protect Ender."

"You?" Gillian demanded.

Eric shook his head emphatically. "No way. My power doesn't mean much against an army. No. We need someone who can blow sh-stuff up." He glanced at Ashley when he almost slipped. She shook her head and indicated he should continue.

"Dad," he said.

"No!" Gillian barked. "No, no, no."

"He was under Exodus's control," Eric spoke over her, trying to stay calm. "He didn't come here to kill Citadel or destroy our house. I don't even think he came here to recruit me to the AU. I think he came here for help. My help."

"Why do you say that?" Mental Block asked carefully.

"It fits. He sneaks into town with a girl who can wipe memories. He stays hidden while he kills three people. Who were those people? They all had a link to D.C., which means there was an opportunity for all of them to be connected to Exodus. Dad, or Exodus, said that he can see through the eyes of people he's touched."

"Exodus' ability to possess the mind of another requires he has at least one moment of physical contact with the target," Mental Block said. "He stores the sensation of the touch in his memory like a catalog. He can call any of them up at will."

"Dad was trying to get around Exodus, but somehow, Exodus discovered his spies were being killed, so Exodus took over Dad's body. I think I saw the moment it happened. Dad hesitated, then the conversation took a completely different turn."

"Your ability blocks telepathy," Mental Block said. At Eric's surprised look, he chuckled. "You've done it to me a few times. So, Steven found out and thought you could protect him from Exodus."

"I can," Eric said. "We just need to find him."

"How?" Gillian asked. "He could have flown all the way back to D.C. by now."

"I don't think so," Eric said. When the eyes of everyone else looked expectantly at him, waiting for this latest deduction, he shrugged. "At least I hope he hasn't."

Gillian put her hand on his arm.

"The question stands," Mental Block said. "How do we find him?"

"The girl," Citadel said.

"I'll find her," Eric said. "I can protect myself if she decides she doesn't want me remembering whatever she says." Mental Block opened his mouth. "I think it's better if I go alone. She might spook if she thinks she's being double-teamed by two SPIs."

Mental Block leaned back in his chair and scowled, but shrugged, accepting Eric's point. Eric tried not to let his relief show. He didn't want to be alone with Mr. Turner right now.

"Well," Eric said, glancing around the room. "The sooner the better." He hesitated. Now that the decision was made and he'd put himself in front of this whole situation, he felt a stab of fear.

Don't worry, Mental Block's voice came into his head before he could block it. *You're not alone. Not—*

Eric shut him out, scowling. Then, he climbed the stairs toward what felt like the most important moment of his life so far.

July 16, 2018 – 7:45 a.m.

After Eric was gone, the meeting broke apart. Ben Turner left silently, not even looking at anyone else. The Williams—Zak, Ashley and Jason—filtered away from the table, Zak and Jason heading upstairs while Ashley moved her chair to her workbench and tucked into whatever project she was working on.

Gillian found herself suddenly alone with Citadel, who had barely moved since joining the others.

"I know who I am now," Citadel said to the empty air.

"You remember?" Gillian asked. Had Mental Block unlocked the rest of Citadel's memories?

"No," he said. "Ben told me. I know, but I don't remember. At least not any more than I already did. I remember my father vaguely, but he was a famous general in the Last War." Citadel shifted uncomfortably. "I remember he let me go. They scrubbed me from history and took me from my family. I never saw him after that. I was a teenager."

"That explains a lot," Gillian said.

Citadel turned his face toward her and cocked his head to the side. "You're doing it again."

"What?"

"Talking like you know me."

Gillian sighed. It might be the right time to tell him. "I met you before," she said. "Before all of this."

Now he turned his whole body toward her. "You never thought to tell me?"

She couldn't tell if his voice sounded angry, or just disappointed. "You were with the group who came to take Russ away. You loomed over the suits as they explained what was going to happen. Your presence...Let's just say it was made clear that no one had a choice in the matter."

"We didn't force Russ..."

"No, you didn't. Russell went willingly enough; he knew the stakes. No one said anything coercive, but it was made plain, and you were the biggest part of that."

"We did what was right. Rumble could have hurt people."

"He did." The words came out of Gillian's mouth clipped short. "He hurt millions. Nothing FORCE did changed that." She felt a surge of anger along with a pressure behind her eyes as tears welled.

"I'm sorry," Citadel said.

Gillian was sure he didn't know what he was sorry for, but his apology was a big step for her. She swallowed the tears along with the lump in her throat.

The Void watched.

If she had a mouth, it would be twisted in disgust. How dare he apologize for the man he'd been? He was a killer. He'd murdered everyone he'd ever known, and he was no different now. Forgetting what you had done didn't erase the deeds. It didn't change who you were.

Mental Block was still alive, but that didn't change anything. Like Void, he'd escaped *despite* Citadel. He was the same as she remembered, though, with a tendency to pontificate and lecture. She never liked him. Just as she loathed Citadel. But Mental Block, at least, had never been a murderer.

"He hurt millions," the woman who cast the shadow Void

occupied said. They were talking about Rumble. Did they blame Rumble for what happened in New York? No! That was all Citadel's doing.

Citadel had no memory of that day and this woman, Gillian, knew nothing of it. She hadn't been there. Void had. Void knew exactly what happened, and she wasn't going to let the lie stand. But as much as Void wanted to rise out of Gillian's shadow and strike both of them down, she hesitated.

Memory was a fickle thing. She knew that even before she became the Void she was now. Was it possible that her memory was flawed here?

She resisted the idea, but she needed to know more. She needed to examine this new possibility.

She had to be right. She had to be just.

Because God knew that Citadel was not.

AUPrimeMovies - In Theaters Now!

THE CELLAR

After getting in a car accident, a woman is held in a shelter with two men who claim the outside world is affected by an apocalyptic SPI invasion.

Outside is dangerous…Inside is terrifying.

July 16, 2018 – 8:00 a.m.

Eric crossed the train tracks and turned his bike into the parking lot of the Ender Motel. It looked deserted, as it always did. Not a single car parked between the faded yellow lines on the gray asphalt.

Still, he approached Room 11 cautiously after laying his bike against a metal pillar that held the roof of the walkway in front of the motel doors. There was no sign she'd see him coming. The thick curtains were closed, the door didn't have a peephole.

What if she did see him coming, though? There weren't back doors in motel rooms. She wouldn't be able to escape. She couldn't attack him; he was immune to her power.

For the first time he could remember, he prepared himself for the confrontation. He thought back to the encounters he'd had with both this girl and Exodus. The buzz of their power in his head was familiar; he triggered his own power to produce the cancellation wave within himself. He wasn't going to be blindsided if she struck quickly.

He paused at the door. What if his dad was here? What if the girl and his father were partners or something? Well, then… that would be it, right? He'd either have a happy reunion or be on his way to D.C. in the next few minutes.

He realized he was giving himself excuses to hesitate. That was a mistake.

Eric ghosted through the door. First, he was in the hot, sunlit walkway, then his vision was occluded as he moved through the door. In the next moment, he could see again, but the room beyond was soaked in gloom. It was hot and stuffy inside. All of the heat from outside was trapped in here with nowhere to go for a long time. It crept into his nose, plugging it with stale warmth.

It took a moment for his eyes to adjust. Light seeped through the window, filtered by the thick curtains meant to keep out light. He scanned the room. There was nothing but furniture and shadows. The girl wasn't here.

Nothing was like it was when he was in here last. The beds were neatly made, the bags were gone. Everything was neatly put away and cleaned as if it had never been disturbed. This girl was used to hiding her trail. She was a pro.

And she was gone.

Eric went back outside and double-checked the room number. It was eleven. He sighed and turned a circle. Where would she go?

He tried to think of everything he knew about her. She could make memories disappear, so she claimed. She'd hidden herself from everyone except Eric.

Where would she go?

He looked briefly across the tracks toward the bowling alley. They'd first met there. She'd had a reason to be there. She'd wanted to make him forget Kristin...*No*.

She'd wanted to *help* him forget Kristin. She'd given him the choice.

Was that what she did? Did she see herself as some kind of hero?

If she left the motel, especially right after Citadel and Steven fought, then she was probably leaving town. Had he missed her already?

No. He didn't know why he felt that way, but he did. She was still around. Why, though? Why would she stick around?

He tried to put himself in her shoes. It would have been easy if Kristin was here. She'd probably be able to tell him exactly what this new girl was doing.

But Kristin wasn't here, and he had to figure this out on his own.

Okay, the facts.

This girl had come to Ender with Steven. Steven had come to see his family again. After the confrontation at the house, Eric suspected the girl might have been working with Steven against her will. If she was a prisoner, then maybe Steven came back for her after the fight with Citadel. Had he taken her away?

No. The motel was fixed up. That took time. They hadn't left in a hurry.

He mounted his bike and looked around. He might have to ride all around town to find them. He started the bike, rolling through the motel parking lot.

Them. Did he think they'd be together when he found them? Not necessarily. She'd been alone at the bowling alley. She wasn't tied to him, but she might have heard the battle at the house and gone to investigate.

He turned his bike toward the cul-de-sac and his house. He rode slowly, watching both sides of the street as he moved along. He turned onto Saints Drive. Even from this distance, he saw the huge gap in the buildings where his house had been. There were a few people gathered around. Eric recognized Dr. Posey, one of the council, loitering with the others, most of whom had their mouths hanging open.

He almost didn't see her. He was focused on the distant scene at his house; he almost didn't look toward Saints Drive Park. He almost didn't see the small woman, almost appearing as a child, rocking slowly back and forth on the swing set.

Eric turned away from his house and rolled across the grass toward her. She looked up just before he reached the benches. He dropped off his bike and laid it against a bench as he had many times over the years. She stared at him as he approached, like a scared rabbit on the verge of flight.

"I'm just here to talk," he said as his hand left the handle-bars.

"You're the telepath from the bowling alley," she said.

"My name's Eric." He took a few steps closer to her. He didn't want to disabuse her of the notion that he was a telepath. Not yet.

"Lilly," she offered her name nervously. "I guess I can't stop you from learning that much, at least. And I can't make you forget it, as much as I'd like to. I don't want to talk. I just want to leave. It was a mistake coming here."

"Three people are dead," Eric said.

The girl laughed. "Why do you think I want to leave?"

"Sometimes," Eric said, taking a step toward her, "what you want isn't what you get."

Yeah, that was the wrong thing to say. She picked him up and threw him toward the monkey bar dome. It was like nothing he'd ever felt. He wasn't gripped or lifted like a hand, but it was as if something powerful touched the bottom of one of his feet and jumped upward, throwing him sideways. The world flipped around him. He had no time to recover from the confusion before his body hit the metal bars.

His power activated on first contact as it always did when he didn't have time to react. He fell through the bars and landed in the middle of the dome, padded by the subtle shift of his vibration. Before he could stand, he was pressed on either side by something immense and he rose from the ground slightly. He rotated to face Lilly. She stood on the other side of the bars.

"You're not a telepath, are you?" Lilly asked. "How did you do that?"

The bubble of force that encased him pressed tightly, threatening to crush him. Then it relaxed, and Eric coughed.

"I can sift my atoms through the spaces between the atoms of other objects. It's all very complex and scientific. I can explain it if—urk!"

The bubble crushed him again, his breath pressed from his lungs. The girl's face was a mask of frustration.

Eric focused on the telekinetic barrier. He had to escape it. He tried to feel it, to sense its vibration, so he could produce a counter vibration to negate it. It was incredibly thin, but infinitely hard. There was a lot of power behind it. It wasn't matter. It was a force field. There were no atoms or molecules to ghost around.

With a terrifying shock, he realized there was no way he could ghost through it. She could easily crush him if she wanted.

"I'm losing my patience, kid," she said. "Stop with the dumb stories."

Eric tried to shake his head. He took a gasping breath to speak. "Steven Sumner is my dad," he croaked.

All at once, the field was gone. Eric fell to the woodchip covered ground, wheezing for breath. He rested on hands and knees for a while, trying to decide if any of his ribs were broken. His chest felt bruised, producing a dull ache with every breath.

He looked up to find the girl draped over the bars, her head inside the dome and covered with her hands.

"Shit, shit, shit."

Eric dropped back onto his rear end. He glanced toward the cul-de-sac and the people wondering over the empty lot that had been his house. The roll of the land hid them from his sight, which meant the people probably hadn't seen the two of them, either.

"Where is he?" Eric asked. She looked past her hands at him. "What is your relationship with him?"

She shook her head. "Kid…" she sighed. "God, your life is fucked up."

Eric couldn't help laughing. It was such a ridiculous understatement that he found it infinitely amusing.

"Girl," he responded in the same condescending tone she used, "You have no idea." He reached toward her with one hand. She took it and tugged to help him to his feet. He sent his power out through her. Her body slid through the bars to join him inside the dome. When she was clear, he let her go.

"Not stories," he said. She gaped from him to the metal bars and back again. She even reached out and touched them to be sure they were solid.

"This town is seriously cracked..." She breathed. "First Citadel, now..."

"Ghost," Eric said. "Citadel calls me Ghost. My real name is Eric Sumner."

"Lilly Tate," she said. "Trench called me Recall."

"Trench...My dad?"

She nodded. "It's a long story."

"Then you're going to tell us all about it."

"Us?"

July 16, 2018 - 8:45 a.m.

"I'm from Miami," Lilly started. She sat on a chair at the head of the table in the Williams' basement, the focus of everyone's attention. The entire Williams family was there, staring dumbly at the young woman. Citadel leaned against the wall farthest from her, not appearing to be listening. Gillian watched Lilly suspiciously, while Ben sat next to her, studying the girl intently. Eric paced on the far side of the table, unable to sit still.

"I grew up in a gated community," she continued, her lips twisting in irony. "Spoiled rich girl. I ran away three times before I was sixteen. I guess that life wasn't for me. But my parents had the resources to come looking for me and I wasn't all that good at hiding."

"When did you discover you were a SPI?" Eric asked.

"Three years ago. Things started moving on their own. I couldn't control it. At first, I didn't even realize what I was doing. Something I wanted would just be there when I turned around. Then it happened when I was looking. Then when my dad was looking."

She took a deep breath, clearly remembering something bad. Eric could imagine what might have happened. Some parents were afraid of SPI powers. Others thought they could do something about it.

Instead of letting out a sigh, Lilly chuckled. "The next day, he didn't even mention it. It was like it never happened. Later, I realized that I used my other power on him. He didn't remember, but as it was happening, I didn't know what was going on. I thought maybe he wanted to ignore it."

"I hid it all through high school. I think there were times when I slipped, but I would always, somehow, make people forget about it."

Eric glanced at Gillian. It would be nice to have had that ability last year. He could've avoided the entire episode with Leonard. Things might be better. No, they would be better. Ender wouldn't be cut off from the AU, Kristin would still be here. Just that one difference would've changed everything.

"Steven," Gillian said suddenly, impatiently. Lilly looked at her. Introductions hadn't been made yet, but Lilly's face suddenly grew pale. She realized who Gillian was. She glanced between Eric and Gillian, making the connection.

Then she licked her lips nervously and nodded. "Yeah, okay. I was in my sophomore year of college. I was familiar with my powers by then. Comfortable with them, even. I was careful. I didn't think I ever exposed myself without wiping the memory of everyone involved. I made extra money helping people forget…Well, whatever they wanted to forget. Usually childhood trauma or bad breakups. You know, the things that can really screw you up." She glanced at Gillian again, nodding her head in quick, short jerks. "Okay, Steven Sumner. He never told me his name—I called him Trench when I had to call him anything, 'cause of the coat. But, telepath, you know? I'm not all that good at reading minds, but sometimes I do on accident."

"What did he want?" Eric asked, noticing his mother's agitation.

"He told me he was a recruiter from the government. You know, like the old CIA. I chose political science as my major, with a focus in foreign affairs. Frankly, I wanted an excuse to get the hell out of the country. My grades were good enough, Trench said, and he wanted to talk about what I was going to do after graduation."

"When was this?" Eric asked.

"Just a few months ago. January, maybe?"

Right after Citadel outed himself. Was there a connection?

"I knew what was really going on," Lilly continued. "No offense, Mrs. Sumner." She looked at Gillian. "Your husband has a rather weak mind. He was an open book, even for someone as bad at reading them as I am."

Eric furrowed his brow. It explained how Exodus was able to control a SPI as powerful as Steven. If Steven was able to cause as much destruction as they'd seen yesterday, he should've been able to make Exodus a pasty spot on the wall. It pointed to Eric's father being under Exodus' control—perhaps against his will.

"What did he want from you?" Eric asked.

"Exactly what he told me he wanted. He wanted me to join the government. He was just going about it in a roundabout way. He never once mentioned my abilities. I thought I'd been careful, you know? No one should have known about me. Or no one should have remembered."

"Are your powers maybe temporary?" Eric asked.

At the question, Lilly squirmed a little in the chair. She grabbed it in both hands and reset herself in it. She licked her lips again. "No, they aren't." She glanced across the room at Citadel. "I can take memory away. I can give it back. But it's always permanent."

"How do you know?" Zak asked.

"My parents haven't come looking for me."

There was a long silence. Eric glanced at Gillian and shuddered. What would it take to make a parent forget about their child? That would be the biggest mind-warp ever. Not to mention the physical evidence of Lilly's existence that must still be in her old house. How would they reconcile that in their minds? What had Lilly done to them?

"Where is he?" Gillian asked. Her voice was not kind. It wasn't like anything Eric heard from her before. He'd heard angry, drunk, desperate, but never this—hard and cold. Emotionless. "Where did Steven go?"

Lilly shook her head, her shoulders rising in a shrug. She glanced at Eric for help.

"Let her finish with why he was here," Eric said. "That might tell us more."

Lilly looked from Eric to Gillian. Finally, Gillian sat back and nodded her head. Exhaustion was beginning to show on his mother's face.

She looked like she wanted a drink.

"I didn't know if I wanted to go into the government. I didn't know why they wanted SPIs there. I knew Trench was one, like me, but we never talked about it. We talked about political stuff. I felt like he was quizzing me on my knowledge and my opinions. Like he was actually testing me for a position in a legit government office. But his mind was telling me otherwise. They wanted fighters. They wanted spies. They wanted SPIs." She said the two similar sounding words with different emphasis, making it clear she was talking about both.

"Finally," she continued, "he broke the ice. He told me he knew I was a telekinetic. I told him I knew he didn't want a covert operative. At least not like he'd hinted. He didn't even think I would be able to read his mind. Not too smart..." She glanced quickly at Gillian, perhaps thinking she'd offended Eric's mother, but Gillian's lips twisted into a smirk at the comment. "He was surprised I knew. He asked me more about what I could do, and I told him. He got real interested about the memory thing. He quizzed me on it at length. He wanted to know how immediate it was, how permanent it was. It was like he *needed* it, you know? I got the feeling he was never sent after a telepath before. He stopped wanting to talk about my telekinesis, which is strong—just ask him." She indicated Eric and he nodded. He'd realized halfway through this stretch that she wasn't talking to him anymore. She was looking at Gillian almost exclusively now, talking to her about Steven.

"You see," Lilly said, "he didn't want me in Chicago anymore. He wanted to use me to get here. He told me about a place where SPIs weren't persecuted, where we were protected. He said it wasn't the EUP where we would be used by the government. It was here in the AU. I could live openly and not worry about getting busted. It sounded good. I don't know how many people I made forget. I was seeing the effects of it. I lost friends. People who couldn't even remember me anymore. I wanted to live a life where I didn't need to do that to get by, so when he said we were going there, I said yes right away. That was two weeks ago."

She closed her eyes and breathed. Eric thought maybe she was tired. She'd done a lot of talking under duress. Maybe she needed a break.

Then a rattling came from up the stairs. Glass against glass.

Zak started and moved toward the stairs to investigate. Everyone was down here, but at the foot of the stairs, he froze. Eric watched his jaw drop open as a glass full of water floated down the stairs and across the room to Lilly's open hand.

She took a drink and sighed.

"That's better."

Everything Eric knew about telekinetics was rattled, then. Telekinesis was supposed to only work in line of sight. Lilly shouldn't have been able to get a glass and fill it with water from the Williams' water bottle without seeing what she was doing.

Lilly looked back at Eric's startled face and smiled. "What? You've never done something by touch before?"

"That's not how it works…" Ben said in a breathy whisper. His eyes were wide.

"That's alpha-level shit right there," Jason said, looking at his parents. Ashley scowled at him. "Stuff," he corrected himself under her glare. "I meant to say stuff. Stuff. Alpha-level stuff. Okay, I'll shut up now." He slinked to the back wall across the stairway from Citadel.

Lilly shifted in her chair to face Gillian. She didn't seem concerned about her show of power.

"Everything he said and thought he wanted from me, up until I told him about my memory powers, went out the door at that moment. He no longer cared about bringing me into the government. His only thought was getting here. I didn't know what had him so bent up at first, but as we left Miami, heading west, I learned more about him. He had plans running through his head. He had me block out his memory every night, so he'd think he was still in Miami when he woke up in the morning. Then I'd have to explain it to him before we moved on. I made everyone we met forget about us, blocking off the time of our interaction so it didn't do too much damage."

"Which is why he needed you," Eric said. "You allowed him to move in secret. Just like you hid your powers for so many years. Anyone who saw the two of you would forget. How many people did you mind wipe on your way here?"

"It's not a mind wipe," she protested.

"Same thing. You said it yourself. You screwed up a lot of people. How many more did it take to get my father here?"

"It's worse than you think," Lilly said. "There were times I couldn't do the job. Some people are difficult to manage. Trench had to…" She couldn't continue.

Eric looked at Gillian, who wore a horrified expression on her face.

"I thought when we got here, it would be over. I got scared of him. He was driven. He did things I never want to see again. When I found out what he could do, it was like when a happy dog turns on you and mauls your best friend. We got here and I thought he wouldn't let me go. I had come to believe I was his captive. I nearly cried when he told me we were done, that he didn't need me anymore."

She took another drink from the glass in her hand and looked at Eric.

"This Exodus guy is controlling him, isn't he? You're immune to telepathy or can make yourself immune. Trench thinks you can make him immune, too. That's why he's here. He's desperate to free himself from what he sees as slavery."

"Yeah," Eric said. That was the only explanation that fit. Steven had made a run for Eric. He'd heard that Eric was able to eject Exodus from Rockhide and thought Eric could do the same thing for him.

"Then why did he run?" Gillian asked. "You freed him, Eric,

but he still ran. Exodus can get him again now. Why did he run?" She looked from Eric to Lilly, sure one of them had the answer.

Eric didn't. He shook his head.

That was a piece they were missing.

"I don't know," Lilly said, but she looked to the floor self-consciously.

"He's gone," Ben said into the silence following Lilly's words. He was staring at Lilly, revealing her lie. "Exodus won't let him run free. As soon as he's able, Exodus will take control and pull him back to D.C."

"Which means there is a period of time where Exodus *can't* do that," Eric said.

"Probably," Ben agreed. "But that's nothing that's been explored. It could be a few minutes, which is why Steven ran. He knew he'd get taken again and didn't want to be around when it happened."

A heavy scuffle from the back of the room drew their attention. Citadel pushed himself away from the wall. But instead of moving closer to them, he turned and climbed the stairs.

Eric noticed that the limp he had since Eric met him was gone.

AUPrimeHistory: True Conspiracies

(Airdate: 6/24/2010)

THE MARSHALL COUP

\<Photo: Andrew Marshall, 21, 1987\>

Every young student in the American Union learns about the Marshall Coup in school, but there is more to the story than we teach our young ones.

Andrew Irvine Marshall was born to a farmer in Iowa in 1966. He was a bright man and a natural leader from a young age. He ran for several community positions in Iowa and Missouri throughout his twenties and thirties, until he was elected to the U.S. Senate in 1999. He was serving as the Junior Senator from Missouri when FORCE, led by Citadel, destroyed New York City.

\<Archive video: AU Army Training, 2006\>

Marshall was instrumental in uniting the three North American nations into the American Union. However, the state of unrest and anarchy in the former United States was not going to be solved just by electing a new president. A military force was raised in 2006 and trained for urban combat. It was the first well-trained unit to operate in central North America since the 1960s.

<Archive video: The Siege of Washington D.C. 2007>

Not everyone wanted the American Union to succeed. U.S. government holdouts remained in Washington D.C., calling out promises that the U.S. would rise again and remain a sovereign nation. To ensure unity, Marshall's Army was called on to remove these naysayers. The sacking of D.C. was quick. When the Army moved in with its armor and artillery, the poorly trained remnants of the US military surrendered. To prevent the United States from rising again, Marshall ordered the destruction of the old monuments and state houses in the city. Those of Marshall's former colleagues in the US House and Senate who threatened the American Union were arrested and tried for treason.

<Photo: Chicago capitol construction, 2007>

As Marshall prosecuted the liberation of the states, the AU government formed in Chicago and began drafting the new constitution that would bring together three very different nations into one. As Marshall rode with the army, he had no idea that he would become the American Union's first head of state. All he cared about was the freedom and safety of his people.

More when we return.

<Commercial Break>

July 16, 2018 – 12:15 p.m.

The engine screamed and coughed in protest. It refused to start.

Citadel dragged himself out of the RV's driver's seat and grabbed the toolbox from under the dashboard on the passenger side. Moving felt like dragging around a bag of rocks slung over his neck. The majority of his strength was gone, but he was still as large and heavy as he'd always been. He ambled to the back of the cabin to the little room that held his bed; he muscled the mattress off, laid it against the side of the room, then hefted the bedframe up until the engine compartment was exposed underneath. He propped the frame on the mattress, balancing both together so he had both hands free to work.

An inspection of the engine revealed the corrosion of ten years of inactivity. He'd started the thing up occasionally to make sure it still worked, but he'd never been able to afford parts or much else other than fresh oil.

The oil had been sitting in the pan for a year, at least.

He found a half-full bottle of oil in a cabinet next to the engine compartment. Then he resigned himself to begin the process of opening the engine so he could coat the moving parts with new oil. He wasn't an expert, that he remembered, but he guessed lubing the pistons might free them up to get the engine started and get the oil pump working.

"Citadel?"

The voice came from outside the RV. The kid.

Good, he could use the help.

He lifted himself from the floor, pausing on his knees to catch his breath. He'd never imagined how much he'd relied on his strength to even move. Now, he was an overweight old man. At least the hip didn't hurt anymore.

He opened the side door to find Eric waiting for him under the awning.

"What are you doing?" Eric asked.

"Preparing for the worst. Wanna help?"

Eric hesitated. He looked around at the RV and saw the signs that Citadel had tried unsuccessfully to mount the huge tires. He hadn't been able to lift the tires, let alone the chassis to get it off the blocks.

"I'm getting her road-worthy, just in case. If we need to leave, you and your mother can get out of town. Steven destroyed your car, so this is all we've got." He neglected to say that he was the one to throw the car at Steven first.

"I'm not going to abandon the town. I told you, it's all I have left."

"Well…" Citadel started. He looked up and down the length of the RV. "I just want to be prepared. Can you give me a hand?"

Eric shrugged, then nodded. "Okay."

Citadel showed Eric the engine and explained how he wanted to run oil over it to try and unfreeze the parts.

Eric grinned and took the oil bottle in one hand. He bent over the engine and shoved his free hand into the engine block. Citadel raised his eyebrows.

"Feeling around," Eric said. "Just to see if there's anything wrong besides stuck parts." After a minute or two, Eric pulled his hand out. Then he regarded the oil bottle. "The oil's probably not gonna want to ghost. Water's like that, too. Liquids are hard." With his free hand flat on the top of the engine, he stuck the spout of the bottle into the engine. "So, we ghost the engine instead of the oil. Just the cylinder head cover; the head gasket keeps the entire thing from ghosting and dropping through the floor." He ran the bottle along the length of the cylinder head, pouring the oil evenly over the full length of the machine.

When he was done, he nodded to Citadel. "Give it a try."

Citadel went back to the front of the RV and turned the key. The engine protested once more but sputtered and churned instead of screaming its dry-metal scream.

"Hold on!" Eric said from the back. Citadel craned his neck and saw Eric once more with his arm inside the engine. He couldn't imagine what the kid was doing in there. "Okay!"

Citadel turned the engine over again. This time, the RV shuddered, and the engine jumped to life. He let go of the key and gave it a little gas. The RV rumbled as the motor began to chug more rhythmically.

Eric came up to the driver's compartment. He didn't at all look like he'd been elbow deep in metal, rust, and oil.

Neat trick, that.

"How do you know anything about RV engines?" Citadel asked.

"How else?" Eric replied with a grin. "A book and a near-photographic memory. I had to feel around a bit to work out what went where in that thing, but I figured it out."

Citadel sighed. "Must be nice, being that smart."

Eric shrugged, then the smile fell off his face. "You're thinking of going to Washington, aren't you?"

Citadel looked at him out of the corner of his eye. "What makes you think that?" He wasn't sure if he was thinking it. But when the boy said it, he felt the yearning to go back to his old home. He wanted to confront Exodus and...

What? Talk to him? Rip his head off? Both?

"I want to go," Eric said. "If my dad isn't here, that's where he'll be."

"What happened to this town being all you had? What happened to fighting to protect your people?"

"It's my dad."

Citadel was silent for a while. He didn't remember having a father. He only knew he had one because Mental Block told him who he was. Well, and the basic understanding that everyone had a father. But then Omar Bradley Sr. had abandoned him to Project Brooklyn. He'd chosen duty to his country over his own son.

What kind of a man did that?

Citadel thought about that. What would he do if he had a son? The question was moot. Citadel had no loyalty or duty to a country—not anymore. The United States, if he ever held that kind of loyalty to the U.S., was gone now. The AU was Exodus' monster.

It all boiled down to a lack of understanding. He didn't know what Eric was feeling. He had no frame of reference. He probably wouldn't even if all his memories were intact. But he did know Eric. The boy cared about this more than anything else. Steven's disappearance was the singular event that shaped his life up until last fall. Now his return was just as significant.

"If I go to Washington, you can go with me," he said, nodding his head. Eric peered at him suspiciously. "I'm not planning on it now. I'm with Mental Block on this. If the AU is coming for Ender, it won't end well, even if we SPIs do nothing. They will punish this town for helping us."

Citadel made sure the gear shift was in park and set the parking brake before turning off the engine.

"Now, help me get the wheels on."

July 16, 2018 – 4:35 p.m.

The sub-basement facility in the Pentagon never really closed.

After the Marshall Coup destroyed most of D.C., the Pentagon served as a temporary base of operations for Marshall's military leadership. The DSA chief and hand that moved Marshall like a chess king, Edward Bradley, continued operating out of the sub-basement that once housed Citadel and the other operatives of FORCE. From this location, Edward began planning for the future of SPIs in America and the reconstitution of FORCE.

Now the facility, which was almost as large as the Pentagon itself and utilized two full floors a hundred feet below the ground, was the home to the new FORCE, a secret cadre of Super-Powered Individuals, whose mission it was to hunt down others of their kind. They were tasked with either bringing those SPIs to justice or recruiting them.

The team currently boasted three members with six others in the roster of former members. Those six had proven untrustworthy or too dangerous and were put down.

The facility also hosted the most advanced medical research center in the world. SPIs generally didn't get sick or injured—even non-endurance SPIs rarely got ill. SPIs did need studying, though. Even seventy years after Project Brooklyn finally bore fruit, little was known about how genetic enhancements worked. Most of the materials from the wartime Project Brooklyn were destroyed when the experiment was thought a failure. The administration at the time hadn't wanted the truth of the experiment revealed at any time in the future. It was bad enough that Manhattan had delivered the first true weapon of mass destruction. If the public learned that the military had tinkered with the health of American heroes, there would have been political backlash.

Now, the Department of Supernormal Affairs tinkered every day with those who didn't exist. Most of those were "undesirable" SPIs that FORCE rejected, who "died" on national television, and ended up in the lab of Dr. William Murray, a geneticist who spent a lifetime cleaning up after Project Brooklyn after it was reclaimed with the discovery of Omar Bradley Jr.

A.K.A. Citadel.

Murray's mentor, Dr. Jacob Morrow, was the primary researcher from the 60s until his death in 1976. Murray took over as lead researcher, a young man of just twenty-seven, but he proved to be a dogged researcher and brilliant geneticist.

Since Edward turned the DSA toward the AU's goals, Dr. Murray worked toward the goal abandoned by Dr. Morrow in the early days of FORCE: to recreate the Project Brooklyn serum and rediscover how to create SPIs. The original formula was lost, and no one knew which recovered serum of several was the one administered to men like General Bradley, who was one of the few confirmed recipients of the gene-altering dose. Human trials had been forbidden by JFK and the complete succession of U.S. presidents since. The USA had been reluctant to repeat the past—a reluctance Edward and the AU government didn't share.

"Are you sure, Doctor?" Edward asked. He stood alongside the older man in his lab. Edward came down personally as Dr. Murray claimed progress. But there was bad news as well.

"As far as I can tell," Dr. Murray said in a nasally voice. "From the sequencing I've performed myself and the back trace of records from all the soldiers who served at Normandy—the original test pool for Brooklyn, he didn't share any familial markers."

"He's not a product of Brooklyn, then?"

"Unless the Sumner family came from a subject whose records were lost, then no."

"But it's a possibility?"

"I went through the conventional records as well. The project records were lost, but we still have the war records from the 40s."

"They didn't take genetic samples back then."

"True." Dr. Murray didn't look up at the sample he was examining at any time during the discussion.

"Or someone tinkered with a completely different subject," Edward mused. "Could Morrow have done some side work we weren't aware of?"

"Dr. Morrow died before Russell Sumner was born. There were no off-the-books experiments, if that's what you're asking."

Edward considered Dr. Murray for a moment. The man was telling the truth, but he was also adept at guarding his surface thoughts. Edward could only get general impressions from him, which let him judge deception at most. He'd never been good at reading emotion like Mental Block. Murray was too inoculated to telepaths in general after his forty-plus years working for the DSA and FORCE.

At Edward's silence, Dr. Murray finally looked up. "Exodus, why would we be doing off-the-books experimenting when this entire program is off-the-books?" He gave Edward a wry smile.

Murray wasn't a funny man, and his attempts at humor often fell flat. At this new, poor attempt, Edward scowled.

"But," Murray said, standing up straight and stretching his aging back for a moment, "there is some good news."

"Rockhide?"

"Rockhide." Dr. Murray gestured and led Edward through a warren of hallways flanked with labs and offices. They finally arrived at a large room. On a steel table lay a corpse covered in a white cloth. For a moment, Edward thought Murray finally learned to tell a joke, but the form on the table was much too small to be Rockhide. One of the failed experiments, then.

On the far wall of the lab stood a cylindrical tank with a glass observation panel stretching the upper third of the tank.

Roger Hamilton lay submerged in a clear liquid, an oxygen mask covering the lower part of his face. He was festooned with sensors, wires, and IVs that stretched out from his body to the walls of the tank. Parts of his dark skin were discolored and cracked.

He didn't look well.

"He's responded to the serum I administered yesterday."

"You mean he didn't immediately die," Edward said.

Dr. Murray shrugged. "It's a positive development," Murray insisted.

"What's in the bath?"

"Various supportive nutrients that are best absorbed through the skin."

"But will his skin absorb them? His endurance enhancement."

"The enhancement has been nullified for the time being. Severe trauma will do that, even to those with Citadel-level endurance. The nutrients will speed the healing process and allow the enhancement to repair the damage quicker, thereby restoring the enhancement's normal function." Edward frowned.

"He'll be restored better than he was before?"

"That's the hope. I know that's not a very scientific word. The serum I injected was designed to target his enhanced strength and endurance genes—those we understand, anyway. Both should be boosted beyond the levels they began with, should he ultimately survive."

"When will we know?"

"Several hours, based on his previous enhancement level," Dr. Murray said thoughtfully. "Twenty-four, at the most. If he dies, we'll know sooner."

"If he didn't have the nutrient bath, how long do you think it would take for him to recover? From the trauma you inflicted. Exclude the serum factor."

"I'd say two days, maybe three."

"That leaves us no more than twenty-four hours. I want to know when Rockhide is stable enough to release. Get him up and conscious in twelve hours. I want him ready to fight in less than twenty."

"There's no guarantee…"

"Then we'll have to do without him. Do it, doctor. As fast as is safe."

"I'll try."

Edward nodded, suddenly excited. He had a window—a very short window, but a window nonetheless. He had preparations to make, orders to pass through Chicago. If he moved quickly, he could take Ender and get rid of the Sumner boy in one coordinated move.

He might even be able to finish off Citadel.

Off in the distance, Edward was aware of a mind quickly approaching on a plume of sound.

Perfect!

Alec Gunn

AUPrimeMovies

THE X-FILES: TRUE CONSPIRACY

The truth is found!

What does Roswell, Project Brooklyn, and the attempted Kennedy Assassination have in common? Only the most important secret ever uncovered. But not everyone is happy for it to see the light of day. Can Scully and Mulder uncover the truth before it's too late?

The X-Files: True Conspiracy is now showing at a theater near you!

July 17, 2018 – 11:15 a.m.

Gillian dropped into her seat in front of the computer. She'd just returned from checking the gas in the generator. It wouldn't do to have it fail in the middle of the day, which would cut the power to her computer.

She had too much to do.

Working on spreadsheets and meeting minutes was hard enough on a good day. The work wasn't literally hard, but it wasn't the kind of work that kept one focused, so it went slow. Add to it a worry for her son, and the town in general, and it was hard to even remember which column the revenue forecast went.

She shouldn't even be doing this, but it was what she could do to help the town. She wasn't a SPI; she wasn't a hero. She was a worn out drunk, too old for her years. She hadn't even hit forty, yet sometimes, she felt like she should be pushing around a walker.

She looked at the spreadsheet on the screen. "Revenue Forecast…" She almost laughed. There was no revenue. The only businesses still running in Ender were the grocery store, the gas station, and the bowling alley. Every week, Piggy Wiggly reported an increase in prices passed on by the corporate office and their suppliers. Paychecks dwindled as people lost their jobs in the city due to government pushback. Just like Henry Matthews spoke of before they left for Chicago, others were seeing the same in their careers.

The AU was slowly cutting every string that kept Ender tied to the outside world. Maybe that was the danger Ben spoke of. That would surely be enough to cause a slow fear to build among the people.

Gillian looked up as footsteps entered through the open front door. Chunky walked alongside Trevor Frey, the owner of the grocery store.

"Can we get them together soon?" Trevor asked Chunky. "I mean, this is an emergency, right?"

"You got a phone?" Chunky snapped back irritably. "No, of course not. I'll get the word out, best I can. It might take a while, though. Sit here." Chunky motioned to a narrow couch in the foyer. He didn't watch to make sure Trevor obeyed, but he strode toward Gillian.

"What's going on?" Gillian asked.

"Where's that boy of yours?" Chunky replied. "Can he run? Of course, he can. We need to get the council here. Have him gather them."

Gillian bristled. She didn't move. "What's going on?"

Chunky stared at her with heat in his eyes, then sighed. "Deliveries to the Wiggly have been canceled."

Gillian's eyes widened.

"Now, you get it? Go get your boy. I'll round up Samuel."

Gillian nodded and clicked the button to shut down the computer. There would be no revenue at all anymore. Before she got out the door, Ben strode in, quickly.

"What's happening?" he asked urgently. She had a hard time remembering that he was a SPI, too—had been this entire time.

"There won't be any more deliveries to the grocery store. Trevor Frey is panicked."

Ben glanced at the man fidgeting on the couch. "I can tell. Get Eric and Citadel. I don't think we have any more time left."

He didn't have to elaborate. If the AU planned to lay siege

to Ender, it would start by starving them out. Then they'd close the roads so no one could get out for supplies.

Or would they close the roads first?

When the people found out there would be no resupply for the grocery store, there would be a panic. People would try to get out of town, go to McAlester or elsewhere to stock up on necessities before they ran out here. If the AU wanted Ender to starve out, they wouldn't allow that. The roads would already be closed.

"You get it," Ben said. "This is it."

"But Citadel..." Gillian said in a hushed voice.

"I know that man, Gillian," Ben said, laying a hand on her arm. "He will find a way to fight. Trust me."

She felt an odd comfort at the touch of his hand. For a moment she wondered if he was soothing her with his power then realized she didn't care. She needed it now, whether it was real or not.

He nodded to her, and she left to go find her son, who she knew would be with the man she most feared in the world.

"My dad can fly," Eric said. "What if that means I can?"

"How?" Citadel said. The wheels were on the RV and it started normally. The gas tank was at three-quarters and—most importantly—there were ten cans of Coca-Cola in the RV's mini-fridge.

They were ready.

It was the day of the week Eric usually tested his conditioning by running the length of the field. He almost had the boy do it, but he'd promised not to train the boy.

"If I knew that, I'd do it."

Citadel shrugged, then turned thoughtful. "I remember..." He tried to put the words together. "I don't know how much training I had, but one of the first things they had me do, before FORCE was even a thing, was clear a path up a river toward Hanoi, Vietnam, with a military unit coming behind me to sack the city."

"'Clear a path?'" Citadel stared at Eric. Finally, the kid said, "Oh."

"I was your age. I was just learning what I could do. I learned a lot about myself on that trip. How much damage I could take. How much damage I could dish out. Well, at least in those days. I wasn't fully mature yet. My enhancements were nowhere near their peak."

"You're saying I'm nowhere near my peak yet?"

"I doubt it."

"How long until you were?"

"I don't remember."

Eric sat thoughtfully. Citadel could almost see the gears turning in his head. He wondered if the kid would eventually think himself stronger. Would he come up with scientific explanations for something, then do them? Or would it be like his "super strength," coming in a moment of intuition, then remaining unexplained?

Dangerous.

"Rumble didn't have intellect enhancements," Citadel said. "I don't think your father does either. Neither of them had the option of thinking through their abilities, at least not on the level that you can. I want you to promise me that you'll tread carefully. Think it through before you do anything dangerous."

Eric nodded. "I'm still not sure where the atoms go..." He trailed off, then looked up at Citadel. "I'm not sure I can promise exactly that, but I'll be careful."

"I guess that's all I can ask for."

The trees at the edge of the field rustled and Gillian appeared through the long grass. She paused at the edge of the field, scanning the scene. The RV on its wheels and the man and boy, sitting enjoying Cokes. After a moment, she continued toward them.

The location of the RV wasn't really a secret, but it still irked Citadel that Gillian had found it and appeared to be coming in like she was invited.

Eric stood when his mom approached. "Mom, it's not what it looks like. We haven't been..."

"I know," Gillian said. Then she looked at Citadel. He could see it in her face. Damn, he might as well be a telepath.

"It's time," he said. "Come on, Ghost, let's go see what we can do about protecting your home."

He crushed the empty can in his hand. By muscle memory, he rolled it into a tiny spike of aluminum and pinched it between two fingers before he stopped. He huffed a laugh. The skin of his palms was whole and unharmed by the sharp metal.

He tossed the dart at the pile of wood Eric stood from. He felt his hand twitch at the last second and the piece of metal hit the wood on its side, bouncing off and landing in the dirt. He scowled.

"Well, we'll see…"

July 17, 2018 – 12:20 p.m.

The RV was turning onto Main when Eric saw the plane in the sky. There were rarely any planes that flew over Ender, except for the occasional airliner flying so high only the trail was visible from the ground.

This plane was flying low, and as it approached, Eric could see it was large.

"Citadel," Eric said and pointed up through the windshield.

Citadel bent over the steering wheel to get a better look. "Military. I wouldn't have expected paratroopers."

The RV rolled over the train tracks in front of the motel and finally stopped in front of the Council hall.

"Eric," Gillian said as she descended the steps out of the RV, "find the council. They'll probably be…"

"That won't be necessary," Ben Turner said as he exited Samuel Blue Hawk's house. "I found them and had them come." He tapped his head to indicate he used his powers.

The buzz of a distant engine slowly became a roar as the plane descended low over the town.

Citadel and Eric joined Gillian on the sidewalk. Citadel kept his eye on the plane.

"Did you get Lilly?" Eric asked. "She's a telekinetic—she could help."

Mental Block cocked his head for a moment before saying, "She's still at the motel. She doesn't seem too motivated to help."

"Not for long," Citadel said. He pointed up at the plane. Eric looked up and saw it was a cargo plane, one with the back end that slanted up. But now, the ramp was lowered, and someone stood on the end of it. With the person standing there, Eric suddenly felt like his sense of proportion was warped. Either the plane was much smaller than he thought, or the person filling the cargo ramp was a lot larger than a normal man.

The man stepped off the ramp as the plane passed overhead. His trajectory dropped him straight down on the motel. There was an explosion of wood, metal, and dirt at he struck.

"They're making this into a SPI incident," Mental Block said. "They're—" He cut off suddenly when there was another explosion from the motel as something large was ejected in an arc toward the railroad tracks.

"That would be Recall," Citadel said. He took a step toward the tracks.

"Citadel!" Eric called, a spike of fear ripping through him. "You're not—"

Citadel stomped on the ground. The concrete of the sidewalk cracked beneath his foot. He seemed to suppress a wince, though.

"I'm not a hundred percent, but I can fight," he said.

Eric moved to follow Citadel as the big man began to jog toward the tracks. But a hand on his shoulder stopped him. He turned to see Mental Block pull his hand away. Eric couldn't help but see Mr. Turner, his science teacher, standing there. That had been a lie.

Or had it?

"Recall and Citadel are heavy hitters," Mental Block said. "They can handle whatever that is."

Eric opened his mouth to protest, but he suddenly couldn't think of a reason. Had Mental Block...?

"The AU military and the AUSS will be here soon. They'll use the excuse of a SPI attack to move in along with *AUPrime* cameras. We need to defend the town."

"How?" Gillian asked. "Just the two of you?" Eric saw the naked fear in her face. Mental Block turned to her and she calmed instantly. The man was using his powers liberally now, but Eric saw the necessity. Calm and logic would be needed to solve this problem.

Mental Block smiled at Gillian. "No, not just us, but we have to mobilize our army."

"Our—" Gillian stopped as Mental Block closed his eyes. Almost instantly, doors along the streets began to open. Men and women emerged onto the street, every one of them armed. Some held pistols, others hunting rifles. Others held assault weapons and military-style munitions.

Eric then remembered the story Mr. Turner told him last year. The one about how Ender protected itself from the raiders and gangs that had threatened every other town during the Chaos Years. Ender was the only town in Oklahoma to remain unmolested during those years. There was a reason for that.

Every citizen of Ender was armed. Everyone old enough to remember the Chaos Years had combat experience. It hadn't been just the show of force that had deterred hardened criminals from Ender. The people had fought for their town.

Now Mental Block was using his powers to urge them to do so again.

Samuel Blue Hawk rushed out of his front door, followed by Dr. Posey and Chunky. Each was armed with a rifle. Chunky's even had colorful feathers tied to it.

"What's happening?" Samuel asked. Mental Block opened his eyes and pointed toward the motel.

"The AU just dropped a SPI into town. They're using it as a pretense to attack the town, which means the AUSS will be here any minute."

Samuel eyed Mental Block for a moment, suspicious, but then a roar echoed through the air from the train tracks and the squealing rip of metal resounded toward the gathered councilmen.

Eric saw the change in Samuel instantly. He became the

commander he'd once been. He glanced right and left and saw the people standing in their yards, armed.

"Gather what fighting men and women we have and have them muster at the school parking lot. Piggly Wiggly is too close to…that." He glanced at Posey and Chunky and barked. "Now!"

As the council moved away, the people around them began moving toward the school. Eric looked at Mental Block, who had a small smile on his face.

"Are you controlling them?" Eric asked. Gillian's mouth opened in shock.

"No," Mental Block said. "I don't have that power. I can only push a few buttons. Get them moving with subtle urges and emotions. From here on out, they're on their own."

"You're not going to help them?" Gillian asked.

"I don't think I can beyond what I've done already," Mental Block said, "Besides, I don't think the AU's FORCE operation will limit itself to that." He pointed toward the motel and the growing sounds of a super-powered fight. "Exodus won't leave it to chance that his beast can do the job alone. We," Mental Block indicated Eric and himself, "have to prepare for the others.

"Follow me."

The air resounded with the blow that threw Citadel twenty feet across the railroad tracks. He felt every crack of his ribs, every scrape from sliding across the asphalt road. He rolled over and paused, catching his breath, bleeding hands flat on the hot surface.

The sound of ripping metal drew Citadel's attention. He looked up and gasped.

The creature that had dropped from the airplane only vaguely resembled Agent Roger Hamilton. The man now stood taller than Citadel. His shoulders were twice as broad as they had been, and his arms were thick and ridged with hard muscle. His dark skin was now a smoky gray, cracked and split, revealing pink flesh beneath. The raw skin on Citadel's knuckles attested to the hardness of that skin.

This monster was no longer human. He wasn't even a SPI.

He was a science experiment.

Only his face reminded Citadel of the man who led the AUSS investigation into Leonard Strange. It was that face Citadel had looked into when Exodus triggered the old memory he had once suppressed, the bomb and the pain.

The thing that was no longer Roger Hamilton, but Rockhide in truth, ripped one of the thick train tracks up from the ground. The rail split from its welded join, giving Rockhide a ten-foot-long iron bludgeon to bear against Citadel.

Citadel took stock of his body, the burning and pain of his injuries, and felt fear.

Then another a familiar feeling. A tingling that started in his sternum and spread through his ribcage. His endurance enhancement was healing his broken ribs. The skin on his hands smoothed and the blood on them flaked.

He pushed himself to his feet and felt the ungodly weight that had slowed him the last two days melt away.

Then the iron train track slammed into his back.

A new pain flashed through Citadel's body as he was driven face first into the road. He slid several feet on his face and chest before he twisted around to look up at Rockhide, who had the bent metal rail lifted over his head, ready to bring down on Citadel again.

The rail came down...and slammed into an invisible barrier inches above Citadel's face. Rockhide reeled with the unexpected collision. The rail jumped out of his hands and cartwheeled away from both combatants. For a moment, Rockhide stared down at Citadel in naked shock.

Then, he vanished.

Almost faster than Citadel could track, Rockhide was thrown into the air in the direction of the residential area of south Ender.

Citadel rose, the pain in his back and face washing away as

he moved. He glanced toward the motel and saw Recall watch him.

"Thank you," he called to her.

She nodded. "Are you okay? He kicked the crap out of you."

Citadel nodded. He stretched his back by swinging his arms. "Adrenaline," he said, giving her a twisted smile. Then he turned in the direction of the lot that once held the Sumner house. "Time to return the favor."

AUPrimeHistory: True Conspiracies

(Airdate: 6/24/2010)

LIBERATION OF THE STATES

<Archive video: War on home soil, 2007>

Once united, the fractured states of America had fallen to criminal and terrorist forces. Its liberation was not going to be clean, or without cost. Andrew Marshall rode with his men as they flushed out the largest of these criminal enterprises.

<Animated map: Marshall's journey>

Atlanta, St. Louis, Denver, and Las Vegas. The battles were hard and casualties on both sides, including civilians, were great. Criminal elements in these cities and more had co-opted and trained themselves in the use of military vehicles and weapons seized from National Guard armories and federal military bases. Marshall had the advantage of air support, which was used judiciously throughout the campaign.

As Marshall moved west, units separated to spread to smaller hotspots: Springfield, Kansas City, New Orleans, Detroit, and others. With close air support from the main unit and units based in Canada and Mexico, this three-pronged approach liberated all major cities in less than a year. It would be another two years before the last remnants of the criminal element were chased west to the coast.

\<Graphic: Flag of the Estados Unidos del Pacíficos\>

These criminals would soon infiltrate the people of California, Oregon, and Washington, where they would form the separatist criminal state known as the EUP.

More on that when we return.

\<commercial break\>

July 17, 2018 – 12:30 p.m.

"What can the two of us do against FORCE SPIs?" Eric asked as Mental Block led him down Wall Street. People were streaming toward the school, so they weren't completely alone.

"True," Mental Block said in a voice Eric remembered from countless science lessons. "You are young and not fully into your abilities yet." He paused. "And me? I've never been much of a fighter. I was always the backup. I helped contain the situation, kept innocents out of harm's way. My role in FORCE never put me on the front lines…Well, almost never."

"Almost?" Eric asked, suddenly curious. Mental Block's lips turned up in a sad smile.

"Wichita Falls. The cluster to end all clusters. But that's a story for another time." He pointed across the street to prompt Eric to cross. "To answer your question, the two of us can't do much, I don't think, but we have backup."

Eric saw it as his feet stepped onto the street. They were heading toward the Williams house.

"What is the weakness almost all SPIs share?" Mental Block asked in a way that definitely reminded Eric of Mr. Turner's science classes. He wondered if Citadel was right. Maybe Mental Block was Mr. Turner after all.

"Electricity," Eric said. "It's in every weapon the AUSS uses against SPIs."

"Exactly. We're going to—" Mental Block suddenly stopped in his tracks just as his feet touched the sidewalk in front of the house. His face suddenly went ashen. "We're too late. Eric, ghost—"

Eric's instincts latched onto the abrupt panic in Mental Block's voice. He felt his body phase out as something passed through him at incredible speed. Despite being mostly out of phase with the physical world, he was still buffeted by the experience. He stumbled a few steps before looking in the direction the object went.

Half a block away, a figure stood in a slick bodysuit that glistened in the sunlight. The bodysuit was black except for two bright white lightning bolts running down either arm. On the breast of the suit was the familiar Vitruvian Man patch, identical to the one Eric had seen in his father's bag.

The symbol of FORCE.

The speedster grinned as he settled himself in the street. He wore tinted goggles, probably to keep the wind from his eyes while moving at speed. Still, Eric would never forget that face. His heart shuddered and he felt a spike of pure terror at seeing this man again.

"Leonard Strange," he breathed, disbelieving. His old high school bully looked older somehow, as if he aged years in just the few months since Eric saw him last. Strange had been executed on live TV on Christmas Day last year. Eric hadn't watched it himself, but now he wished he had. It must have been faked.

"I thought maybe I'd catch you off-guard," Leonard said as his body swaggered, unable to stand still. "And paste you to the street without a hassle. I'm kinda glad it wasn't so easy."

"Metabolism," Mental Block said. "Look at him." Mental Block noticed the aging, too. "Speedsters age faster than normal. Without endurance enhancements, the more they move faster than normal, the quicker they age. He's probably spent the last few months training non-stop, so he looks a decade older." Mental Block spoke quickly and softly as he moved away from Eric.

"Mr. Turner," Leonard said. "Smart move. Once I finish with Eric here, I might even let you live."

"Can't you do anything?" Eric asked Mental Block. The telepath shook his head.

His obsession is more powerful than I can overcome, Mental Block sent him telepathically. *He wants you more than anything. I'll do what I can. We came here for a reason.*

Eric looked toward the Williams house. How long would he need to hold off Leonard before Mental Block could get whatever he came here for?

Gillian stood by Samuel Blue Hawk as he stood in front of a crowd of several hundred people—the whole town of Ender, Oklahoma. She didn't know how she ended up here with him, but it seemed like the right place. She wanted to help, and this was where it felt right.

She wondered how much of that feeling was Ben Turner—*Maxwell's*—influence. Mental Block was a self-described empath and could manipulate feelings. Was she doing this because Ben was making her? Did she truly understand the level of danger they were all in?

"We're here," Samuel began, his deep voice booming over the crowd without amplification, "because we've just experienced a SPI attack."

There was a murmur through the crowd and heads turned, looking for the attack. They were far enough away from the motel that they couldn't hear Citadel's struggles. Samuel held his arms up to get their attention. His old hunting rifle swung from his shoulder.

"We are protected. Citadel and," Samuel glanced at Gillian, "*other* SPIs are here to counter the threat. But we cannot let them fight alone. This attack is a feint by the American Union—a pretense for them to move in and take our town."

That statement caused a renewed murmur, this one laid over a general growl of unease and anger.

"If we want Ender to survive this, we must fight," Samuel said. He seemed to be manipulating the crowd as well as Mental Block, amping them up, then soothing them with assurances and solutions. "Just as we did in the Chaos Years, we must protect our land, our families. The AU will not stop at putting down Citadel and our SPI allies. They will wipe Ender from the map because we stood up to them. We rejected their propaganda. We see the AU for what it really is: a hypocrisy made flesh. They hunt down and murder SPIs—human beings —while also using SPIs in secret, just as the United States did. Everything they have told us in the last decade has been a lie. What more is a lie?"

Gillian couldn't stand by and stay silent. She had to answer that question.

"The AU," she said, mimicking the tenor and volume of Samuel's voice, "is run in secret by a telepath named Exodus. Last winter, Citadel and my son..." She trailed off, suddenly realizing that she was outing Eric as a SPI. "My son, Eric, faced Exodus after Eric put down Leonard Strange." She paused. *There. The truth is out.* She watched the crowd. Their eyes were on her.

Some of them had mouths that hung open. Others shook their heads in disbelief.

"Exodus can control minds and possess bodies. He was possessing the body of Roger Hamilton, his SPI agent within the AUSS, when Citadel defeated him, but he is still a danger to everyone. Ender must remain free. It must remain a bastion against Exodus and the AU. Ender will be the place where the liberation of the American people begins."

Silence followed her words. She glanced at Samuel, who looked at her with a light smile. He didn't seem surprised at all by her statement, by the revelation that Eric was a SPI. After a moment, he turned back to the crowd.

"While Citadel, Eric, and their friends defend us against the AU SPIs, we must defend Ender against the AUSS, which we expect to arrive at any moment. If you were with us before, please find your units and muster."

Samuel waited as the crowd shifted. The crowd separated into four groups. They were the four units of the Ender militia, the force that had held Ender against all threats for five years. It was as if they never disbanded. Gillian noticed then that the people who were together were those she usually saw together in town. The unspoken bonds that had formed in those five years had lasted a lifetime.

There was a fifth group of stragglers, mostly young men and women who would have been children a decade ago. But soon, that group vanished, absorbed into the units of their families.

"We will defend the roads out of town," Samuel said. "North, South, East, and West. Just like before. I know it's been a long time and we all thought these days were behind us, but this isn't the kind of thing you forget. Pass on your knowledge to the young folk. Keep everyone alive, and show those bastards that Ender is our town!"

Then the parking lot behind the crowd exploded in a shower of asphalt and concrete.

July 17, 2018 – 12:30 p.m.

It started in Saints Drive Park. Just as it always did.

Citadel and Rockhide collided in the woodchips, falling together into a fierce wrestling match that scattered wood and tore into the earth. Their bodies fell into the metal and plastic of the playground equipment, crushing it.

Rockhide snatched the chain from one of the swings and tried to wrap it around Citadel's neck. Citadel snapped the chain in two places until it fell away, the short lengths useless in Rockhide's hands.

Citadel gripped one of Rockhide's wrists in both of his hands and flipped the giant over, crashing him into the metal bench where Eric once sat, drawing in his sketch pad. With Rockhide on his back, Citadel pounded him with jackhammer blows to the head.

In response, Rockhide kicked up, launching Citadel over his head and into the heat-browned grass of the sledding slope. Citadel landed and spun to his feet, his speed and agility enhancements kicking in.

Rockhide rose slowly, grinning.

"Now, this is more like I imagined it would be," Hamilton said. He grabbed a scrap of twisted metal that had once been part of the swing set and threw it at Citadel, then leaped into the air, arcing over the trees toward town.

Citadel caught the structure and it ripped in two, throwing the scraps to either side into the dirt of the hill behind him. He marked Rockhide's trajectory, then ran to catch up. He favored his speed enhancement over the strength Rockhide was using to traverse the distance. In a straight line, it would have been no contest, but Citadel had to navigate the streets and other obstructions that Rockhide merely leaped over. As it was, he saw Rockhide rise into the air twice more, heading for the center of town before he found the man again, landing with a crunch of concrete in the parking lot of the Piggly Wiggly.

As Citadel approached at what might have been thirty miles per hour, Rockhide ripped a light pole from the ground and swung it in his direction, trying to connect with a baseball swing, hoping to rocket Citadel back the way he came. But Citadel was done matching his strength and endurance against Rockhide's. Citadel wasn't the model of physical SPIs just because he was stronger and tougher than anyone else.

He also had the speed and agility that few physicals possessed.

With those enhancements, he ducked under the light pole, reaching up to grab it at the same time. He borrowed its momentum, holding tight as he spun around a new axis, feet planted deep into the concrete.

Rockhide was lifted off his feet and thrown into the brick and glass of Murphy's Speedy Eats at roughly the same speed as a home run baseball. Brick crumbled, steel screeched, and glass shattered. Citadel threw the rest of the light pole into the hole after Rockhide. The collision of steel and concrete hit the building like a wrecking ball, and the entire structure collapsed.

In the movies, there would be a moment of silence as the crumbled structure settled and the audience thought the villain finally defeated.

Rockhide didn't want to give anyone that sort of suspense. Before the dust could settle, the pile of rubble shuddered and flexed. Rockhide burst from the wreckage and began using it as munitions against Citadel.

Unfortunately for Rockhide, the projectiles he threw—clumps of concrete, brick, and steel—moved toward Citadel in slow motion. Citadel's speed and agility made it simple to dodge each one.

However, they flew past Citadel and crashed into the front of the Piggly Wiggly. Glass shattered as the front doors of the grocery store were crushed in the onslaught. Citadel fervently hoped there was no one inside. Had Mental Block used his powers to evacuate the town?

There was no time to think about that now.

Citadel ran as fast as he could toward Rockhide. Speed and agility were his advantage now. Whatever had been done to Rockhide, it made his endurance and strength at least a match for Citadel's own.

It was strange. Usually Citadel was the brute, the one with overwhelming force. He was used to using that force alone to solve his problems.

Now, he was the smaller, faster combatant.

He struck Rockhide's flank before the monster knew he was coming. His fist connected with unholy force—his natural strength enhanced by the speed at which he struck—in Rockhide's kidney. Such a punch would cripple a normal man, even most SPIs.

Rockhide merely grunted, his arm swinging around instinctively to counter. Citadel ducked under the blow. The back of Rockhide's forearm brushed the top of Citadel's head.

In the slow motion of Citadel's perception, Rockhide's body began to twist in the direction of his swinging arm. Citadel spun and struck Rockhide's opposite kidney. This blow wasn't quite as hard; it didn't have as much speed behind it. Even still, Rockhide's body contorted toward this second strike.

Citadel noticed the cracks in Rockhide's skin flexed and widened as he moved. Between the cracks, the black-gray flesh faded to pink. It was some sort of bare skin or scar tissue caused by whatever Dr. Murray did to Hamilton.

Citadel had a sudden memory of Murray, a man who, even in his thirties, had a high forehead and round, rosy cheeks. He rarely smiled but had a brash voice that seemed to come from a happier man even when he was angry. He was a little insane, Citadel remembered. He didn't like his work, and he took it out on the SPIs in his care. This...thing was just the sort of joke Murray would tell, an Endurance SPI pushed to the limits of physical possibility—and broken because of it.

Citadel almost felt sorry for Roger Hamilton.

Murray had given Citadel what he needed to stop this beast from rampaging any—

Citadel felt the blow before he realized he'd been thrown from his feet. His mental distraction cost him. His head rang as he tumbled head over heels across the Piggy Wiggly parking lot. It seemed every part of him made contact with the ground until he slammed into the wall of the grocery store. Concrete and steel buckled under the force of the impact, but this was a much larger building than the Murphy's, so it didn't completely collapse on top of Citadel.

"I think you need a lesson in respect, Citadel," Rockhide said.

Citadel shook his head to keep the ground from spinning around him. He looked up, toward the voice, but Rockhide was gone. Recall was running toward him, her eyes wide, looking from the Murphy's to Citadel laying against the grocery store in a heap.

"Doesn't seem like the debt is settled," she said.

"He's tougher and maybe smarter than he looks," Citadel said as he rose to his feet. He felt the tingle of his endurance healing him; this time it was centered around his head. "He damn near took my head off there."

"Oh, I thought you were just learning how to do cartwheels."

Citadel scowled at Recall. "You could help, you know. You're powerful."

Recall's face went white. She swallowed hard. "That's not why I'm here."

Citadel felt a flash of anger. He wanted to throttle this girl, but he wasn't that man anymore. Had he been that kind of man at one time? Had he led FORCE with an iron fist like everyone believed?

No, he wouldn't force her to do what he wanted. He had to be better than what he once was.

"Fine," he said, probably with more force than he meant. "Did you see where he went?"

She pointed toward the better part of town.

The schools.

He set himself to run, but turned his head toward Recall. "You have to decide one day what is worth fighting for, Lilly. You've used your powers for yourself for so long that maybe you don't know what it's like to fight for others. You can't run forever."

Suddenly, the air chattered with a sound Citadel never imagined he'd hear in the quiet little town of Ender, Oklahoma.

Gunfire.

Alec Gunn

EUP News Analysis

(Posted 10/22/2015)

IS THE AU LYING TO ITS PEOPLE?

Chicago/Los Angeles — A recent investigation into the American Union's (AU) Department of Supernormal Affairs (DSA) has revealed that the AU may be lying to its people. Our reporters have discovered that up to 80% of the reported Super-Powered Individual (SPI) activity in the AU is fabricated by the DSA. This includes a recent report released by the AU in September.

In that report, eight individual SPI events were reported, in which someone was captured and subsequently executed for being a SPI. However, only two of those events could be verified by local witnesses and interviews with AUSS personnel willing to speak to EUP News. The two events that were confirmed, the so-called Jackie Robinson Day Massacre, and a smaller scale, telepathically-induced mass suicide in Florida, were verified by independent sources.

However, a follow-up look into both these events revealed that the bodies of the two SPIs executed could not be found. Were they taken for scientific research, or could the executions themselves have been faked? The AU frequently live-streams SPI executions, but it's very possible that these "live" broadcasts could be doctored recordings.

This is an ongoing investigation, and we will have more for you as it progresses.

July 17, 2018 – 12:35 p.m.

Samuel Blue Hawk shouted over the sound of gunfire as the beast rose from the crater it had created in the parking lot of Marshall High. Gillian ran for cover, but she could hear his voice behind her.

"North, East, and South, move to your positions! West, lay down cover fire for the retreat!"

The air exploded in the popping rattle of nearby gunfire.

The giant SPI brushed off the onslaught of projectiles as if wiping at gnats. Gillian shuddered at the monstrosity that barely resembled Roger Hamilton, the AUSS agent who had stalked her son for months.

Samuel pulled at Gillian's sleeve. "We have to go."

Gillian realized she was planted to the ground, staring at the oncoming beast. She wondered if she was frozen in fear or awe. Maybe both?

Rockhide charged the unit firing on him. His swinging arms threw human bodies into the air. Most landed dozens of feet away and didn't move again. Some rolled over and screamed in agony.

The remaining men and women in the West unit fled.

Gillian wasn't in the path of Rockhide's destruction, but her heart fluttered all the same. She marked at least six unmoving bodies—corpses—on the ground around Rockhide. The giant SPI slid to a stop when the defenders broke away in all directions. He turned and Gillian saw his cracked-skinned face grinning, his strangely human teeth shining behind peeled lips.

Then he saw Gillian and Samuel watching him. Samuel's pull on Gillian's arm grew more insistent, and Gillian broke from her immobility as a spike of fear triggered her flight instinct. She let Samuel pull her toward the school building. They ran together, the old man surprisingly spry.

A shadow passed over them and Rockhide landed hard, forcing them to skid to a halt. He turned toward Gillian and Samuel, his grin never lessening.

"You're that kid's mom, aren't you?" Despite the drastic changes to his body, his voice was normal. "I bet Citadel is going to love it when I—"

Rockhide never finished the sentence. Something hit him low in the body at amazing speed, knocking him over and back toward the school building. Gillian felt a breath of wind in her hair moments after the object—Citadel—passed by her.

Two forms rolled over and over, struggling for control over each other. They struck the wall of the gymnasium and tore through it like tissue paper. The sound of SPI pounding on SPI was unlike anything Gillian heard before; it was like construction equipment pounding through stone without the noise of engines or crumble of rock.

As the two SPIs vanished behind the walls of the Marshall High School gym, Gillian heard Citadel howl in pain.

Citadel reached for the cracks in Rockhide's skin, but as his fingertips brushed at the edges, Rockhide's fist connected with his head and shoulders. Citadel was forced to abandon his efforts for a moment as he wrestled with Rockhide, taking the blows as only he could, but feeling every one as sharp stabs of pain. Bones broke and healed just as quickly. Muscles bruised and tore, only to regrow in moments.

Citadel felt it all.

He couldn't hold back an expression of pain any longer, but he turned the scream of agony into a howl of rage. As he'd done long ago in Vietnam, he pushed passed the pain and discomfort and fought. To some, pain was a wall—a barrier between them and the person they could be. It was a signal that something was terribly wrong, that the cause of the pain should be avoided.

For Citadel, one who rarely felt pain in his life, it was no barrier. He reached up to the top of that wall and pulled himself up and over. He leaned into the pain and cried out as he reached to grip Rockhide's shoulder. A ridge of tough hide at the edge of a crack gave him a hand hold. He braced himself and hammered Rockhide's chest with his other fist, calling on all his strength and speed to make the giant…thing, feel it. He connected six times in less than a second before Rockhide ripped him away, producing his own cry.

Citadel let himself be thrown away from Rockhide but didn't let go of that ridge of flesh he clung to. Rockhide's enormous strength was his own weakness. Citadel was thrown across the polished wood floor of the basketball court, but he maintained a hold on Rockhide's skin.

Rockhide's cry turned into piercing scream as a patch of black-gray skin tore away from his shoulder, revealing pink scar tissue beneath.

Citadel rolled to a stop and cast aside the bloody scab he ripped off. As he stood to face the monster again, he saw Rockhide's own endurance enhancement regenerate the hard plate of skin in moments. But Rockhide's eyes skewered Citadel with hate.

Now, Citadel knew how much time he had—he had to move faster. But fast wasn't enough. He needed to be vicious. He needed to be more of a monster than Rockhide.

To win this fight, Citadel needed to become what he feared most.

As he braced himself to move, he heard in his memory screams of pain and terror of young men dying, and the curses of Ho Chi Min before Citadel ripped his head off.

July 17, 2018 – 12:35 p.m.

Eric knew Leonard Strange better than anyone else. Leonard was simple, single-minded. When he wanted something, he got it, or kept trying. Leonard had spent weeks taunting Eric in an attempt to get Eric to out himself as a SPI.

Leonard hated Eric more than anyone else. As a simple school bully, Leonard was only ever brought down by one person. Eric. As a super-powered killer, Strange again faced Eric.

And lost.

Leonard was simple, straight-forward in every way. His powerset was limited. He had a speed enhancement rarely seen; he might be the fastest man alive, even though there were two speedsters Eric knew about in the EUP—they even had their own trading cards.

But Leonard lacked a significant agility enhancement. This meant his ability to change direction or stop himself was limited. He could literally strike like the lightning emblazoned on his arms, a single flash of speed in one direction. Then he had to stop, slow for a second. Only then could he strike again.

Eric prepared himself for the strike. He felt the atoms in his body change; he shifted his phase so Leonard would pass right through him. Once that happened, he would turn part of himself ultra-dense and catch Leonard's arm, possibly ripping it right off his body with the sheer momentum.

Leonard wasted no more breath—he gave no warning. One moment he was there, then he wasn't. Eric couldn't even see the speedster move.

This was it.

Eric's mind felt the sudden shock before the rest of him did. There was no feeling of Leonard passing through Eric. Instead, Leonard hit him like a freight train. Eric was already trying to calculate his mistake, figure out the science of what happened before he felt his ribs crack. The state of his matter cushioned some of the blow. If anyone else was hit like that, they would have been torn apart like a bug on a windshield.

Instead, Eric was thrown into the air. He passed through a parked car and landed on the sidewalk on the other side. His body rolled along the concrete and into the lawn of someone's front yard. As the agony of the hit finally began to wash over him, causing him to writhe in the grass, Eric heard Leonard laugh.

"I've learned a few things, Sumner," Leonard called from across the street. "People much smarter than you have you all figured out, and they made me into a weapon to destroy you."

A chill joined the pain in his bones as Eric realized Leonard was talking about Exodus. The telepath with a mind as enhanced as Citadel's muscles had figured out how Eric's ability worked. Exodus probably knew more about Eric's powers than Eric did.

No, that was impossible. Exodus couldn't possibly have the information he needed to make such conclusions.

It was a trick.

Eric pulled himself to his feet, trying to ignore the sharp pain in his chest. The parked car he'd passed through lay between him and Leonard, as if Leonard had positioned himself there on purpose.

No. Exodus didn't know everything, did he?

Eric leaned against the car as if exhausted or defeated. Leonard's smile widened. Eric wouldn't have time to judge when Leonard moved. If he waited until Leonard tensed his body, it would be too late. He used Leonard's smile as his cue.

He flowed his power through the car and pushed with all his strength.

The car phased out for a split second, becoming light as a feather. Eric's push threw it away, toward Leonard across the street. The instant it left Eric's hands, it became solid, a half-ton hunk of metal hurtling toward its target.

Eric had an amused instant to notice that the chassis was thrown, but the tires still stood in the place they were parked.

Then it all went to shit.

If Leonard was shocked by Eric's new power, he must have recovered at super speed. Again, Leonard vanished, but this time, the effect of his movement was visible. The car was ripped in half as Leonard passed through it. The two halves of the chassis careened to either side, one crashing into the large shade tree, the other tumbling into the yard beyond, tearing up the grass and dirt like a plow.

Leonard stopped a few feet from Eric. He brushed off the bodysuit he wore, running his hands over the white lightning bolts on the sleeves.

"That's impressive, Sumner!" Leonard said, nodding his head. "But like I said: I've learned, too. Did you know if you move fast enough, the air hardens around you? I'm the first speedster able to do it, apparently. It's the bubble of air and sound that forms around a jet moving at just the speed of sound."

That was how he'd done it, then. It was like a forcefield around him when he moved at a high enough speed—but that air wasn't like his body. When he was hit just now, he hadn't been preparing for air. He'd been preparing to pass through flesh.

Eric didn't know if he could change his frequency fast enough to counter that. He'd either get hit with the forcefield or by Leonard himself.

His chest began to vibrate. It was the same feeling he'd had when his powers first began to manifest last year, but he knew what it was now.

It was fear.

Stark, raving terror manifesting as a loss of control over his ability. He didn't have a solution to this problem. There was no scientific way he was going to get out of this. He was going to die the next time Leonard Strange moved.

Leonard moved.

July 17, 2018 – 12:40 p.m.

"Yeah," Rockhide said, rolling the shoulder Citadel tore through. It was healed now, the motion more to ensure the pain was just a memory than anything else. "That hurt."

Blood was splattered over the basketball court around both Citadel and Rockhide, yet neither of the combatants was injured…anymore.

"You know this could just go on forever," Rockhide said. "I hurt you, you heal. You hurt me, I heal. Neither of us can die." He shook his head, saddened by the fact.

Citadel nodded. "I survived a nuclear explosion—I'm not going anywhere. But are you sure your endurance enhancement is equal to mine?"

"For what I went through to get it…" Rockhide shrugged.

"Why are you doing this?" Citadel asked. He was stalling, he knew. He didn't want what had to happen next. "You could walk away from this. Walk away from the AU, from FORCE. Like you said, you can't die. Find a reason to live."

Rockhide looked at him as if he were crazy. "I have a reason to live," he said. "Exodus is my friend. He gave me this." He slammed a fist against his own chest, producing a thud that echoed through the gym. "Sure, it was a risk, but I am his right hand. His fist when he needs me. I won't abandon him."

Citadel gaped at Rockhide. He expected some resentment, some urge to escape slavery. But Rockhide wasn't a slave to Exodus.

There was nothing more to be done. It had to end here.

Citadel looked around—he didn't want anyone to see.

Then, without looking back at Rockhide, he moved.

Despite his speed, Rockhide had an instant to move in defense. The giant raised his arms to meet Citadel's charge, but there was nothing the big SPI could do. Citadel moved around arms the size of telephone poles. He reached past them and gripped the edge of one of the thick skin plates on Rockhide's chest. He ripped it out like he was removing duct tape from a hairy man's chest.

Immediately, with his other arm, he punched through Rockhide's exposed flesh. The wound was already beginning to heal, but Citadel didn't stop moving at his best speed, with all his strength.

Rockhide fell as Citadel began digging out his internal organs. Those, too, began to heal as soon as they were removed, regenerating from the traces of cells remaining in the body.

Citadel felt sweat break out on his brow—or maybe that was blood splattering in his face. He knelt on Rockhide's body that lay prone on the floor, his hand digging into the mutant's chest. Blood was *everywhere*. Citadel was swimming in it. As Rockhide lost it, his endurance produced more; it seemed like there would be no end.

Citadel raced Rockhide's endurance enhancement, ripping him apart as his body struggled to heal. Citadel tried to deafen himself to Rockhide's echoing screams.

It wasn't a nuclear explosion. It wasn't so clean. Citadel's speed was the only thing that allowed him to make progress. Soon, he was standing over Rockhide's open chest cavity, tearing through his ribs to get to his heart, ripping away bone and thick skin as it regrew.

This part, however, was just to weaken Roger Hamilton, to overload his enhancements as Steven Sumner did to him. It would never kill the mutated SPI.

There would be only one way to do that.

As long as Rockhide's endurance wasn't as strong as Citadel's.

Citadel ripped at the collarbone, throwing away the second ribcage he tore out, then he punched through to crush the spine behind. He gripped the broken spine and pulled as hard as he could.

The spine, cord, and part of Rockhide's brain came out through Rockhide's chest. Citadel threw that to the other side of the gym. Then he pummeled Rockhide's head, turning what was left to mush.

The regeneration slowed, then stopped. Bones ceased knitting back together, blood stopped flowing.

Citadel staggered back from what he'd done. His throat constricted. He fell back, landing on his backside on the bloody floor. He stared, his vision blurring.

"And here I thought you might have changed," said a woman's voice from across the gym.

Citadel was on his feet before the speaker finished, expecting Gillian to be there, watching what he'd done with horror. Instead, there was nothing.

Nothing, at first.

In a far back corner, untouched by the light of lamps or sun, something moved. A dark shadow within the other shadows.

A void.

It climbed up the ceiling and approached the halogen lamps hanging from the rafters. Before it reached them, they burst into sparks and went dark. It only moved forward through the dark places in the ceiling, destroying the lamps as it went. Soon, the room was all in shadow, save a thick shaft of light filtering through the gap in the wall where Citadel and Rockhide entered.

Then, the shadow, darker than the darkness around it, dropped to the floor. It struck like a glob of viscous liquid, but nothing around it—not blood, nor entrails—was disturbed by its appearance. It rose from the floor, forming into a wholly black shape. It became the silhouette of a woman, small and shapely. It walked toward Citadel in a way that was horrifyingly familiar.

"There is nothing more for you to do here, Love," the shadow said. "It's time to come join me. Join me in the dark. Come, Omar." Its voice grew cold. "Pay for your sins."

It reached out a single, small hand.

Citadel shook his head. "No, no..." It was all he could muster, the only word that would come to his mind. This had to be a hallucination—some psychosis brought about by what he did. What he was seeing was impossible, by any standard.

"Yes, Omar," the shadow said. Then, it expanded around him, the darkness engulfing him. He could do nothing to fight it. As it embraced him and took him, he felt the truth. It was real.

She was real.

"Jitter..."

The silence was sudden and complete. After a moment, Gillian became afraid. She'd pulled herself from Samuel's grasp when the screaming started. She stood there at the edge of the parking lot, watching the gaping hole in the gym wall.

Now, it was quiet. As if in response to the horror that must have happened inside, the lights within the gym popped and shattered.

Then...nothing.

She waited. Waited for either Citadel or Hamilton to emerge from whatever the hell was inside.

No one did, though.

They'd killed each other. That was the only explanation. Somehow, the two SPI titans killed each other and left no survivor.

Gillian approached the gym hesitantly. Samuel called to her, but she paid him no heed. Some part of her marked the rattle of gunfire coming from the edges of town.

The AUSS had arrived.

Finally, she peered into the darkness of the gym, lit only by reflected light from the hole she partially obscured.

The smell hit her first. It was the most horrendous thing she'd ever experienced—just the smell. That was compounded by what little she saw within the pool of light. An indescribable violence was done here.

"Citadel?" She called. If what she saw *was* Citadel, then she would die in just a few moments. But she knew it wasn't.

Rockhide would have burst from this place as soon as Citadel was dead.

She climbed through the hole and made her way along the edge of the basketball court. There were still some clean patches, but not many. When her eyes adjusted to the poor light, she saw the body. Much too large to be Citadel, it lay unrecognizable, save for the fact that it had a torso and four limbs. The head was gone. The blood-soaked black and grey limbs verified that this was Hamilton.

Citadel was nowhere to be found.

The only trace of him was two large footprints in the center of the bloody floor. Two clean marks in the shape of boot soles, with no mark to tell which way their owner had gone. Only…

Gillian looked up to the ceiling, but all that was there was an impenetrable darkness.

Citadel was gone.

AUPrimeHistory: True Conspiracies

(Airdate: 6/24/2010)

THE LEGACY OF THE CHAOS YEARS

<Archive video: Los Angeles, 1997>

If anything remains of the Chaos Years, it can be found here: Los Angeles, California, the capitol of the Estados Unidos del Pacificos, or the United Pacific States. Known colloquially as the "EUP," this splinter nation was founded as a rejection of all the values held by the American Union. Freedom. Security. Morality. The EUP knows none of these.

<SFX: Super-Powered Terror>

This shocking footage comes from within the EUP, acquired by brave patriots in January of this year. Streets are patrolled by SPI terror squads in the name of "security." People live in fear of the SPI elite, a ruling class that no civilian revolution could defeat. When the people aren't in terror of physical SPIs, they are controlled by powerful telepaths who broadcast their mind control through television signals.

<File Photo: Mental Block - FORCE Presentation 1999>

These criminals are led by this man, known only by the code name Mental Block. This nefarious person has the power to control many minds at once, an ability he uses to keep an iron grip on the EUP government, effectively becoming its master.

<Animation: AU Flag>

Only the American Union can stand up to the SPI threat from the EUP. Our AUSS has the technology and training to combat both physical and mental SPIs using the latest in electronic and robotic advancement.

<Video: AUSS Strong>

We are your shield against the inevitable EUP invasion. We stand strong…for you.

<End Credits>

July 17, 2018 – 12:37 p.m.

Eric willed his body to protect itself however it could. He'd done it before. Sometimes his instinct was better than his brain when it came to controlling his powers. Maybe this time it would be fast enough?

Almost the instant after Leonard vanished, he reappeared with a thud, followed by the thunder of the barrier of air breaking in front of Eric's face. The thud came from something he hit not even a foot away. Leonard was thrown back by a combination of his collision with the force field and the shattering of his bubble of air. Eric felt nothing, though he should have felt the hammer thud of air when he heard it.

Eric's head snapped around, looking. Then he saw her.

Lilly stood at the end of the block, a look of relief on her face. Eric's own relief could have drowned hers out.

"Hold him," Eric called to her. He didn't see her move or act, but Leonard suddenly let out a scream of frustration. Leonard thrashed against Lilly's power as she pushed him to the ground, his body blurred as he struggled to use his speed against the telekinetic force field that imprisoned him. Eric knew from experience that the force field was not something even this speedster would be able to break through.

Finally, Leonard was forced to his hands and knees. He

shouted, cursing and spitting. Eric kneeled next to him.

He indicated Lilly. "You think you're special, Lenny? It helps to have friends. Where are your friends?"

"Um, Eric?" Lilly said, her voice strained. Was she having trouble with the field? He looked up at her, but she wasn't looking at him or Leonard. She was looking toward the horizon.

Eric looked, too. That was when he noticed the deep thrumming that must have been building over the last few seconds.

"Yeah," Leonard said, grinning. "I got here a little early. I'm not good with patience and he can't keep up with me."

Eric felt the blood leave his face. He looked at Lilly. She shook her head, as pale as he must be. "I can't do shit if you expect me to hold him," she said, jerking her head toward Leonard.

"Let me talk to him. Maybe I can get him to stop."

Leonard laughed. "Sonic licks Exodus' feet like the rest of us, Sumner."

"He's my dad," Eric said. That wiped the grin off Leonard's face.

The thrum became a scream as Sonic flew closer. The power required to propel him through the air caused a blast of sound louder than anything else Eric had ever heard. He shifted the vibration in his ears to cancel out the sound, and it became a dull hum that buzzed against his skull.

Eric moved away from the others, toward the figure that was now visible in the sky. Sonic slowed when he saw Eric, keeping a distance.

"Which are you?" Eric said in a normal tone. Anyone who could manipulate sound, he figured, could hear through anything. "Exodus or my dad?"

"I stopped being your dad a long time ago, son." The voice came to him on a strange wavelength, probably designed to reach through the jet engine sound of his flight power. It warbled, giving Steven's voice a strange, otherworldly quality.

"I can help you," Eric said. "I can protect you from Exodus, like I did at the house."

Steven shook his head as he descended to the ground half a block away in the middle of the street. The pounding screech stopped, and the silence made Eric feel like he'd lost all hearing. But then Steven spoke again in a normal tone.

"I made a mistake coming here. I'm too dangerous, Eric. I denied it for a long time; I'm too much like my brother. I can hurt people—I can hurt a lot of people. Exodus' control is the only thing keeping me in check."

Eric wrinkled his brow. That made no sense. Steven—Sonic, whatever—had more control over his abilities than anyone Eric had ever seen. Surely more than Rumble had.

"I don't think that's you talking, Dad." He almost called the man before him "Exodus," but he wasn't sure he was actually facing the telepath this time. "You risked everything to see me and Mom again. You wouldn't have gone through that if you didn't think it was worth it."

Steven walked toward Eric, his long trench coat swirling around his ankles.

"I'm not being controlled this time, Eric, but I know what I am. I'm worried about what you are. If you are like me and your uncle, you could be just as dangerous. If you're the next generation, like Exodus fears, do you have the power to destroy the planet like Russ destroyed New York?"

"Are you here to kill me, then?"

"No. I'm here to bring you and Citadel in. The girl, too." Sonic glanced over Eric's shoulder toward Lilly. Eric followed his gaze.

Lilly shrugged with a self-conscious grin. "He doesn't remember me."

"That won't be easy," Eric said to his father, "if we decide we don't want to go."

"Easier than you think," Sonic said. "Like I said, I'm dangerous. As dangerous as Russ ever was. If you think those sounds," he pointed to the air where Eric could faintly hear the rattle of gunfire, "mean that the people of Ender are defending their town from the AUSS, you're mistaken. The AUSS is already in town." He pointed to himself. "And they set a bomb in the middle of it."

Again, he pointed to himself.

"You'll destroy Ender just to get us?" Eric asked, incredulous.

"If I get you, there's no point in destroying Ender, is there?"

"Eric..." Lilly said behind him, a warning. Eric held up his hand—he had to think.

There had to be a way out of this.

"Give me proof," he said to Sonic. "Proof you aren't speaking in Exodus' voice right now."

"I don't think he is," Lilly said.

"Proof," Eric repeated, reaching out his hand, palm up.

If this was Exodus using Sonic's body, there was no way he'd submit to Eric's power. Steven Sumner took the dozen steps to Eric and took his son's hand. Eric instantly sent the pulse he knew would break any telepathic waves Exodus was using. He felt the buzz pass into Steven and wash through him.

He prayed.

Steven took a step back, then nodded. "A bomb, Eric."

Eric's heart dropped into his stomach. His eyes welled as he shook his head.

"We have to stop you, Dad," he whispered. "*I* have to."

"Even if it means destroying everything you love? Your school, your friends...your mother?"

"I won't let you do that."

Suddenly, Leonard Strange broke into hysterical laughter. Everyone turned to look at him, still crouched on hands and knees beneath Lilly's force field.

"Just burn it all down, Sonic!" Leonard screamed between bouts of giggles. "Do it!"

Eric glanced at Lilly. She seemed to understand—perhaps she read his mind. What she did was exactly what Eric wanted. The field constricted until Leonard was flat on his stomach, arms pinned beneath him. His laughter froze; his eyes went blank and his face went slack. Any sign of cognitive thought was gone. Lilly stared at the young man in disgust.

"You deserve that," she said, almost too quietly for Eric to hear. She looked up at Eric and nodded grimly. "He's done."

Eric turned back to Sonic, who hadn't made a move to stop

Lilly from wiping whatever memories she could in order to neutralize Leonard.

"*You* deserved that, Eric." Steven said. "For what he did to you and your friends."

Not for a moment did Eric think that changed anything.

"Will you come with me now?" Sonic asked.

Eric could only shake his head silently.

"Then you'll have to try and stop me."

With a sudden boom, Sonic took to the sky again.

July 17, 2018 – 12:45 p.m.

Eric felt the shockwave of Sonic's launch go through him, dampened by his powers. He looked around desperately, hoping Citadel would come out of nowhere to tackle his father, or that Mental Block would emerge from the Williams house with a secret weapon that would solve all his problems.

Lilly stood over Leonard, who sat bewildered, staring up at Sonic in sheer terror. Leonard didn't make a move or try to run—he looked almost like a child. Eric suspected Lilly made Leonard forget he was a SPI. That would be the most immediate way to solve their problem.

Eric's mind raced. How could he stop his own father, a man who had over a decade to hone his powers? Unless Eric figured out how to fly in the next minute, he wouldn't even be able to reach him. He'd defeated Leonard Strange by pulling him out of phase, but that wouldn't be possible for this.

Eric had reflected before on the nature of his powers and their relationship with his father and uncle. Rumble was able to vibrate solid matter, but the true secret of his ability was that he could tap into the potential energy of the objects he touched, causing them to explode in some cases. But he had to be touching something for his powers to work.

Sonic could vibrate the air, creating sound. But that wasn't all. Pure sound couldn't vaporize houses and generate the thrust necessary for a man to fly. He was doing something else with the air—perhaps related to Rumble's ability to tap into potential energy.

Did air have potential energy?

Eric had discovered just days ago that his powers had a secret, too. He could somehow shift atoms in and out of existence, take them away and make things lighter, add to them to make things denser and heavier. It was how he made himself dense. But like Rumble, he could only affect objects he touched.

Eric stood up straight, a smile coming to his face. No, Eric wasn't Rumble's son. He was Sonic's. Why wouldn't his powers lean more toward Steven's?

Sure, maybe he could only affect atoms he could touch. But air had atoms, didn't it?

This realization both gave him hope and scared him to death. If it was true, Sonic was right. Eric really might be able to destroy the planet. But that wasn't going to happen today

Right now, Eric only needed to stop his father from destroying Ender.

An instant after putting this all together, Sonic released a blast of sound that might have deafened everyone within several miles. It might have shattered buildings and torn people to shreds. It might have been the end of Ender.

But Eric touched the soundwave.

His outstretched hands took hold of the vibrating air. He felt his power pulse from the center of his chest and ripple along the surface of the sphere of sound Sonic created. The air solidified into something that looked like wavy glass. Sunlight refracted off of it and burst into color.

Then the sphere hummed and shattered.

At the center, Sonic hovered over the ground. He stared at Eric, his mouth open. Then it closed and Eric received a glare he imagined he might have received several times during his childhood if his father had been there to discipline him.

"Don't make me kill you, son," Sonic said, his voice modulated to counter the thunder of his flight.

"What do you think you were just about to do?"

"You might have survived that, but I can destroy you if I need to."

"Just stop, Dad. Then you don't need to kill anyone else."

"You'll come with me? To D.C.?"

Eric just shook his head.

"Then I can't stop."

Sonic opened his mouth and released a deafening scream. The vibration lanced toward Eric like a spear, visible in the air. Eric ghosted, letting the lance of near-solid air pass through him and rip through the asphalt below. Gravel peppered the air around Eric, but that, too, passed through him.

It was true—Sonic's power didn't just vibrate the air. It did something similar to what Eric had done, but on a more active level. Sonic used air as a weapon.

The sound was just a by-product.

Eric, solid once more so he could breathe, reached out to the air and chained together the atoms of air between him and Sonic. A spear of glass-like air shot back at Eric's father. Sonic shot away higher into the air as he simultaneously shattered Eric's spear with a thumping boom.

Sonic's ascent didn't last long—he suddenly veered off and arced laterally, hands outstretched.

Eric felt it the same as Sonic did. They were suddenly surrounded by a stoppage of the air. A dome of impenetrability. Eric glanced quickly at Lilly.

"Finish it, Ghost!" Lilly shouted from outside the dome. "I can't hold it forever."

She was containing the fight; Sonic wouldn't be able to flee this time.

The dome covered most of the block, including the street which Eric stood and several of the yards in front of the houses here. Sonic finished his circuit, realizing there was nowhere to go. He landed on the far side of the dome from Eric.

"'Two men enter, one man leaves.' Is that it?" Steven said.

"You're lucky you scare her," Eric said. "She tried to crush me yesterday—she could have done it. If she thought she could get away with it, she would have swatted you like a fly."

Steven shook his head.

"Listen, son," he said. "I don't want to have to do something I'll regret."

Eric laughed. "Like destroy your hometown? Like kill everyone I've ever known?"

"Not everyone."

Eric froze. "What do you mean?"

But he knew the answer.

"The girl. In Chicago. You know her, don't you? So does Exodus."

Eric stayed silent, afraid what he might say next would be a mistake.

"That's what Exodus does, Eric. He takes what you care about and uses it against you. Don't ever make the mistake of thinking Exodus is ignorant."

As he spoke, Steven walked toward Eric. He showed no threat.

"He has her. Maybe not in a dungeon somewhere, but he can get her at any moment he wants. He has you by the short hairs, just like he has me."

"What could he have on you? You've stopped caring about anything."

"No, I haven't. Do you realize that if I destroy Ender—kill you, kill Gillian—I'm free?" Eric saw a tear fall from Steven's eye. "If I do that, the next thing I'd do is tear the Pentagon apart looking for that bastard. Until he took control of me again and never let me go."

Steven now stood within arms' reach of Eric. Neither of them made a move to attack the other. "You see, I'm stuck. I can't get free; I realize that now. Any move I make digs me deeper into his control. He's watching us right now, through my eyes."

Sonic's arm suddenly reached out and grabbed Eric's shoulder.

"Now, son!"

Eric knew instantly what the man meant. He pulsed his

power through Steven's body, washing away Exodus's telepathic presence.

"We need to act fast," Steven said quickly. "There is only one way this ends if I don't take you back with me. If I don't destroy Ender, Exodus will do it for me. *With* me. Do you understand? Either I do it of my own free will or I do it as a puppet. There is no way out of this. We have two choices. Get your mother out of Ender and let me do what I have to do…"

"Or kill you," Eric finished. Eric glanced at the Williams house. *I hope you're listening, Mr. Turner.* "How many people will you kill to save me and Mom?"

"I don't care. I only care about you."

"I can't let that happen. If you care about me, you'll get as far from here as possible and never come back."

"Aren't you listening? I don't have a choice."

Eric reached up and laid his hand on top of Steven's on his shoulder. "Then I'm sorry, Dad." It was the only logical choice—he'd tell himself that for years, if he had to.

A small comfort.

Eric squeezed his father's hand, then reversed the flow of his power. Steven stiffened, his body becoming ultra-dense, almost solid. Eric then touched the air around Sonic and solidified that, too.

Steven Sumner fell away from his son, frozen arm outstretched. He dropped to the ground with a crunch of hardened air. An umbilical of glass seemed to stretch between Eric and Stephen, maintaining the suffocating shell around the elder.

"Eric, what are you doing?" Lilly came up behind him cautiously.

"The only logical thing," Eric said. "The only logical thing." The phrase repeated in his head like a mantra. He counted off the time. Seven minutes should do it. He'd read somewhere that a person could survive without air for seven minutes.

"Eric, don't do this." Lilly put a hand on Eric's shoulder. "This will not end well for you."

"You can take the memory away when it's done," Eric said.

"I won't do that."

One minute. Eric didn't realize how long seven minutes really was.

"Eric," Lilly begged. "He's unconscious. Leave him that way and we can get out of here. He won't wake up before we can get away. Just do what he said. Get us out of here and he can demolish a bunch of buildings."

"There are people here, too."

"Ender is evacuating," said a new voice. Mental Block was coming from the direction of the Williams house, followed by Zak, Ashley, and Jason Williams, all with bags slung over their shoulders. "Let him go, Eric."

Eric was actually surprised that he didn't feel the buzz of Mental Block's powers in his head. He was letting Eric make his own decision. Eric held Sonic frozen, wrapped in useless, solid air as his count reached three minutes.

Then he let go.

Steven slumped back onto the street, unmoving except for the slight rise and fall of his chest. Eric cried out, falling into Lilly. She held him up, small as she was. His face buried in her shoulder as he sobbed into her hair.

Then, Gillian arrived, driving Citadel's RV.

July 17, 2018 – 12:50 p.m.

Everyone packed into the RV: Zak, Ashley, and Jason Williams, Ben Maxwell, Lilly Tate, and Eric Sumner. It was a close fit, but they made it work. Ben took the seat next to Gillian in the cab, as he quickly explained what had just happened. Eric, red-eyed and wiped out, sat in a narrow swiveling seat just behind the driver's seat. The others spread out on the benches, and Lilly retreated back to the bedroom.

Gillian stared out the window at the prone body of her husband.

"Is he…?" She asked.

"No," Ben said gently. "But we have to leave him. He has a job to do. We have to leave."

"Which way?" Gillian asked.

"West," said Ben.

"North," said Eric, right on top of him.

Both adults turned to look at Eric.

"Exodus knows about Kristin. We need to go to Chicago."

"Damn it," Gillian said.

"If we get to Los Angeles, we can go back to Chicago with better backup," Ben said.

"I'm not waiting that long," Eric said. "If you want to go west, drop me off in McAlester and I'll go north myself."

"I'm not dropping you off anywhere," Gillian said.

"Just drive," Ben said. "We don't have much time."

"Where's Citadel?" Eric asked. "We need to pick him up."

Gillian shook her head as she put the RV in gear and hit the gas. "Citadel is gone. He took out Hamilton, then vanished. I don't know what happened."

"Are you sure?"

Ben slumped in his chair, staring straight ahead. After a moment, he nodded.

"She's sure," he said. "Citadel isn't in Ender, that I can see. It's like he's been swallowed up and taken into a void."

"Is he dead?" Eric asked. They reached the railroad tracks and rumbled over them. Eric noticed they were headed west.

"If he were dead, there would have been a body," Gillian said.

"Besides," Ben added, "if something killed him, we have bigger problems than your father or Exodus."

Gillian crossed herself, a gesture Eric had never seen from her. It was so out of place that he felt like he'd fallen into another dimension or something.

They were twelve miles out of Ender when the RV shuddered. Eric raced to the back of the RV and tore aside the bedroom curtains. Lilly sat next to him and they both watched the end of Ender. A cloud rose over Ender, Oklahoma, shaped like a dome.

"Debris," Lilly said, her voice quiet in awe. "That's all that's left."

Jason joined them and watched silently. Not even a *dude* coming out of his mouth.

The cloud rose a little over the horizon, then began to flatten again.

"I wonder how *AUPrime* is going to explain that," Jason finally said when it disappeared.

"Something SPI related, of course," Eric said. "I can't imagine what, but whatever it'll be, it's going to make people even more afraid."

They drove in stunned silence until they were far enough

away for it to feel right to speak again. Still, no one did. Then, without warning, Gillian turned the RV onto the Indian Nation Turnpike heading north.

"Tell me you're heading 40-West to Oklahoma City," Ben said quietly.

"Tulsa, and 44-East to St. Louis, then 55-North to Chicago."

Eric grinned. He thought he would have to fight them on this. He never loved his mother more than at this moment.

"Thank you, Mom."

"Don't thank me yet, kiddo. We have three SPIs heading into the capitol of the AU. We're putting all of you at risk."

"It's Kristin, Mom."

"I know." Then she glanced at Ben. "I can drop you and the Williams' at 40-West if you don't want to do this."

"I'm sticking around," Jason called from the couch. Eric turned to look at his best friend. He gave Eric a smile, though his eyes looked haunted.

"You're coming with us," Zak said. "To Los Angeles."

"I'm going with them, Dad," Jason said in a firm voice. Zak's face darkened and he opened his mouth to argue, but Ashley put her hand on her husband's arm. She didn't say anything, but Zak leaned back against the wall in resignation.

Eric was stunned. He'd have thought Ashley would be on Zak's side, and that was one person Jason wouldn't stand up to. Jason seemed to be thinking the same thing, because he gaped at his mother in shock.

"What about you, Ben?" Gillian asked.

Mental Block shrugged.

"Recall?" Mental Block called to the back of the RV. "Are you coming with us to California?"

Eric watched as Lilly stirred on Citadel's bed. She rose and came to the door of the room. Her face was thoughtful—she was struggling with herself for the answer.

"No," she said as if angry with someone. "I'm going to Chicago. I can't stand by anymore. I think my fight is with them." She made a gesture that indicated Eric and Jason.

Mental Block nodded. Then he turned to Gillian.

"Chicago is one place I can't go. The risk is too great, and people know what I look like. In a small town like Ender, I could use my powers to conceal myself after a fashion, but I won't be able to do it in a city the size of Chicago."

Gillian nodded silently.

"When you're done in Chicago, drive straight to Los Angeles. We'll be waiting for you."

Gillian nodded, keeping her eyes on the road.

Mental Block turned to stare at Eric. "Make no mistake," he said. "You are about to face your greatest challenge if you want to get Kristin out from under Exodus' nose. He'll have placed people close to her; he may even control her to some extent, if he's had the opportunity to touch her. You need to master your powers. Not just know them but *master* them. I wish you would come to L.A. to we can work out how best to do that, but I understand the urgency. Do what you need to do."

"What are you going to do?" Jason asked.

"We need to find out what happened to Citadel. If he's still alive, we need to find him and bring him to us. I don't want another seventeen years before we see him again."

AUPrimeNews Now

BULLETIN

TERROR IN THE HEARTLAND...AGAIN!

This is Sheppard Smith with a late breaking bulletin.

Just six months ago, the town of Ender, Oklahoma was savaged by the SPI terrorist Leonard Strange, who was captured and executed right here on AUPrimeNews.

Now, the little town of Ender has suffered another SPI attack. Unknown SPIs ripped through the little village at about noon today. This admittedly grainy cell phone video shows the attack as two of the terrorists came to blows over a disagreement.

Their battle destroyed the entire town of Ender as AUSS forces converged on the town. Both SPIs were killed by our heroes, but not before leaving thousands homeless:

<City Manager, Jacob Lane>

"It was terrible...What are we going to do now?"

AU Emergency Management officials will assess the damage and provide support for those affected.

When we return, we'll discuss the repercussions of this incident on public policy. Will this mean an all-out war against the SPI menace?

Epilogue

Citadel burned.

It was the bomb all over again. He writhed within the fireball, though it never burned itself out as it should. Pain roiled along his skin, which burned away, then repaired itself only to burn away again. His hair was melted from his body— he breathed in the fire and felt his lungs burn.

This is what you left for me, Jitterbug's voice said in some blocked off, peaceful corner of his mind. *This is all I am, now. Power and consciousness wrapped around a core of nuclear fire.*

He heard the voice faintly against the backdrop of his anguish, which he couldn't express in screams when all around him was the bomb.

Then it stopped.

Mercifully, he floated in a blackness and silence for a moment before being dumped unceremoniously onto a concrete floor.

He lay on the cold floor as his body repaired itself. He sobbed, even after the pain was gone from his skin and lungs. He wept on the floor as the Void rose above him, again taking the basic shape of the woman he loved.

She had no face; he could see no features. Only a small silhouette in the shape of her body. She crouched over him in the dimly lit room and stared at him, unmoving, as he cried.

What do you have to cry about? She asked. *The pain is temporary. It's nothing to you.*

"I thought you were dead," he managed.

I AM DEAD! She screamed in his mind so forcefully that a spike of pain crashed through his head. He gripped his skull in both hands until the pain subsided, the damage to his brain healing in seconds.

You've been living your life with a blank slate for the last sixteen years, Omar. You think you can avoid the consequences of your actions by forgetting what happened. What you did. But I won't let you forget. I've worked hard these last few weeks to piece together your memory.

Citadel realized now that all the memory he'd regained: Vietnam, the Pentagon, Jitterbug...it all came from her. He wasn't healing from the bomb; she was putting his brain back together like he was Humpty Dumpty.

We aren't done. You need to remember it all. You need to relive the pain of your past. You will remember all of those you have killed, all you have allowed to die.

"Thank you," Citadel grunted. He still lay on the floor. His body didn't want to obey his will. Or rather, his will didn't want to move his body.

No! You will not thank me when it's over. It will be painful. It will be a special kind of torture. When you remember it all, you will want to die all over again. When you realize how unforgivable you are...

She reached out and touched his face. He flinched. The Void's darkness was a cold that reached even Citadel's buried nerves. She was as cold outside as she was hot inside.

Then, she continued, *you will beg me to kill you. I haven't decided yet if I will let you die.*

She drew him into her again, as she had in the high school gym.

And he burned.

The Greatest Gift

The greatest gift you can give an author isn't your money. Yeah, we love money just as much as other people, but the true currency in the literary world is and al¬ways has been

THE REVIEW

If you are enjoying the Heroes of FORCE, and you want to show your appreciation, head on over to the online store where you purchased it (or the online version of the physical store where you picked it up), and leave a positive review. Feel free to reveal the flaws and give your honest opinion. I hope you'll write good things, but I want you to be honest above all (in reviewing this book, and in life in general).

I am grateful for every review. Every review means someone will make an informed decision whether or not to buy this book (and thereby give me money — see how that works?).

Stay True, Believers!

—ALEC GUNN

The Truth is HERE

The Heroes of FORCE were once American Legends.

Now their legacy burns in the nuclear fire that engulfed New York City.

Discover the truth about FORCE! Read the
Top Secret Project Brooklyn Documents
featured in this story and discover the secrets of FORCE.

Find it now at:

pencastlebooks.com/alec-gunn-heroes-of-force-force-feed/

www.ingramcontent.com/pod-product-compliance
Lightning Source LLC
Chambersburg PA
CBHW052037240626
47153CB00006B/2122